Praise for bestselling author Kathie DeNosky

"Kathie DeNosky's *Lonetree Ranchers: Brant*
takes readers on a thrilling and adventurous ride."
—*RT Book Reviews*

"Cowboys are Ms. DeNosky's specialty,
and she scores again with hunk Morgan Wakefield.
Lonetree Ranchers: Morgan is sure to delight readers
with its hot, sensual and emotional intensity."
—*The Romance Reader's Connection*

"Ms. DeNosky always has a way of
making her secondary characters just as loveable
as the main ones. So if you love babies,
cowboys and romance you need to get to a copy of
Remembering One Wild Night, because
it will be one book you will remember."
—*Writers Unlimited*

KATHIE DeNOSKY

lives in her native southern Illinois with her big, lovable Bernese mountain dog, Nemo. Writing highly sensual stories with a generous amount of humor, Kathie's books have appeared on the Waldenbooks bestseller list and received a Write Touch Readers Award and a National Readers' Choice Award. Kathie enjoys going to rodeos, traveling to research settings for her books and listening to country music. Readers may contact Kathie at P.O. Box 2064, Herrin, Illinois 62948-5264, or e-mail her at kathie@kathiedenosky.com. They can also visit her Web site at www.kathiedenosky.com.

KATHIE DeNOSKY

Lonetree Ranchers: Brant

Lonetree Ranchers: Morgan

HARLEQUIN®

TORONTO • NEW YORK • LONDON
AMSTERDAM • PARIS • SYDNEY • HAMBURG
STOCKHOLM • ATHENS • TOKYO • MILAN • MADRID
PRAGUE • WARSAW • BUDAPEST • AUCKLAND

PLEASE RECYCLE · THIS PRODUCT IS RECYCLABLE

Recycling programs
for this product may
not exist in your area.

ISBN-13: 978-0-373-68804-3

LONETREE RANCHERS: BRANT & LONETREE RANCHERS: MORGAN

Copyright © 2010 by Harlequin Books S.A.

The publisher acknowledges the copyright holder of the individual works
as follows:

LONETREE RANCHERS: BRANT
Copyright © 2003 by Kathie DeNosky

LONETREE RANCHERS: MORGAN
Copyright © 2003 by Kathie DeNosky

CONTENTS

To professional rodeo bullfighter Joe Baumgartner,
for sharing his experiences and knowledge with me.
And a special thank-you to the
Professional Bull Riders, for showing me
a behind-the-scenes look at this exciting sport.

LONETREE RANCHERS: BRANT

Chapter 1

Her sensible black pumps held tightly in one hand, Anastasia Devereaux plastered her back to the brick wall behind her, took a deep breath and waited for the fog to clear from her glasses. "Don't look down," she whispered when the haze evaporated. "You can do this if you don't look down."

She closed her eyes in order to gather her courage and slow the erratic pounding of her heart. How on earth had she—an intelligent, totally unadventurous librarian—managed to find herself inching along the outside ledge surrounding the fourth floor of the Regal Suites Hotel in downtown Saint Louis? And at midnight, no less.

Glancing to her left, she gulped. There was no turning back now. If she did, she'd be trapped. She cautiously turned her head to the right. Her only option was to continue to the next balcony.

She took a deep breath and focused on the side of the building across the alley to keep from looking down as, inch by slow inch, she cautiously moved closer to the safety of the platform to her right. The rough brick behind her pulled at the twisted knot of hair at the back of her head, snagged her silk blouse and shredded the backs of her nylons. When the cold February wind whistled around her, she shivered. She wished she'd had the presence of mind to grab her coat and purse before she'd impulsively escaped Patrick's hotel room. But she hadn't, and there was no sense lamenting her short-sightedness now.

Her hip came into contact with the iron railing of the next balcony and she automatically reached out to wrap her hand around the cold metal. It felt like a lifeline and she held on for dear life as she tried to steady her frayed nerves. Her grandmother would never forgive her if she fell and her lifeless body was found in the Dumpster below. It would be terribly undignified. And a Whittmeyer woman—even one with the surname Devereaux—never lost her dignity. Ever.

"Forgive me, Grandmother, but there's no ladylike way to do this," Anastasia muttered as she tossed her shoes onto the balcony, then hitched up her khaki skirt to throw her leg over the wrought-iron railing.

Scrambling over the barrier, she fell onto the rough

concrete floor. The surface bit into her knees and palms, but she ignored the pain. There was a light on inside and she thanked her lucky stars that she'd found her way to a room that was occupied. She prayed the person inside hadn't fallen asleep or gone out without turning off the lamp.

She gathered her shoes, took a deep breath and tentatively tapped on the sliding glass door. Silence.

Now what? Patrick could discover her missing at any moment, and if he walked out onto his balcony, he wouldn't have any trouble spotting her. Doubling her fist, she hoped the glass didn't break as she pounded on it for all she was worth. The sound of a muttered curse, then the slamming of a door was followed by silence.

"Please let me in," she called, feeling panic begin to claw at her insides.

"Where the hell are you?" a male voice inside the room shouted back. He didn't sound very sociable.

"I'm on the balcony. Please hurry," she added, glancing toward the platform outside Patrick's room.

When the drapes were suddenly yanked open, Anastasia blinked. She found herself staring through the glass at a man with the most extraordinary blue eyes, wearing nothing but a towel knotted at his waist and a formidable frown. Straight, sable-colored hair fell low on his forehead, softening his expression yet lending a ruggedness to his extremely handsome features that she found quite appealing.

She watched him disengage the lock and pull the

door aside. "What the hell are you doing out there?" he demanded.

She dropped her shoes and took a step back. But her foot came down on one of the pumps and sent her reeling backward. The man lunged forward and, wrapping her securely in his arms, drew her to his bare chest before she toppled over the railing and fell to the alley below.

"Whoa there, sweetpea." His voice rumbled up from deep in his chest and sent an answering shiver straight up her spine. "That's a long way down and unless you're an angel with wings, I don't think doing a backflip off this balcony would be a real good idea."

"I don't." Anastasia shook her head. "Have wings, that is." She glanced over the wrought iron and shuddered at how close she'd come to falling. "And I'm afraid my landing would be anything but graceful."

The man continued to hold her as he backed them into the room and closed the balcony door. "You're safe now," he said, his voice suddenly sounding much more gentle than it had moments before.

A shiver coursed through her, but she wasn't sure if it was from being cold or the sound of his sexy baritone. And she couldn't discount the impressive muscles holding her to him, either. He had the widest shoulders and his chest looked exactly like the models on the boy-toy calendar her assistant, Tiffany, had tacked up in the storeroom at the library. The thought that the man holding her probably didn't have a stitch on beneath the towel caused her to shiver again.

"You're chilled to the bone, sweetpea," he said, obviously misinterpreting the reason for the tiny movement. His arms tightened around her.

This time she was sure the tremor running the length of her was due to the man holding her to him. Her cheek was pressed to his warm, bare chest and his hands were rubbing slow circles over her back. What woman with a pulse wouldn't shiver?

"Th-thank you…for letting me in."

"How long have you been out there?" he asked, his voice sending a fresh wave of goose bumps along her arms.

"I…I'm not sure." How long had she been out on that ledge? It seemed like hours, but it couldn't have been more than a few minutes. "Five minutes. Maybe ten."

As she continued to ponder the man's question, she realized he still held her firmly against his warm bare flesh. She pushed herself free, but the sight of blood on his smooth chest caused her to stop and glance down at her palms.

"Let me see," he said, taking her hands in his. He led her over to the bedside table and held them under the lamp for a better look. "What happened?"

"I fell when…I climbed over the rail of the balcony," she said, realizing her knees were about to give way.

"How the hell did you get out there?"

"I walked—" she shuddered at the thought of what she'd done "—along the ledge."

Whether it was the thought of how easily she could

have fallen to her death or from the tingling sensation radiating where his warm hands held hers, she wasn't sure, but if she didn't sit down, and soon, she was in very real danger of falling on the floor at the man's big bare feet.

Sinking onto the side of the bed, she sucked in a sharp breath at the pain radiating down her shins. "Ooh!"

Without asking for permission, the man shoved her skirt up to just above her knees. "Damn! You're skinned up pretty bad, sweetpea." He reached over to a big red-and-black gym bag sitting on the end of the bed. "Take off your panty hose."

Before she could tell him she'd do no such thing, there was a loud pounding on the door in the outer room. She jumped at the sound.

"Were you expecting someone?" she asked cautiously.

He looked through the doorway into the sitting area of the suite, then at her. "No." Grinning, he shrugged. "But I wasn't expecting you, either."

"It's Patrick." Panic welled up inside her as she stood up and looked around the room. "He can't find me. I have to leave."

Brant Wakefield watched the woman desperately look for a way to escape the bedroom of his suite. She was as skittish as a pasture-raised colt. If he didn't reassure her, and damn quick, he had no doubt she'd be crawling back out onto that ledge.

"Hey, sweetpea, don't worry. I don't know who Patrick is, or why you're trying to get away from him, but I won't give you away." He walked to the door. "Sit tight. I'll get rid of whoever's out there, then we'll take care of bandaging those scrapes."

Pulling the bedroom door almost shut, Brant walked across the sitting area. As soon as he got rid of whoever was on the other side of the outer door, he intended to get some answers from his unexpected guest.

Another knock, this time harder, came from the other side. Brant squinted one eye and looked through the peephole. A man wearing a dark-gray, pin-striped suit stood with his fist raised to impatiently pound on the door again.

Aw, hell. The guy was a "suit." If there was one thing Brant despised, it was a "suit." You just couldn't trust them. And Brant would bet good money that the slick-looking suit on the other side of the door was the one the lady in his bedroom wanted to avoid.

Brant sized up his opponent. He was at least six inches taller and outweighed the guy by a good thirty pounds. And unless the little weasel held a black belt in martial arts, Brant could take him in a fight. Easy.

Sure his expression reflected his irritation, as well as his disdain, Brant released the locks and threw the door open wide. "What the hell do *you* want?" he demanded.

The suit took a step back. "I…uh, I'm sorry to disturb you, but I'm looking for my fiancée." He held a picture up for Brant's inspection. "I was wondering if you've seen her."

Brant didn't like lying. It was dishonest any way you

looked at it. But he was well aware of his state of undress. It wouldn't be his fault if the guy assumed that Brant had been playing some kind of bedroom game with a willing little filly.

"The only woman I've seen lately is the one taking off her panty hose in the bedroom," he answered truthfully. He folded his arms across his bare chest and stared down at the man. "And I was right in the middle of helping her when *you* interrupted us."

The man's grin made Brant immediately drop his arms to his sides and clench his hands into tight fists. He'd like nothing more than the pleasure of wiping that lecherous smile off the man's pasty face with a good right hook.

Brant was once again reminded of why he disliked most of the suits of the world. They used their expensive clothes to hide their unscrupulous nature. But the guy standing before him was one, Brant knew for a fact, he'd despise no matter what kind of clothes he wore. He just had a shifty look about him that set Brant's teeth on edge and said louder than words that the guy was as crooked as a barrel of fishhooks.

"I'll let you get back to your evening's entertainment," the man said, pulling a card and an ink pen from the inside pocket of his suit coat. Scribbling on the back, he handed it to Brant. "Here's my name and room number. If you see a rather plain-looking woman wearing a khaki-colored skirt and an off-white blouse, give me a call."

Brant had to hold himself in check to keep from punching the guy right square in the nose. The woman might not be a beauty queen, but she deserved to be thought of by her fiancé as more than just "plain-looking." He turned the business card over in his hand and noticed that it read Patrick Elsworth, Esquire, Certified Public Accountant. Shrugging, Brant reached to close the door.

"She wears black, plastic-framed glasses," the man added as Brant slammed the door in his face.

Securing the locks, he walked over to the wastebasket by the desk and tossed the card inside, then pushed the door open to the bedroom. The woman was nowhere in sight.

"Lady?" Nothing. "Hey, lady?"

Where the hell could she have gone? Was she outside on the balcony? Or worse yet, walking the ledge around the building again?

His heart pounded at the thought. Although he didn't know the woman, he sure as hell didn't want to see anything happen to her. Just when he decided to check the balcony, the bathroom door opened a crack.

"Is he gone?" she whispered.

Brant nodded. "We won't be hearing any more from him tonight."

She opened the door wider and stood there looking uncertain. With her black-rimmed glasses and the dubious look in her green eyes, she reminded him of his first-grade teacher, Mrs. Andrews, when he'd tried to tell her that he hadn't meant to slip a grasshopper down the back of Susie Parker's dress—that it had jumped there all by itself.

"How do you know he won't be back?" the woman asked, sounding as doubtful as she looked.

"Because I made it clear that I didn't appreciate being disturbed," Brant said. Grinning, he innocently splayed his hands and shrugged, hoping to put her at ease. "I can't help it if he thinks I'm in here getting up close and personal with a buckle bunny."

"What's that?" She shook her head as she limped toward the door. "Don't tell me. I think I have a pretty good idea already."

Brant followed her into the sitting room. She'd taken her straight, pale-blond hair down from the twist at the back of her head and he was amazed at how much younger she looked. When he'd first seen her staring at him through the balcony door, he'd have judged her to be somewhere in her mid to late thirties. But now? Shoot, she couldn't be more than twenty-four or twenty-five years old.

He also noticed that she'd removed her torn panty hose. Swallowing hard, he tried to wipe the image of her trim calves and slender ankles from his obviously overtired brain by averting his gaze to her feet. It surprised him to see her toenails were painted with fire engine-red polish. It just seemed out of place, considering the rest of her attire was so—he refused to use the word *plain* to describe her—conservative. Yeah, that was the word. Conservative.

As she walked across the room, Brant decided it was none of his business what color the lady painted her toenails, or that she was hiding great-looking legs beneath that oversize skirt.

"Have a seat and take it easy while I go throw on some clothes." Focusing on the injuries he'd noticed when he first escorted her from the balcony into his bedroom, he added, "Then I'll take care of patching up your knees."

She nodded and sank down on the couch. Staring up at him for several seconds, she pushed her glasses up with a brush of her hand and cleared her throat. "I didn't mean to be nosy, but I couldn't help noticing that you have several jars of greasepaint on the counter in your bathroom. Are you some type of clown?" she asked politely.

"Not exactly." He almost laughed out loud. From the cautious tone of her voice, it sounded more like she was asking if he was some kind of crook who used greasepaint for his disguises. "I'm a bullfighter."

"A matador?" She looked doubtful again. "I didn't think they painted their faces."

"Wrong kind of bullfighting," he said, unable to keep his smile from breaking through. "I work rodeos and bull riding events. I'm in town this weekend with the PBR."

"What's that?"

"Professional Bull Riders."

"That's very…interesting, Mr…." She paused, her cheeks coloring a pretty pink. "I'm so embarrassed. You've gone out of your way to be kind to me and I don't even know your name."

"Brant Wakefield."

"I'm Anastasia Devereaux," she said, politely extending her hand.

"Glad to meet you, Miss Devereaux." He reached out

to shake her hand, but the moment her soft palm touched his, a jolt of electric current zinged up his arm and exploded in his chest. He swallowed hard and, pulling his hand back, flexed his fingers. He must be getting a case of that carpal tunnel something or other that everyone was talking about having.

Incapable of speech, he turned and walked into the bedroom. He'd been getting ready to take a shower when she knocked on the balcony door, but that could wait until after he'd taken care of her scraped-up hands and knees. The way she'd limped when she crossed the sitting room, he'd bet her knees were getting sore as hell.

He tugged the knot of the towel loose at his waist, pulled on a pair of underwear, jeans and a T-shirt, then reached back into his heavy-duty canvas bag for the first-aid kit he took everywhere he went. Heading back into the sitting room, he stopped short at the sight of her huddled on the couch, her arms wrapped around her middle, shivering uncontrollably. A knot formed in his gut and he could have kicked himself in the rear for not offering her a blanket or his coat.

Pulling the coffee table out of the way, Brant knelt in front of her, set the first-aid kit on the carpet beside him, then rubbed his hands up and down her arms in an attempt to warm her. Unless he missed his guess, her reaction had more to do with walking along the ledge than with braving the freezing temperature outside.

"I'll get my jacket for you," he said, rising to his feet.

He went back into the bedroom, then returned to

drape his heavy, leather-and-wool varsity-style jacket over her shoulders. As an afterthought, he lifted her hair from beneath the collar. The thick shoulder-length strands flowed over his hands like golden silk threads and he had to fight to keep from tangling his fingers in them.

"That should warm you up in no time," he said, taking a step back. It for damn sure raised his temperature several notches and had him wondering what the hell had gotten into him.

"Th-thank y-you," she said through chattering teeth.

Kneeling in front of her again, he lifted her skirt above her knees and tried not to notice the lovely expanse of smooth feminine thighs mere inches from his fingers. He took a deep breath, uncapped a small bottle of antiseptic and hoped the smell would clear his head.

"Would you like to tell me what this is all about?" he asked as he soaked a piece of gauze with the antiseptic, then dabbed it on her scraped skin.

"No," she said quickly. She hesitated for several seconds before she finally spoke again. "I'm sorry, but I don't think that would be a good idea."

Brant stopped tending her wounds to study her expression. He could tell she wasn't sure she should confide in him. All things considered, he could understand her hesitation. After all, she didn't know him or anything about his character.

"You can trust me," he said, looking directly into her wide green eyes. Eyes that if a man wasn't careful, he could get lost in. He suddenly had to clear his throat before he could speak. "I just want to help you out of whatever trouble you're in."

"What makes you think that I'm in trouble?" she asked, sounding defensive.

"Something drove you out onto that ledge." He turned his attention back to the abrasions on her knees. "And I'm betting it wasn't that you just wanted to get a breath of fresh air." He capped the small bottle of anti-septic and reached for a tube of antibacterial ointment. "Why don't you start by explaining why you're running from your fiancé?"

Her hand shook as she pushed her glasses up on her nose again. "I don't know you."

"That's true," he said, nodding. "But under the circum-stances, I don't think you have a choice. It's clear you need help and since I don't see anyone else volunteering for the job, I'm your best bet." A sudden thought caused him to glance up at her. "Did the suit get rough with you?"

If he had, Brant had every intention of finding old pasty-faced Patrick and making him sorry he'd ever been born. No man abused a woman when Brant was around to put a stop to it. Bar none.

"Not exactly," she answered, shaking her head. "He was too busy threatening—" Snapping her mouth shut, she sat there staring at Brant for several long moments. "I…don't think it would be wise to involve you," she finally said, sounding tired.

"Why don't you tell me what's going on and let me

make up my own mind?" He applied the salve to the scrapes on her knees as he waited for her to decide what to do. Just when he thought she was going to decline his offer, he heard her take a deep breath.

Glancing up, he caught her watching him. The apprehension in her big green eyes twisted his gut. Anastasia Devereaux was up against a wall and scared witless.

"You've been more than kind, Mr. Wakefield. But—"

"The name's Brant."

She nodded. "Patrick is running out of options. And desperate men resort to desperate measures. I don't want to involve you in my problems, Brant."

The sound of her soft voice saying his name did strange things to his insides and quickened his pulse. He concentrated on placing squares of gauze on her wounds and tried to ignore the feeling. He must have landed on his head earlier in the evening and just couldn't remember it. The lady in front of him wasn't his type. Not by a long shot.

Aside from the fact that the women he normally found attractive wore makeup and their clothes fit more snugly, Anastasia's demeanor and manners practically shouted culture and refined living. For that matter, so did her name. And although his bank account proved that he was quite successful at bullfighting, and his degree in ranch management attested to the fact that he was far from being a country bumpkin, he sure as hell wasn't the refined, academic type.

Besides, she was engaged to that slick little weasel, Patrick. And Brant wasn't one to tread on another man's territory, even if the guy wasn't good enough to breathe the same air she did.

"It would be best if I found a way to escape the hotel undetected and leave you out of this," she said, reminding Brant that whether she was his type of woman or not, the lady was in a heap of trouble and needed help.

"I can take care of myself," he said, unwrapping a roll of gauze. He wound it around her leg, then secured the bandage with tape. "And I give you my word that your fiancé will have to come through me before he lays a hand on you, Annie."

Anastasia sucked in a sharp breath. The only people who had ever defied her grandmother's decree that she be called anything but Anastasia had been her parents, Jack and Christine Devereaux. They'd called her Annie, and she'd forgotten how much she missed the informal shortening of her name.

A deep sadness knifed through her as she thought of her parents. Even though they had died nineteen years ago—just after her fifth birthday—she still remembered them and couldn't help but wonder how different her life would have been if they'd lived to raise her.

She took a deep, steadying breath to chase away her sense of loss. It was nonproductive to spend time dwelling on what might have been. Even if her grandmother had never allowed her to experience anything even remotely adventurous, she'd had a very nice childhood. Her grandmother said so. And whatever Carlotta

Whittmeyer said, well, that's just the way it was. No one dared contradict one of her grandmother's edicts. Ever.

Turning her attention back to the man tending her wounds, Annie bit her lower lip. Brant Wakefield seemed trustworthy. And heaven only knew she could use a friend right now.

"I…don't know where to start," she said, not at all certain she should be telling a stranger why she'd fled from the room next door and taken the uncharacteristic risk of walking along the narrow ledge surrounding the hotel. Or why it was imperative that she avoid Patrick Elsworth for the next week.

"Why don't you start at the beginning?" Brant asked, winking at her.

His smile was encouraging and her heart skipped a beat at the gesture. She refused to acknowledge it as anything but a case of nerves from the evening's harrowing events. She never had been, and never would be, the excitable type.

"Patrick is my grandmother's accountant," Annie said, choosing her words carefully.

"Is that how the two of you met?"

She shook her head. "No. He was a regular borrower at the library where I work. He'd been coming in for several weeks before he asked me to have dinner with him. That was a little over a year ago."

"So you've been seeing him for some time?" Brant asked, one eyebrow raised in question.

"Yes." Suddenly feeling as if all the strength had been drained from her body, Annie leaned her head against the back of the couch. "And before this goes any further, I think I should set the record straight. Patrick Elsworth never has been, nor will he ever be, my fiancé."

Chapter 2

Brant sat back on his heels to stare at the sparkling diamond on the third finger of Annie's left hand. "Then what's that?" he asked, pointing to the impressive ring. "Last time I heard, a rock like that is a man's way of branding a woman as his."

"It's the engagement ring Patrick *tried* to give me," she answered, as if that explained everything.

"This guy asked you to marry him, you took the ring, but you aren't engaged." Brant wanted to make sure he had things straight.

"Correct."

Brant turned his attention back to the first-aid kit as he pondered her explanation. Maybe it was logical to a woman, but it didn't make a damn bit of sense to him. Unless she…

He shot her a glance. The diamond had to be worth several thousand dollars. Had she stolen the expensive piece of jewelry?

As if she'd read his mind, she shook her head. "Before you ask if I'm a thief, the answer is no. The ring rightfully belongs to my grandmother and I have every intention of seeing that she gets it."

Brant was more confused than ever. "You mean this guy was trying to give you an engagement ring that belongs to your grandmother, and you're wearing it, but you didn't accept it and you're not going to marry him."

"Exactly."

"Are you sure you started at the beginning?" he asked. "Either I've missed something, or you've left out a bunch of pretty important details."

She fidgeted with the hem of her skirt before she pulled it down over her bandaged knees, blocking his view of her shapely thighs. "I've been seeing Patrick socially for the past year—"

"I got that much," Brant said, rising to his feet. He pulled the coffee table back into place, then sat on it, putting himself directly in front of her. Reaching for her right hand, he began cleaning the abrasions on her palm. He tried to ignore the fact that her skin was possibly the softest he'd ever felt. "Why don't you fast-forward to the events that led up to your being in his hotel room and what drove you out onto a ten-inch ledge?" he asked to distract himself.

"We'd been seeing each other for a few months when Patrick started giving my grandmother tips on investments and tax shelters, even though she already had a very competent accountant," Annie explained.

Brant wrapped gauze around her hand. "Let me guess. It wasn't long before she switched bean counters."

She nodded. "Correct. Grandmother dismissed Mr. Bennett, the CPA she'd had for years, to hire Patrick. At first, everything seemed fine. But then I started noticing a change in him."

Brant replaced the contents of the first-aid kit. "What was different?"

"It wasn't anything overly obvious, at first," she said, fingering the expensive engagement ring. "Patrick started wearing nicer, more expensive clothing, and I thought he might have been put on retainer by a few more clients." She shook her head. "But in the last couple of months he's replaced his economy car with a BMW, bought a new home in a prestigious subdivision and furnished it with pricey antiques and original art. I thought he might have gone into debt for all of it. Then he started bragging that he'd paid cash for everything but the house. That's when I realized something was seriously wrong. An accountant who opened his firm on a shoestring budget in a town the size of ours, couldn't possibly afford to do those things in less than a year's time."

"You aren't from Saint Louis?"

"No. We live in Herrin, a small town southeast of here. Over in Illinois. The population is somewhere around ten thousand, so I'm certain he hasn't been making *that* kind of money."

Common sense told Brant that it took a lot longer than a year to build a business to the level where it paid that well, even in a city. "It does sound pretty suspicious," Brant admitted, snapping the lid shut on the medical kit.

"That's what I thought." She continued to twist the diamond ring around the third finger of her left hand. "But until this evening, that was all I had—suspicions."

Brant jerked his head up to look at her. "So now you have proof?"

She nibbled her lower lip before she finally answered. "Not exactly."

"Then how can you be sure he's been stealing money from your grandmother?" Getting her to give him all the details was like pulling teeth.

She suddenly stood to pace the room. As he watched her, he found the sight of his big jacket dwarfing her small frame oddly endearing. He sucked in a sharp breath. Where the hell had that come from?

Now he knew for certain that he must have landed on his head sometime during the first round of the bull riding event. He reached up and ran a hand over his scalp. But there weren't any lumps or tender places…

"I know Patrick has been embezzling from Grandmother because he admitted it this evening just before he asked me to marry him," Annie said as she walked the perimeter of the sitting room.

"You mean this jerk admitted to stealing from your

grandmother, then wanted you to marry him?" Brant asked incredulously.

"Yes."

He shook his head. "I'll give the little weasel this much, he's got a set of solid-brass balls."

She stopped pacing to look at him. "That's exactly what I thought. But when I told Patrick that I'd rather die than marry him—" She closed her eyes and shuddered. "He said that could easily be arranged."

Brant was on his feet and standing in front of her in a split second. "The guy threatened your life?"

"Yes."

"Do you think he meant it?"

She nodded. "Yes, I believe so." Nervously adjusting her glasses, she sighed. "In fact, I know he did. He's just that desperate."

Brant's gut burned with anger and he found himself regretting that he hadn't buried his fist in the suit's face when he'd had the opportunity. Placing his hands on her shoulders, Brant tried to ignore the current that seemed to radiate from her body to his as he stared down at her. "You have to call the police, Annie."

"And tell them what?" she asked, her green eyes shadowed with doubts. "Even though Patrick admitted to stealing money from my grandmother and threatened me, I have no proof and no witnesses. And we both know if the authorities inquired about either incident, he would deny everything." She shook her head. "They couldn't do anything, because it would be a case of he said, she said—his word against mine."

Mulling over what she'd said, Brant had to admit that Annie was probably right. The police couldn't do anything without some type of solid evidence.

"If you suspected him of being that big of a snake, what were you doing in his room?"

"I've asked myself that same question about a thousand times since dinner," she said, sounding disgusted. "All I can come up with is naiveté or sheer stupidity. And at this point, I'm leaning toward the latter."

"You're being too hard on yourself, Annie," Brant said, slipping his hands beneath the jacket to massage the tension he felt in her slender shoulders.

"I should have known better." She shrugged. "But Grandmother has a couple of accounts in the banks up here, and when Patrick told me he had a business meeting in Saint Louis with one of the bankers, and asked me to come along, I thought I might have the opportunity to find something to incriminate him."

"I take it you didn't find anything?" Even though her silk blouse lay between his palms and her satiny skin, Brant enjoyed the feel of her softness beneath his hands.

"No, I didn't find out anything because there was never a meeting scheduled." Closing her eyes, she shook her head. "It was nothing more than a ploy to get me to accompany him to this hotel and get me to take a trip down the aisle. He said that he'd known I was getting suspicious and that it was just a matter of time before I told my grandmother. So he bought this ring with more of my grandmother's money and here I am."

Brant stopped rubbing her shoulders. Now he was really confused. "How would the two of you getting married solve anything? You could still tell your grandmother and she could have him arrested."

Annie opened her eyes and shook her head ruefully. "Patrick knows how Grandmother is. She would never file charges against her only granddaughter's husband, no matter what he'd done. It would create too much of a scandal." She shook her head. "And anything that casts a bad light on the Whittmeyer family is to be avoided at all costs."

Brant detected a bitter undertone to her quietly spoken explanation. Anger twisted his gut to think that her grandmother would sacrifice Annie and her happiness for the sake of the family name. Stepping away from her, he stuffed his hands in the hip pockets of his jeans before he did something stupid like pull her into his arms to offer her comfort. The trouble was, he wasn't sure comfort was all he wanted to offer. Which, all things considered, was ridiculous. He'd known the woman less than an hour.

"Why not call your grandmother, fill her in on what you know and let her get an auditor to go over her accounts?" he asked, wondering why his voice suddenly sounded like a rusty hinge. He cleared his throat. "Or maybe she can just fire this character and chalk all of it up to experience."

Annie's soft sigh sent a streak of protectiveness straight through him. "I can't. Grandmother is on a tour of European museums and won't return for another

week." She walked over to sink down on the couch.
"And to tell you the truth, I'm not even sure which
country she's in right now."

"Is there anyone else you could get hold of?" Brant
asked. "What about your parents? Or maybe an aunt or
uncle?"

Annie shook her head. "My parents died nineteen
years ago. All Grandmother and I have are each other."
She pulled his coat more closely around her. "Walking
that ledge wasn't the smartest thing I've ever done, but
it was all I could think of. I wasn't about to marry
Patrick, and I have to stay alive until Grandmother
returns so I can explain what's going on."

Annie looked so small and lonely sitting there in his
big coat that it was all Brant could do to keep from
sitting down beside her and pulling her into his arms.
Instead, he ran a hand across the back of his neck and
tried to get his mind off the way she looked and return
to the business at hand.

"How did you manage to get away from him long
enough to crawl out there and make it over to my
balcony?" Brant finally asked, deciding it was best to
let her do the talking. Otherwise, he might end up acting
on his first impulse.

"Patrick had gone into the sitting area of his suite to
make phone calls to reserve a chapel in Las Vegas and
make airline reservations. That's when I grabbed the
ring and escaped." She shuddered and Brant figured she
was remembering how scary it had been out on that
ledge. "Now all I have to do is find some tangible proof

of my suspicions and figure out a way to avoid him for the next week," she said, looking tired.

"Going home is out of the question," Brant guessed, thinking out loud. "I'm betting that's the first place he'll look for you."

She nodded. "Hiding out in Herrin would be next to impossible. Everyone in town knows me." Taking her glasses off, she rubbed the bridge of her nose with thumb and forefinger. "But I really have nowhere else to go and no money to get there. I left my purse in Patrick's suite, along with my coat."

Brant had to concentrate hard on what she was saying. Without her glasses, she looked completely different. And although she wouldn't be considered pretty by conventional standards, she was *very* attractive.

"Don't worry about where you'll go or the money to get you there. I'll take you with me," he blurted out before he could stop himself.

Time seemed to come to a complete halt as they stared at each other. But the more Brant thought about the idea, the more it made sense. He might have met Annie Devereaux only an hour ago, and they might come from completely different walks of life, but it just wasn't in him to leave a woman to fend for herself when she was in trouble. No siree. He could no more walk away and leave her alone to deal with her problems than he could stop the sun from rising in the east every morning.

"I truly appreciate the offer, Brant. But I can't involve you any more than you already are," Annie said, standing to remove his coat. She handed the leather-sleeved jacket to him. "I'll find a way—"

"Too late, sweetpea," Brant interrupted. Smiling, he hooked his thumb over his shoulder toward the bedroom. "I got involved the minute you knocked on my balcony door."

"But—"

"But nothing. I have the way." He chuckled. "And believe me, I have more than enough means to get you out of here and keep you safe until your grandmother returns from her trip. And that's just what I'm going to do."

Annie blinked as she tried to comprehend what Brant was saying. "Stay with you? For a week?"

"Yep."

"I can't do that."

"Why not?"

"Because…because…I just can't," she stammered. "I don't know you or anything about you."

He nodded. "I understand that. But we can remedy that right now."

As she stared at him, Annie couldn't seem to focus on anything but how handsome he was and what a nice smile he had. Brant Wakefield was—as Tiffany, her teenage assistant at the library, would say—really hot. His eyes were quite possibly the bluest she'd ever seen and radiated an integrity that she'd never seen in Patrick's pale-gray gaze.

But that was only the beginning of Brant's rugged appeal. The sound of his sexy baritone would take the breath of every female who still had a pulse. And his touch was…magic. That's the only word she could think of that even remotely described how it had felt when he'd cleaned and bandaged her skinned knees and hand. His fingers brushing her leg as he tended the scrapes had sent tingling sensations straight up her thigh to the most feminine part of her. The fact that he had a body to die for didn't hurt her impression of him, either.

"What would you like to know about me?" Brant asked, interrupting her introspection as he placed his coat back around her shoulders.

Annie sucked in a sharp breath at his nearness and the mingled scents of spicy cologne, leather and man swirling around her. Brant Wakefield was too male, and much too close for her peace of mind.

She sank back down on the couch in order to put distance between them. "What was the question?"

He once again seated himself on the coffee table directly in front of her. Resting his forearms on his knees, he patiently repeated his question. "What would you like to know about me?"

How your lips would feel as you kissed me? How your body would feel pressed to mine if we…?

Annie gulped and glanced down at her tightly twisted hands, resting in her lap. What on earth had gotten into her? She wasn't in the habit of fantasizing about men she dated, let alone a total stranger. Which Brant was.

"I…uh, what do you want me to know?" she finally managed to ask.

His smile was so darned charming that her stomach
fluttered wildly. "Let's see. You already know my name
and that I'm a bullfighter in town with the PBR." He
paused for a moment. "I'm thirty-two, I own the
Lonetree Ranch in central Wyoming with my brothers,
Morgan and Colt. And when I get too old to dodge
bulls for a living, I intend to raise bucking horses for
rodeo. Anything else you'd like to know?"

Her gaze flew to his left hand. He didn't wear a
wedding band, but that didn't mean he wasn't commit-
ted to a relationship. "Won't your girlfriend object to
my being with you for the next week?"

"I don't have one."

"Oh."

He grinned. "Now, don't go getting the wrong impression there, sweetpea. I like women. A lot. I just
haven't found the right one yet."

"I never thought…" Heat flooded her cheeks.
Anything she said would end up embarrassing her
more. Deciding to change the direction of the conversation, she asked, "But how would you get me out of
the hotel without Patrick seeing us?"

"Leave that to me," Brant said, rising to his feet. He
walked over to the phone on the desk and picked up
the receiver.

Annie couldn't believe she was actually contemplating going along with his crazy scheme. But as she
watched him punch in a phone number, she realized
that as scary as the idea was of spending the next week

with the most handsome cowboy—make that the only cowboy—she'd ever met, it was also oddly exhilarating.

"Hey, Sarah. It's Brant. I need your help with something," he said into the phone. He paused. "Yeah, I know what time it is." Grinning, he held the receiver away from his ear and winked at Annie. "Sarah's the on-site event coordinator. She's just a little bent out of shape right now over my waking her up at one-thirty in the morning."

"Maybe this wasn't such a good idea," Annie said, hearing the woman's raised voice all the way across the room.

He chuckled. "She'll get over it." Placing the receiver back to his ear, he nodded. "Yeah, I know you'll get even. Now jot this down. I need you to pick up a woman's hat, shirt and jeans in size…" He turned back to Annie. "What size do you wear?"

"Ten, but—"

"Shoe size?"

"Seven."

"Make the shirt and jeans a size eight, a pair of boots in a ladies' size seven and a hat that would fit you." He listened a moment, then laughed. "Yeah, I know I owe you, Sarah. Just charge everything to my room and have it here first thing in the morning. Oh, we'll also need a PBR varsity jacket in small added to that order."

As soon as he hung up the phone, Annie shook her head. "I can't wear a size eight or anything in a small size. They'll be too tight."

His charming grin made her lower stomach do that strange little fluttering thing again. "Trust me, sweetpea. They'll fit just fine."

The next morning Brant checked his watch for the fifth time in as many minutes. As soon as Sarah dropped off the things he'd asked her to buy, Annie had spoken to the woman privately, then waited for Sarah to return with some undisclosed item, grabbed the packages of clothes and disappeared through the bedroom door. That had been a good half hour ago and he hadn't seen her since.

Just when he decided she'd probably drowned in the shower, or crawled back out onto the ledge to escape him the way she had the crooked little bean counter, Brant heard the bedroom door open. Spinning around, he opened his mouth to ask what had taken so long, but the sight of the woman standing uncertainly in the doorway brought him up short.

He grinned. "Damn, sweetpea. You clean up real nice."

She gave him a doubtful look over the top of her glasses. "I'm not too sure about this."

"What's wrong?" He didn't see a single thing wrong with the way she looked. Far from it. In the figure category Annie Devereaux was about as perfect as a woman could get.

"These jeans may be made of stretch denim, but they're still a lot tighter than I'm used to," she protested. "And the blouse is a bit too snug."

When she twisted to look at her behind in the mirror above the desk, the fabric of the red and blue western-cut blouse pulled tight over her breasts, causing Brant's mouth to go bone dry. The shirt was snug all right, but in a good way. A damn good way.

Turning, she bent over to pick up a tag that she'd dropped on the carpet. His heart stopped, then took off at a gallop. Did she have anything on under those jeans? He'd seen more women in stretch jeans than he could count and they'd all had a little ridge where their panties went around their legs. But Annie didn't have any kind of detectable line to indicate that she did or didn't have on underwear. The thought that she might not have on anything inside those jeans sent his blood pressure up several notches.

Averting his eyes to the top of her blond head, he cleared the rust from his throat. "The clothes are perfect. You'll blend in with the crowd and Elsworth won't recognize you if he walks right by you."

She nibbled at her lower lip. "I suppose that's what we want, isn't it?"

Brant nodded. "That's exactly what we want, sweetpea. It's your ticket out of here."

"I guess you're right." Lifting her long hair and twisting it as if to put it up in a bun, she shrugged. "Once we get out of the hotel, I'll find somewhere to change back into my skirt and blouse."

"Not unless you want to stick out like a sore thumb," he said bluntly. He adjusted his black Resistol, then picked up the matching one Sarah had bought for Annie. Handing it to her, he said, "Leave your hair down and put this on."

She stared at the wide-brimmed hat in her hands. "I've never worn anything like this."

"All the more reason to put it on." He took the hat from her and positioned it on top of her head. "Elsworth won't be looking for a shapely blond in jeans, boots and a black Resistol. He's going to have his eye out for a little wren in baggy clothes."

"A what?"

Brant chuckled. "In that oversize tan skirt and off-white blouse you looked like a frightened little wren."

"I did not."

"Did, too."

"My clothes are not baggy," she said defensively. "They're just not formfitting. And neutral colors are quite fashionable."

He snorted. "If you're trying to look like a wren." Stepping back, he allowed his gaze to travel from the top of her hat to her new boots. He frowned. "Can you see without your glasses?"

"Not well." She pushed the black frames up with a brush of her hand. "I'm nearsighted and things at a distance are kind of fuzzy."

"But you won't walk into a wall or anything like that if you take them off?"

"No."

"Then let me have them," he said, extending his hand. "I'll put them in my shirt pocket and give them back once we're out of here and on the way to the arena."

Annie dutifully removed her glasses and handed them to him. "I've thought about getting contacts, but

I've worn glasses so long, I'm not sure how I would look without them."

He grinned. "Trust me, sweetpea. You'd look just fine."

Was that appreciation she detected in Brant's eyes? The kind of look a man had when he found a woman attractive?

Her heart skipped a beat, but she quickly abandoned the silly notion. Whether she wore glasses or not, she never had been, nor would she ever be, the type of woman that men noticed for longer than it took to acknowledge her presence, then dismiss her.

She watched Brant move around the room as he packed the rest of his things in the big red-and-black duffel bag. The glint she thought she'd seen in his deep blue gaze was probably nothing more than an illusion due to her blurred vision from not wearing her glasses.

"Get the clothes you had on before you changed," he said as he scooped up a handful of coins and his wallet from the desktop. "When we leave the Savvis Center this evening, we'll go straight to the airport."

When she retrieved her skirt and blouse, with her underthings hidden safely within the folds, he stuffed them into the bag and zipped it shut. The sight activated the butterflies in her stomach. There was something oddly intimate about having her clothes packed with his in the duffel bag.

"Are you ready to go?" he asked, holding the varsity jacket he'd had the event coordinator bring along with the other clothes for her. Thankfully the woman had been understanding when Annie requested she make another trip to the store for the change of underwear that Annie had been too embarrassed to request the night before, and that Brant hadn't thought of.

"Not really," she said, unable to stop a nervous giggle from escaping as she slipped her arms into the waist-length coat with the PBR logo on the back. "What time does the bull riding start?"

"In a couple of hours." He shrugged into his own jacket, then picked up the duffel bag and guided her toward the door. "But we need to catch a ride to the Savvis Center and grab a bite to eat in the VIP lounge before I have to get my clothes changed and my face on."

"Your face?"

He laughed as he released the locks and opened the door. "The greasepaint."

Annie had to force her boot-clad feet to step out of the safety of Brant's room and into the hall. To her relief, there were no other hotel guests in the corridor.

She must have looked as apprehensive as she felt, because Brant reached down and took her hand in his as they walked to the elevator. "Hang in there, Annie," he said quietly. "Everything is going to be all right."

His warm palm securely holding hers was reassuring and she found herself beginning to believe that his crazy scheme just might work. "Brant, I really appreciate everything you've done for—"

But before she could finish thanking him, he suddenly dropped the duffel bag and tugged her into his arms. Reaching up, he pushed the brim of his hat up, then did the same to hers.

"What do you think you're—"

"Hush, sweetpea," he said a moment before his firm lips covered hers in a kiss that made her knees wobble and curled her toes inside her brand-new boots.

Chapter 3

As Brant brought his mouth down on Annie's, he tried to keep an eye on the man he'd seen step off the elevator. Patrick Elsworth was walking right toward them and Brant wanted to make sure he kept her turned so that she wouldn't be recognized.

But the feel of her soft lips beneath his and the slight weight of her pressed against him sent Brant's blood pressure up close to stroke range and made concentrating on anything but the woman in his arms damn near impossible. He tightened his hold to draw her more fully against him and her lips parted on a small gasp. He couldn't have stopped himself from deepening the kiss if his life depended on it.

The silkiness of her straight blond hair flowing over his hands, the sweet taste of her as her tongue timidly met his, had him forgetting all about the man approaching them. Annie kissed like a shy angel, but her full breasts pressed to his chest reminded him that she was a flesh-and-blood woman with a body made for a man's loving. Brant's lower body responded in a way that totally agreed with the thought.

"Good morning," Elsworth said, stopping beside them.

Brant broke the kiss and nodded a silent greeting, but continued to hold Annie close for several reasons. First of all, he was afraid she might panic and turn so that the man recognized her. Second, if he didn't hold on to her, Brant wasn't sure he could keep himself from hauling off and knocking the cocky little weasel into the middle of next week. But the biggest, most distracting reason he continued to hold her was far simpler than the first two. She just felt too damn good to let go.

When Elsworth failed to move on past them, Brant raised an eyebrow. "Was there something you wanted?"

The man nodded. "I'm still looking for my fiancée. I don't suppose either one of you have seen her this morning, have you?"

Brant felt Annie's body stiffen at the man's reference to their "engagement." Shaking his head, Brant tightened his arms around her and lowered his head to nuzzle the side of her neck. "Like I told you last night, the only woman I've seen is the one I'm holding right now."

Brant watched the man's gaze rake Annie's backside,
lingering on her shapely behind and long slender legs
encased in the snug denim. A fierce protectiveness
surged through Brant and he possessively slid his hand
down to her bottom in order to block the man's view.
When he looked back up, Elsworth wore the same las-
civious expression that had set Brant's teeth on edge the
night before, and had him wanting to wipe off with his
fist this morning.

"No wonder you didn't have time to discuss the
matter with me last night," Elsworth said, winking at
Brant.

"And I don't intend to talk to you about it now,"
Brant said, cutting off anything else the man could say.

He concentrated on kissing the hollow behind
Annie's ear in order to hide the intense reaction he was
sure colored his own expression. Patrick Elsworth's
bold perusal of Annie's body had pure fury burning at
Brant's gut. Which was ridiculous, considering that he
was only trying to help her get out of the hotel undetected.

When he was sure he had control of the anger roiling
inside him, Brant raised his head to give Elsworth a
pointed look. "If you can't hold on to your woman,
leave the ones of us who can alone."

To his immense satisfaction, Elsworth's irritating
grin disappeared immediately and without another
word he continued down the hall.

"Is he gone?" Annie whispered when Brant kept on
holding her.

"I think so," he answered.

He tried to tell himself that the reason he held her close, still cupping her cute little rear in his hand, was in case Elsworth returned. But the truth of the matter was, he liked the way she felt against him and he wouldn't have minded picking up where he'd left off with the kiss.

The thought brought him up short. What the hell was he thinking? He'd kissed her for one reason and one reason only. To hide her identity from Elsworth. Nothing more.

Releasing her, Brant reached down to pick up his duffel bag, then ushered her to the elevator. "Let's get out of here before the jerk decides to come back," he said, feeling as if his jeans were a couple of sizes too tight in the stride.

Annie followed Brant to the elevator on wobbly legs. Having him hold her to his hard frame, feeling his large hand caress her bottom, had not only startled her to the point of speechlessness, it had unleashed a riot of sensations unlike any she'd ever known. When he took her into his arms, her heart had started racing and her breathing came out in short little puffs. That had been enough to scare her silly, but it was his kiss that made the world feel as if it came to a complete halt. She'd never been kissed like that in all of her twenty-four years.

His firm lips moving over hers had made her head spin, her knees rubbery and her insides flutter. But when his strong tongue dipped inside her mouth to explore, tease and taste, her body had started to tingle in places that had no business tingling. Most disturbing of all, the sensation hadn't stopped yet. And she refused to even begin to think about what the feel of his hand on her bottom had done to her newly awakened libido.

"Ready to catch a cab to the Savvis Center?" Brant asked, slipping a folded piece of paper into the inside pocket of his coat.

Annie looked around. When had they exited the elevator and walked over to the registration desk? She'd been so lost in thought that she'd completely missed Brant checking out of the hotel.

What was wrong with her? She'd never been this easily distracted before. But with her insides quivering like a bowl of Jell-O and her heart skipping every other beat, she supposed it was understandable. What she couldn't comprehend was why she felt more alive than she had in her entire life.

"Are you all right, sweetpea?" Brant asked, looking concerned. He placed his hand at her back to guide her to the double doors leading outside.

"Uh…yes," she finally managed to say, forcing her legs to propel her forward. "I'm ready to leave whenever you are."

"Hey, Brant, wait up," a male voice called to them as they started through the hotel exit. "I want to talk to you about my draw."

She turned to watch a cowboy hurrying across the lobby toward them. "His draw?"

"The bull he's supposed to ride," Brant explained. He shook his head and swore softly. "This is the last thing I wanted to have happen." By the time the man walked up to them, Brant's easy expression had turned to a dark scowl. "I thought you were advised last night not to ride this afternoon."

"It was only a mild concussion," the man said, grinning. "Doc just cleared me to ride." He glanced at Annie, then seemed to do a double take as his gaze veered back, his grin widening. "Who's this lovely lady?"

Annie barely managed to stifle a surprised squeak when Brant slipped his arm around her waist and pulled her firmly against his side. "This is Annie. She's with me."

"Nice to meet you, Annie. I'm Colt Wakefield, this big galoot's younger, better-looking brother."

He extended his hand and even before he'd spoken the obvious, she could tell that Brant and Colt were related. Both had the same dark hair, the same startling blue eyes.

She heard Brant mutter an oath under his breath as she placed her hand in Colt's. "It's nice to meet you, Colt," she said. Was it her imagination, or had Brant tightened his arm around her waist?

"The pleasure's all mine, Annie," Colt said, enveloping her palm in his much larger one.

Colt Wakefield was every bit as good-looking as his older brother. But curiously, she felt none of the tingling sensations from his touch that she experienced from Brant's.

"We were just leaving for the Savvis Center," Brant said, his voice sounding more like a growl than his usual warm baritone.

"I'll ride along and you can tell me what you know about Black Magic," Colt said, following them through the double doors and out into the cold.

As they stood waiting for a cab, Brant held her close, using his big body to shield her from the sharp wind. Despite the bright noon sunshine, the temperature couldn't have been much above freezing. But surprisingly, she found that she was quite warm in the circle of Brant's strong arm.

"Turn out, little brother," Brant said, his tone more of a command than one of advice.

"You know I can't do that, bro," Colt said, shaking his head. "A turn out won't get me any closer to the finals at the end of the season."

"What's a turn out?" Annie asked.

A cab pulled to a stop in front of them and Brant opened the back passenger-side door and motioned for her to get in. He seated himself beside her before he answered, "A turn out is when a rider decides not to ride the bull he's drawn."

Colt slid into the backseat from the other side. "Yeah, Brant wants me to stand behind the chute while the gate opens and Black Magic walks out into the arena without me on his back." He snorted. "No way in hell I'm going to let that happen."

"Look, little brother, this is Black Magic's first season," Brant said, his expression grim. "He's young and unpredictable. You suffered a concussion during last night's round, and the last thing you need is to have your brains scrambled two days in a row."

Annie looked from one man to the other. Both of them wore the same stubborn expressions, had the same defiant tilt to their chins.

"I can't make the finals if I turn out," Colt said, glaring at his brother over the top of her head.

She watched a muscle work along Brant's lean jaw. "October is a long way off," he argued. "You can make up the points between now and then."

"I missed getting to go to the finals last year after Fireball mashed me against the gate and broke my ankle coming out of the chute in Detroit," Colt said stubbornly. "I'm not going to miss out this year because I don't have enough points." When the cab pulled to a stop at the back entrance of the arena, he threw open the door and got out. "Get used to it, big brother, I'm not turning out."

Brant exited on the opposite side, then extended his hand to help her as he continued to argue with his brother. "Dammit, Colt, you—"

"I'll do my job and make the ride," Colt interrupted, slamming the cab's door. "You just be there to do your job when it's time for me to dismount." Turning his attention to Annie, he touched the brim of his black cowboy hat with one finger. "It was nice meeting you, Annie. I hope to see you again sometime."

Before Annie could respond in kind, Colt's angry strides quickly carried him the distance to a door marked Personnel Only. Pulling it open, he disappeared inside the building without a backward glance.

"Damn fool," Brant muttered. "I swear he's twenty-six going on sixteen."

Annie glanced over at him. "Why don't you want your brother to ride this afternoon?"

His expression grim, he paid the cabdriver, then placed his hand at the small of her back to guide her through the same entrance Colt had used only moments before. "Colt's had three concussions in less than two months. If he doesn't start landing on his feet instead of his head, he's not going to have any brains left."

She remained silent as Brant showed his pass to the security guard. She'd never had siblings and had no idea what it would be like to feel so much concern for their well-being.

Brant led her down a long hall into a huge staging area, and looking around, Annie noticed a wide corridor to her left with signs indicating the training and press rooms were located somewhere beyond. To her right, several of the largest, most intimidating beasts she'd ever seen stood docilely inside a labyrinth of portable pens.

"Could I please have my glasses?" she asked, wanting to get a better look. When Brant handed them to her, she put them on and stared openmouthed. "Are those the bulls Colt rides, and you fight?" she asked, shuddering at the sheer size of the animals.

He smiled. "Yep. Those are the best bucking bulls in the world."

She stared for several long seconds at the bulls, then at the handsome cowboy grinning at her. "You and Colt are both out of your minds. Just how many concussions have you suffered lately?"

After they had helped themselves to the buffet tables provided for the riders, contract personnel and their guests in the VIP lounge upstairs, Brant had taken her to a section of seats reserved for family and guests of the PBR, then left to change into his bullfighting outfit. Sitting by herself as she stared out at the huge arena, Annie began to wonder if she wasn't the one who had lost her mind. She'd never before been the impulsive, adventurous type. But in the last fourteen hours, she'd done things she'd never in a million years have dreamed of doing—things that she hoped her grandmother never learned about.

She shook her head. If Carlotta Whittmeyer ever found out that Annie had walked along a hotel's narrow outside ledge several stories above an alley, and spent the night in a hotel suite with a man she didn't even know, Annie would never hear the end of it.

But she really couldn't fault the woman's need to squelch any adventurous streak Annie might have inherited from her parents. Her grandmother had good reason for being overly protective. She'd been faced with a parent's worst nightmare. Carlotta had lost her only daughter—her only child—when Annie's mother and father had been killed.

From the moment they met in college, until their

untimely deaths eight years later, Christine and Jack Devereaux lived by the adage that life was meant to be experienced, not simply observed from the sidelines. They'd loved climbing mountains, exploring caves and navigating the rapids of the swiftest rivers. And when they weren't off in some remote part of the world pursuing their passion for extreme sports, they were planning their next trip. They'd even taken her with them occasionally, instead of leaving her with the nanny.

Had they lived, they might have instilled the same passion for adventure in their daughter. But a white-water rafting accident had claimed their lives when Annie was five. That's when she'd gone to live with her grandmother.

Annie could remember as if it was yesterday how confused she'd been and how apprehensive she'd felt about going to live with a grandmother she barely knew. They'd both been suffering from the terrible loss and should have turned to each other for love and reassurance to see them through the difficult days following the accident. But instead of reaching out to comfort a frightened little girl who couldn't understand why she'd never see her beloved parents again, Carlotta had begun lecturing her on the foolishness of taking risks. That had been nineteen years ago and her grandmother hadn't missed a day since, cautioning Annie about placing herself in unnecessary danger, of the high price that being reckless and impulsive could cost.

Annie sighed. She was pretty sure her grandmother

loved her and had dealt with the situation the only way she'd known how. But Annie couldn't help feeling that their relationship could have—should have—been so much different.

"Do you mind if I join you?" a female voice asked, bringing her back to the present.

Glancing up, Annie saw a pretty, auburn-haired girl of about twenty standing next to her. "I don't mind at all," she said, smiling. "I'd like the company."

"I'm Kaylee Simpson," the girl said, sinking into the seat next to her.

"It's nice to meet you, Kaylee. I'm Ana…Annie."

The lights suddenly went out, ending the introduction, and a single spotlight came on, drawing attention to a cowboy standing in the center of the dirt-covered floor below. He identified himself as the president of the Professional Bull Riders, welcomed the crowd to the final two rounds of the Saint Louis Open and wished everyone an enjoyable afternoon.

When he finished, Kaylee leaned over to ask, "Are you here with someone?"

"Sort of," Annie said evasively.

She was saved any further comment when a loud boom signaled the beginning of a very impressive indoor pyrotechnics and laser display. Annie and Kaylee rose to their feet with the rest of the crowd when the theme from *Mission Impossible* blared from the loudspeakers, and giant sparklers ignited twin flames. The two trails of fire crawled across the dirt floor to the center of the arena, forming a lane that each cowboy riding in the event walked between as he was introduced to the cheering fans.

When Brant's brother Colt was introduced, Kaylee placed two fingers to her lips and let loose with an enthusiastic, ear-splitting whistle. "There's the man I'm going to marry," she said, her smile radiant.

As the opening ceremony ended, they sat back down and Annie watched the staging crew extinguish what was left of the fiery lane on the floor below. "How long have you been engaged to Colt, Kaylee?"

"Oh, we're not engaged," the girl answered, shaking her head. "Colt Wakefield barely knows I'm alive. He thinks I'm a kid."

"But I thought you said—"

"I will marry him," Kaylee said, nodding. "Just as soon as he wakes up and sees me as more than his best friend's baby sister."

When curiosity got the better of her, Annie asked, "How old are you?"

"I'll be twenty next month," Kaylee answered with a smile.

The announcer chose that moment to introduce the bullfighters, and at the mention of Brant's name, Annie's pulse quickened and she had to take a deep breath to steady her breathing. But the figure jogging out to the center of the floor looked nothing like Brant. Aside from the fact that he had bright pink, blue and yellow greasepaint stripes circling his mouth and eyes, the man's cowboy hat was battered and worn-looking, he wore a gaudy-colored long-sleeved shirt and a huge pair of cutoff jeans that looked like a ragged, denim miniskirt. Suspenders held the garment in place, and when he turned around she noticed that bandannas hung like limp flags from the back of the waistband, and large bright patches, advertising western products, covered the seat. Beneath the outlandish garb, it appeared that he wore bicycle shorts. Thick pads covered both knees, and instead of cowboy boots, he wore athletic cleats.

"That's Colt's brother," Kaylee said.

"Brant," Annie agreed absently.

"You know him?"

"Sort of."

Kaylee laughed. "You sort of came with someone and you sort of know Brant." Her face lit with understanding. "Oh my God! Brant's the one you're with."

"No. Yes." Annie's cheeks burned. "It's complicated."

"I don't think I've ever known Brant to bring a date to one of the events before," Kaylee said thoughtfully.

"It's not like that." Annie watched Brant take his place beside a row of gates at the end of the arena. "We're just…just—"

What were they? Friends?

No. She and Brant really didn't even know each other. "We're…acquainted," she finally said, deciding that was the best definition of their unusual alliance.

Clearly not buying the explanation, Kaylee laughed. "If you say so." The girl's expression suddenly changed to one of concern. "You won't say anything to Brant, will you? You know, about my wanting to marry Colt?"

Smiling, Annie shook her head. "Your secret's safe with me."

"Thanks." Looking relieved, the girl shrugged one shoulder. "I don't want my brother, or Colt, finding out how I feel about him. They'd tease me something awful and never let me hear the end of it."

Their attention was suddenly drawn back to the arena floor with the announcement of the first bull rider.

"There's my man," Kaylee said proudly. "Right now, Colt's in fifth place in the point standings. But my brother, Mitch, is breathing down his neck. Mitch is only two places behind Colt."

Two men—one holding the end of a long rope attached to a gate, the other appearing to hold the closure shut—stood at one end of the arena. The man holding the metal gate suddenly let go, while the other man jerked hard on the rope. Both quickly stepped back as it swung wide and a black bull with Colt on its back exploded from the chute.

As if asking for divine intervention, Colt held one arm above his head, while his other arm extended down between his legs, where his hand appeared to be tied to the animal's broad back. Fascinated, Annie watched the large beast jump, spin and twist in an effort to dislodge Colt. She wondered how on earth he would manage to get loose and make it to safety without being seriously injured.

It didn't take long to find out, when the sound of a horn blew and Colt reached down with the hand he'd been holding above his head to pull on the rope, freeing himself from the bull. As the angry animal continued to buck wildly, Colt jumped from its back and ran for the fence surrounding the arena floor. But instead of the beast ignoring the man running from it, as Annie had hoped would be the case, the bull gave chase.

Annie blew out her pent-up breath when it appeared that Colt would win the footrace to safety. But her relief was short-lived. He suddenly stumbled and fell to his knees. The bull, seeing the object of its fury at a disadvantage, bore down on Colt with its sharp-looking horns lowered to do serious damage.

Annie's heart pounded wildly against her rib cage and fear streaked up her spine as she helplessly watched the horrifying scene playing out before her. But what happened next made her heart stop completely.

The bandannas tied to the back of his costume flapping wildly, Brant jumped in front of the bull and slapped it on the end of the nose. To Annie's horror the bull turned, and with a loud bellow lowered its deadly-looking horns to chase him.

Chapter 4

Time stood still as Annie watched the large, black bull charge Brant, while Colt made it to the safety of the fence. Dodging to one side, then the other, Brant stayed one step ahead of the angry animal as it relentlessly pursued him across the arena.

Then just as quickly as the chase began, it was over. Brant had maneuvered the bull back toward the bucking chutes where a gate had been thrown wide. Obviously seeing a way to escape the noise and bright lights, the beast lost interest in Brant and trotted docilely through the opening and out of sight. One of the cowboys standing close by shut the gate, and the wildly cheering crowd turned their attention to the replay of Colt's ride on the huge four-sided screen hanging high above the arena.

Annie released her pent-up breath and tried to concentrate on slowing the erratic pounding of her heart as she looked around her. No one acted as if Brant had done anything out of the ordinary. Even Kaylee wore a contented smile.

Focusing on the man who had just performed the most heroic act she'd ever seen, she watched him pick up a length of thick rope with a cowbell tied to it and hand it to Colt. The brothers exchanged a high five, and she could tell from their expressions that they'd put behind them their earlier disagreement about Colt riding the bull. Both men looked extremely pleased, and when the score for Colt's ride was flashed across the board, they grinned and slapped each other on the shoulder.

Amazed, Annie sat staring at the two brothers. They appeared to have enjoyed the excitement, the danger.

"Weren't you frightened for them?" she asked, turning to Kaylee.

The girl shook her head. "They both know what they're doing." Smiling, she pointed to a cowboy settling himself onto the back of a bull. "When riders get to this level of the PBR, they're the best in the world. Once they dismount, they all know they have to get to their feet as fast as they can and keep moving to get out of the way while the bullfighter distracts the bull. And Brant has always been the one bullfighter the guys want in the arena when they ride. They know they can depend on him to do everything in his power to divert the bull's attention so they can make it to safety."

Annie stared at Brant jogging over to once again take his position beside the bucking chutes. He'd proven his agility and athleticism by the way he'd adeptly avoided the bull his brother had ridden. And he certainly looked confident enough in what he was doing. She'd have to take it on faith that was the case.

During the course of the afternoon, Annie changed her mind several times about Brant. She couldn't decide whether he was the bravest man she'd ever met, or the most insane. Time after time, she watched him and the other two bullfighters save riders from the angry beasts by putting themselves in the paths of the dangerous animals. And they always managed to emerge from the skirmishes untouched.

But several hours later, after the last bull had trotted from the arena, and the crowd watched Kaylee's brother accept a hefty check for winning the event, Annie felt drained. She'd never witnessed anything as terrifying, exciting or oddly exhilarating as watching the cowboys and bullfighters pit their strength, courage and wits against two thousand pounds of angry animal.

"Well, it's time to find Mitch," Kaylee said, standing up to leave. She politely extended her hand. "It was really nice to meet you, Annie. Will I see you at next week's event?"

"I…I'm not sure," Annie said, joining Kaylee as they climbed the steps leading to the lobby area. "Will it be held here?"

Kaylee laughed. "No. The PBR won't be back here for another year. The guys are scheduled to be in Anaheim next weekend."

Annie didn't know what to say. Brant had said he was taking her with him, but she hadn't given a second thought as to where they would be going.

Suddenly feeling very unsure of her decision, she wondered what she'd gotten herself into. She was going off with a man she'd known less than twenty-four hours and didn't have a clue where he was taking her.

But before the gravity of what that might mean could sink in, a strong hand was placed to her back and a smooth baritone close to her ear asked, "So what did you think of your first bull-riding event, sweetpea?"

A shiver coursed through her at the sound of Brant's voice and she glanced up to meet his incredibly blue gaze. A warm protected feeling surrounded her. She had no basis for trusting him, other than the integrity in his eyes and the fact that he'd been nothing but a gentleman from the moment they met.

He'd changed out of his outlandish garb, removed the greasepaint lines from around his mouth and eyes, and once again wore the wide-brimmed black Resistol that matched hers.

"Hey, there, Brant," Kaylee said from beside Annie. "You sure got your exercise today."

"Hi, Kaylee-Q." Brant reached out to affectionately pull the brim of the young woman's hat down over her eyes. "How's my favorite girl?"

"Happy. Mitch won today," Kaylee said, grinning as

she repositioned her hat. "Now when I tell him I want that buckskin mare for my birthday that Joe Castleman has for sale, he can't use the excuse that he doesn't have any money."

Brant laughed. "You tell Mitch if he doesn't buy it for you, I won't be so quick to save his sorry hide the next time he lands flat on his back."

"I'll be sure to do that." Turning to Annie, Kaylee smiled. "I hope I see you in Anaheim."

"We'll see," Annie answered noncommittally.

As Kaylee disappeared into the crowd exiting the lobby area, Brant steered Annie to a service elevator. "Where are we going?" she asked.

"We're taking the back way out of this place," he said, pushing the down button. "I don't want to take the chance that Elsworth is out front looking for you."

Annie shook her head. "He probably wouldn't think of looking for me here."

"Why?" Brant's grip tightened on the handle of his red-and-black duffel bag. Did she think this type of event was beneath her and old pasty-face?

"Because bull riding wouldn't appeal to him, therefore he wouldn't think it would be something I'd find entertaining." She pushed her glasses up with a brush of her hand as they stepped onto the elevator. The steel doors swished shut and the car began to descend. "Patrick never gave me credit for having any interests other than his."

"And is bull riding one of the things you find entertaining that he wouldn't?" Brant asked, not at all sure why her answer should matter to him.

He watched her nibble on her lower lip before answering. "I'm not sure." She glanced up at him. "I have to admit there were a couple of times this afternoon when I was scared witless."

"Why?"

"Because I was sure one of those bulls was going to run you down," she said, sounding genuinely concerned for his safety.

A warm feeling spread throughout Brant's chest, but he ignored the sensation. From what he'd seen, Annie was kind and didn't want to see anyone harmed in any way. She'd probably felt the same way about all the guys she'd seen in the arena today.

Before he could analyze why that thought disappointed him, the elevator doors opened and they stepped out into the same staging area they'd entered several hours before. Guiding Annie to the exit, Brant helped her into the back of a waiting cab, then gave the driver instructions to take them to Lambert airport.

"I know I should have inquired before, but where are we going?" she asked. He noticed that she nervously twisted the diamond ring she'd swiped from Elsworth the night before around her slender finger.

"We'll take a flight from here to Denver," he said, hoping to reassure her. "Then once we get my truck out of long-term parking, we'll spend the night and drive to the Lonetree tomorrow."

"Why aren't we flying directly to Cheyenne, or Casper, or wherever the closest airfield is to your ranch?" She twisted the ring a little more earnestly.

He placed his hand over hers. "I couldn't get a direct flight out of Cheyenne, so I drove down to Denver," he said, smiling. "It's only about a four hour drive."

"If it's that close, where are we staying tonight, and why?" She looked a little alarmed, and he could see the wheels turning in her pretty little head. Annie was speculating on what he had planned, and she wasn't sure she was going to like his answer.

"We'll get a couple of rooms close to the airport tonight, then after a shopping trip to get more clothes for you, we'll head home," he answered, hoping that his reference to two hotel rooms would put her more at ease.

"I hate for you to go to that expense," she said, gazing at him with guileless green eyes.

His heart slammed against his rib cage. Was she saying she wanted him to get one room, that she wanted to spend the night with him?

Before he managed to find his voice, she went on, "Could you keep a total of what you spend so that my grandmother can reimburse you?"

Brant could have laughed at his own foolishness, if not for the disappointment settling in his gut. What the hell was wrong with him? Annie Devereaux wasn't his type of woman. She'd be about as comfortable doing the two-step in a honky-tonk as he'd be attending an opera where the people trying to sing sounded like cats with their tails caught in the door.

"I'm not worried about the cost, sweetpea," he said as the cab pulled up to the airport's east terminal.

He paid the driver, then helped Annie from the back-seat and headed straight to the ticket counter. Discovering there wasn't another first-class seat available, he exchanged his ticket for business class, purchased one for Annie and checked his bag.

She waited until he pocketed his credit card before asking, "Do you always fly first-class?"

"When I can," he answered, placing his hand at her elbow. He steered her toward the area where the metal detectors were located. "The rows of seats are farther apart and I can straighten out my bad knee."

"You should have kept your seat," she said, stopping to glance back at the ticket counter. "Maybe you can get your ticket back if you—" She suddenly broke off whatever she'd been about to say and spun around to face forward.

Bewildered, Brant stopped walking and turned back to face her. She stood as if she'd been frozen to the spot, her face ghostly pale. "What's wrong?" he asked. When she remained silent, he placed his hands on her shoulders. "Annie?"

"I think I saw Patrick," she said, her voice little more than a whisper. "He's showing a picture to some people over by the ticket counter."

With a quick glance beyond the top of her head toward the check-in area, Brant swore. "That's him all right." The panic filling her pretty, green eyes twisted his gut. "Don't worry, sweetpea. I gave you my word that I wouldn't let him touch you, and I damn well intend to keep it." He held out his hand. "Let me have your glasses."

"What's he doing now?" she asked, handing them over.

"Don't turn around. It looks like he's working his way this direction," Brant said, tucking the black frames in his shirt pocket.

Taking her by the arm, he set his sights on the metal detectors up ahead. Fortunately, there weren't that many people waiting in line to go through the security check. Once they were past that point and into the gate area, Elsworth wouldn't be able to follow them without a ticket for one of the flights.

Before they even reached the detectors, Brant started digging his keys and change from his jeans pockets. He handed their tickets and boarding passes to the guard, then supported Annie by the elbow as she quickly tugged off her boots. While she sent them and her hat through the scanning device, he kicked off his shoes and removed his hat. Having to fly nearly every weekend to the various bull-riding events, Brant was familiar with airport security and had quickly learned that when traveling, jogging shoes were easier to remove than having to pull off boots. He just wished that he'd thought of having Sarah pick up a pair of jogging shoes for Annie, instead of the boots.

Tossing his shoes and hat on the conveyer belt, he emptied the coins and keys from his hand into a small plastic container and followed Annie through the arched detector. He was relieved when neither one of them set off the alarm. That would have required a scan with a handheld device and given Elsworth more time to discover them.

While they waited for their things to clear the scanner, Brant looked over to where Elsworth stood talking to an airport custodian. He was still several yards away. Maybe they'd be out of sight before he got any closer.

No sooner had the thought crossed his mind, when Elsworth turned to stare in Brant and Annie's direction.

"Anastasia!"

At the sound of her name, Annie automatically turned around. "Oh my God," she whispered. "He's found us."

Brant stuffed his keys and change into his jeans, then leaning close, whispered into her ear, "Act like you don't know who he is. Just pick up your boots and hat and start walking." Jamming his own hat on his head, Brant grabbed his shoes, accepted the envelope with their tickets from the guard and ushered her down the causeway where their departure gate was located. "They won't allow him into this area without a boarding pass and ticket."

Annie glanced over her shoulder. Without her glasses she wasn't sure if Patrick's steely-eyed glare was real or a figment of her overactive imagination. But it didn't matter. Whether the look was real or imagined, her heart pounded and it was all she could do to keep from breaking into a run. He was standing just on the other side of the security device and that was way too close for comfort.

When they reached their departure gate, and well out of Patrick's sight, Annie dropped her boots, sank into one of the seats and buried her face in her hands. "What have I gotten myself into?"

Brant sat down in the chair next to her to put on his shoes. "Everything is going to be fine, Annie. I gave you my word that Elsworth won't touch you." He turned to cup her cheek in his big palm, then staring at her with his startling blue eyes, he added, "And, sweetpea, if you knew me better, you'd know that's as ironclad as any contract a lawyer could draw up."

He held her gaze for several long seconds before dropping his hand and leaning down to tie his shoe-laces. Rising to his feet, he turned toward the snack bar across from the waiting area. "I'm going to get a cup of coffee. Would you like something?"

Annie shook her head and watched as he strolled over to the kiosk, his gait loose and confident. There was no doubt in her mind that Brant meant every word he said. The only problem was, she wasn't sure she was any safer with him than she was with Patrick.

Oh, she knew for certain that Brant would never allow anyone or anything to harm her physically. It was her suddenly unstable emotions that concerned her. Every time he turned his incredible blue gaze her way, she felt things she'd never felt before. Her stomach fluttered as if a herd of butterflies had been unleashed, and heat streaked through her to areas that had no business warming up. If she didn't know herself better, she'd swear she had the hots for Brant Wakefield.

She shook her head to dislodge the unsettling thought. Anastasia Devereaux wasn't the type to have the hots for anyone. She was steady, dependable and never got excited about much of anything.

But what about Annie Devereaux? She'd walked an outside ledge high above the streets of Saint Louis, she'd spent the night in the same hotel suite with a man she didn't even know, and was about to spend the next week traveling, God only knew where, with him.

Annie swallowed hard. She was beginning to wonder if she still knew who she was. She'd always thought she was content with the life her grandmother had laid out for her. But now?

In the past twenty-four hours she'd had more excitement than she'd had in all of her twenty-four years. And, she'd never felt more alive.

Brant pushed the brim of his hat up with his thumb and glanced at the woman's head resting against his shoulder. They hadn't been in the air more than ten minutes, when Annie fell sound asleep. About five minutes after that, she'd moved to lean against him. He checked his watch. And they had another forty-five minutes left before the plane touched down in Denver.

He took a deep breath and the clean scent of her herbal shampoo surrounded him. It took everything he had in him to keep from reaching over to run his fingers through the pale-blond strands. She moved to a more comfortable position and he watched her perfect lips part on a soft sigh. His mouth suddenly felt as if it had been coated with cotton and he had to fight the urge to lean closer and press his lips to hers, to once again taste the sweetness of her.

That thought had him sitting up in his seat and staring straight ahead in two seconds flat. What the hell was wrong with him? Hadn't he learned the hard way that he had absolutely nothing in common with a woman like Annie?

He thought back to his college days when he'd been foolish enough to believe that an eastern, city-bred filly and a western, pasture-raised stud could work out the differences in their backgrounds and find lasting happiness. If not for the lingering pang of regret, he could almost laugh now about what an odd couple he and Daphne had been.

They'd met in an art appreciation class his senior year at the University of Wyoming. He'd needed another humanities course to graduate and she'd taken the class because that was the type of thing that appealed to her. He'd never been able to figure out why Daphne Elizabeth Morrison-Smythe had chosen to attend a state university out West, instead of one of the Ivy League schools closer to her home. Hell, they offered a lot more of that cultured stuff, and one of those schools even had a building named after her granddaddy.

But at the time, Brant hadn't cared. He'd taken one look at the flame-haired beauty and fallen head over heels in love. And he was pretty sure that she'd loved him, too. At least, as much as she had been capable of loving.

Unfortunately, love hadn't been enough to bridge the gap in their backgrounds. She'd quickly tired of dressing in jeans and boots to watch him play chicken with a ton of pissed-off beef. Then she'd tried to convince him that he'd be just as happy dressed in a tux to attend a symphony or art exhibit as he was in his bullfighting gear. And for a while he'd tried. He really had.

But he'd had nothing in common with her highfalutin friends, and it hadn't taken him long to discover that trying to be something he's not just made him miserable. He couldn't change who he was any more than she could change who she was.

When they parted, it had been on amicable terms, but he'd learned a valuable lesson. People were going to have to accept him the way he was, or not. It was their choice. But he would never again try to change himself to please another person.

The ping of the seat-belt sign brought him back to the present. They were getting ready to land in Denver.

"Annie," he said softly, touching her shoulder.

"Mmm." She snuggled closer and smiled in her sleep. His chest tightened with a protective feeling like nothing he'd ever experienced.

"Sweetpea, the plane's getting ready to land."

Brant watched her long lashes flutter, then slowly open. He didn't think he'd ever seen anything quite so sexy.

When she tilted her head to look up at him, it must have registered with her that she'd used his shoulder for a pillow. Her cheeks coloring a pretty pink, she jerked upright. "How long have I been asleep?"

He chuckled. "I think you went out about the same time the seat-belt sign did."

"I'm sorry," she said, finger-combing her hair.

Fascinated by the movement of the blond strands, it took a moment for Brant to realize what she'd said. "Sorry? For what?"

He noticed her finger shook slightly as she pointed to his sleeve. "I've wrinkled your shirt."

"Don't worry about it," he said, pulling her glasses from his shirt pocket. He wasn't going to upset her further by telling her that he'd actually enjoyed having her use him for a pillow. Hell, he wasn't all that comfortable with how much he'd liked it himself.

She put the black frames on, then pushed them up with a brush of her hand. "I've never been this far west as an adult."

Her simple statement reminded him that no matter how good it felt having her lean on him, or how protective he felt of her, they had nothing in common. "I'm sure it's going to be a lot different than you're used to," he said as the plane taxied to the terminal.

"Why do you say that?" she asked, covering her yawn with a delicate hand.

He swallowed hard. How would her hands feel on his body? Would they be as soft caressing and stroking his skin as he imagined?

Barely resisting the urge to cuss a blue streak, Brant gathered their coats and her hat from the overhead storage compartment, then waited until they'd disembarked the plane before he trusted himself to answer her. "There's a lot of distance between towns out here. And they're a lot smaller than where you're from."

"We have some pretty small towns in southern Illinois, too," she said as she walked ahead of him into the airport.

When a man bumped into her as he hurried toward the baggage-claim area, Brant reached down and took her hand in his to keep them from being separated in the crowd. The bandage where he'd tended her scraped palm rubbed against his, reminding him of why she was with him. She was escaping a man that meant to harm her, not to approve or disapprove of the land he loved.

"Bear Creek is about twenty miles from the Lonetree. It's the closest town," he said as they waited for his duffel bag. "And about all there is in town is the grade school, a church, a bar and a general store with a lunch counter and a gas pump out front."

"What about a post office?" she asked, sounding genuinely interested. "Where's that located?"

"In the store." He plucked his red-and-black bag from the rest of the baggage. "The Rancher's Emporium carries everything from canned goods to tractor parts. And that includes a postal window."

"It sounds quite charming," she said, smiling up at him.

He laughed and shook his head as they stepped out of the terminal and waited for the shuttle to take them to long-term parking to get his truck. "I've heard Bear Creek called a one-horse town, a hole in the road, and a bump in a deer trail, but I think that's probably the first time anyone's ever called it charming."

* * *

Brant glanced out the lobby window at Annie, patiently waiting in the front seat of his truck for him to return with her room key. The only problem was, his room key and hers were one and the same.

He slid his wallet into his hip pocket and nodded to the middle-aged man behind the registration desk, then, taking a deep breath, walked back out to the pickup. Sliding into the driver's seat, he put the truck in gear and pulled around to the back of the building.

"We've got a slight problem," he said, cutting the engine and lights. "There was only one room available."

She calmly turned to face him. "How many beds?"

"Two."

"Good enough," she said, surprising him.

He got out and walked around to help her from the passenger's side. "You don't mind?"

"I'm too tired to care one way or the other," she admitted. "Besides, I know you can be trusted."

Inserting the key card in the lock, he held the door while she preceded him into the room, then turned back to the truck to get his bag. He wasn't exactly sure how Annie's statement made him feel. On one hand, he was honored that she trusted him so completely. On the other, he didn't care much for the idea that she thought of him as harmless, either.

He slammed the truck door and headed back into the room. Hell, he was a flesh-and-blood man with a healthy appreciation for the opposite sex, just like any other. And the more time he spent around Annie, the more he appreciated the way her cute little rear swayed slightly when she walked, how her breasts filled out her new, tapered blouse.

"Do you want the shower first?" she asked when he closed the door and secured the locks.

"No, go ahead." He set his bag on the desk, then turned to find her looking at him expectantly. "What's wrong?"

"I need my skirt and blouse."

"Why?"

"It's the closest thing I have to a nightgown," she said as if it was the most reasonable explanation in the world.

Turning, he slid the heavy zipper open on the luggage, then handed her the clothes. "Here you go."

When she took them from him, something fell from between the two garments to land at his feet. Bending down, he picked up a scrap of beige lace with four straps dangling from it and a tiny patch of beige silk attached to an elastic waistband with something resembling a string.

Looking at the delicate items in his callused hands, Brant swallowed around the biggest wad of cotton he'd ever had clog his throat. Annie hadn't worn panty hose last night. She'd been wearing a garter belt and hose. And the mystery from this morning about what she did or didn't have on under her jeans had just been solved. Apparently, Annie had a thing for sexy underwear. *Very* sexy underwear.

Sweat popped out on his forehead and his body tightened in places that within seconds would be extremely hard and all but impossible to hide. "If you—" he stopped to clear the rust from his voice "—don't mind, I think I will take my shower first," he said, stuffing the delicate lingerie into her hands.

He didn't take time to rummage through his duffel for clean clothes. Instead, he picked the bag up by the handles and took it with him, then slamming the bathroom door behind him, dropped the luggage to the floor. Yanking the snaps free on his shirt, he quickly shucked the rest of his clothes, turned on the shower and without hesitation, stepped inside.

Barely suppressing his shocked yelp, Brant stood beneath the icy spray until his teeth chattered and his body felt as if it would never function properly again.

Her cheeks feeling as if they were on fire, Annie stood with her fist clenched around the silk and lace as she watched Brant close the bathroom door behind him. This morning, when the woman he'd called Sarah brought the items that he'd requested, Annie had discreetly told her what she needed. Sarah had understood completely and delivered the new underthings without blinking an eye. And although Brant had looked extremely curious about their whispering, he hadn't been the wiser.

But now, because of her carelessness, he had learned the one thing about her that no one else besides Sarah knew. Annie preferred very delicate, very provocative undergarments.

Sinking down on the end of the bed, she sighed. She'd started wearing sexy lingerie in college as a way of rebelling against her grandmother's strict upbringing. At the time, it had been the only thing she'd had enough courage to do that was even close to wild and daring. And the beauty of it was, it had been her little secret. No one else knew that beneath her sensible khaki skirts and loose silk blouses she wore undergarments that were so sheer, so minuscule, she might as well not be wearing anything at all.

She glanced toward the bathroom. At least until now, no one else had known about it.

Staring at the closed door, she couldn't help but grin. If the look on Brant's face was any indication, the lingerie had been the very last thing he'd expected to fall from her clothes. When he'd picked up her thong and garter belt from the top of his shoe, his sexy blue eyes had widened in utter shock and he'd been absolutely speechless.

Annie covered her mouth with her hand to keep from laughing out loud. Brant Wakefield had just learned that not everything was always as it seemed.

Even a stuffy, plain-Jane librarian had her little secrets.

Chapter 5

The next morning, Annie awoke to Brant's quiet snores coming from the other bed. Turning her head, she noticed that his black hair was slightly rumpled and his square jaw wore the dark shadow of overnight stubble. Instead of detracting from his good looks, it added a sexy ruggedness that sent a wave of goose bumps skipping over her skin. He really was one of the sexiest, best-looking men she'd ever met. And she was going to spend the next week going with him to heaven only knew where.

As she continued to watch him sleep, her gaze drifted lower and her eyes widened. When Brant had finally emerged from the bathroom last night, he'd been fully dressed and she could have sworn he was shivering when he climbed into bed and pulled the covers up to his ears. But sometime during the night, he'd pushed the covers down to his waist and removed his shirt.

Staring at the expanse of his chest as it rose and fell with his deep even breathing, she studied his perfect male body. His stomach and pectoral muscles were well defined, his skin smooth and inviting.

Her pulse quickened and she had to moisten her suddenly dry lips as the memory of what it felt like to be pressed to all that warm, hard sinew came rushing back. He'd held her so securely, so protectively when he'd rescued her from his balcony. What would it be like to be loved by a man like Brant, to have him caress her skin the way she'd touched his? Her lower belly fluttered and a tingling sensation coursed through her.

"That's it," she muttered, throwing the blanket back.

She rose from the bed and quietly crossed the short distance between the two beds. All that smooth, warm-looking male skin was enough to drive a saint to sin. It would definitely be in her best interest to cover him and stop all her foolish fantasizing about something that would never in a million years happen anyway.

But just as she reached down to pull the sheet up to cover his chest, Brant's hand grasped her wrist and tugged. Caught off balance, Annie tumbled forward and landed on top of him with a startled squeak.

"What's 'it'?" he asked, his sexy baritone rough with sleep. The sound sent a tremor coursing through her.

Annie couldn't think straight as she stared down into his vivid blue eyes. "Wh-what?"

He wrapped his arm around her shoulders and turned them until she found herself lying flat on her back with him leaning over her. "You said, 'That's it' before you got up. What did you mean, sweetpea?"

She couldn't tell him that she'd been ogling his perfect body and savoring every luscious memory of what it felt like to touch him. Or that she'd been wondering what it would be like to have him touch her in ways she'd never been touched. "I…I don't remember."

"Liar," he said softly. He pillowed her head on his left forearm while he threaded the fingers of his right hand in her hair. "You were looking at my chest like a starving dog looks at a bone."

"You were watching?" she asked, wondering if that throaty female voice was really hers.

"Oh, yeah, sweetpea. There hasn't been a move you've made since you crawled into that bed last night that I haven't known about."

Her heart skipped a beat. "Really?"

He nodded. "Do you know how sweet you look when you sleep?"

"You were watching me?" she asked incredulously.

"Just like you were watching me." His smile caused the butterflies in her stomach to flap wildly.

Surely Brant didn't mean he was having the same kinds of thoughts about her that she'd been having about him. She just wasn't the type of woman that men wasted their time fantasizing about.

"I thought I'd cover you," she said, thinking fast. "You seemed to be a bit chilled last night after your shower."

His deep chuckle sent a shiver slithering up her spine. "Sweetpea, do you know why I was so cold when I came out of the bathroom?"

"No," she said, moving her head back and forth.

Tracing his finger down her cheek to the fullness of her lower lip, he smiled. "I'd just spent a good ten minutes standing under a spray of ice-cold water."

Was he trying to tell her that she'd somehow aroused him? Not likely.

Her heart pounded against her ribs. "Why?"

He grinned. "I discovered that beige silk and lace can cause a man's temperature to rise considerably."

"It…does?" She'd known the sight of her underwear had surprised him, but she had no idea that it had affected him *that* way.

"You just about caused me to have a coronary last night, sweetpea," he said, nodding.

"Me?" Surely she misunderstood what he was saying.

The gleam in his stunning blue eyes as he nodded told her more than words that he meant everything he was telling her. "And you're doing a damn fine job of getting it jump-started this morning."

"Your heart?"

His deep chuckle sent heat streaking through her. "Among other things." He cupped her cheek with his hand as he gazed down at her. "Last night you told me you knew you could trust me."

"Y-yes." Annie couldn't believe how difficult it had suddenly become to form words.

"I just want you to know that although you can trust me, I'm not a gelding. I'm a man with a man's desires—susceptible to the same temptations as any other." His head slowly descended. "And right now, you're tempting me in ways that you can't even imagine, sweetpea."

"I find…that hard…to believe," she said, trying desperately to catch her breath.

"It's the truth." His firm mouth barely brushed hers. "But since it seems you have doubts, I guess I'll just have to show you." He raised his head to gaze down at her. "Do you want me to do that, Annie?"

She couldn't have stopped herself from nodding if her life depended on it. Heaven help her, but she wanted Brant to kiss her again. "Please."

His promising smile took her breath. "It'll be my pleasure, sweetpea."

As Brant's mouth covered hers, Annie's eyes drifted shut and she brought her hands up to run them over his wide, corded shoulders. His smooth warm flesh, the hardness of honed muscle beneath her palms, was everything she remembered and more.

His lips moved slowly, thoughtfully, over hers for endless seconds, as if giving her the opportunity to call a halt to the caress. But she could have no more stopped the kiss than she could pluck stars from the sky. She wanted Brant to kiss her, wanted to once again feel the exquisite pull of desire that she'd experienced in his arms the morning before.

His tongue traced the seam of her mouth and she answered his request by parting for him, allowing him entry. Strong and masterful, yet gentle and coaxing, his tender stroking created an eagerness in her that made her head spin. Gathering her courage, she tentatively touched her tongue to his and a groan rumbled up from deep in his chest. At the sound, a spark somewhere deep inside her flickered to life, then quickly grew into a flame. Heat spread to every part of her, and her limbs felt heavy and languorous.

Brant pulled her more fully against him, then slowly tugged her blouse from the waistband of her khaki skirt. Lifting the tail of the garment, he ran his callused palm over her skin, caressed her waist, her ribs, then the swell of her breast. When he moved to cup the heaviness, her heart skipped a beat and breathing seemed to be all but impossible.

He broke the kiss to nip and nibble his way to the rapidly beating pulse at the base of her throat. "Do you have any idea how sweet you are, Annie?" he murmured as his thumb chafed her nipple into a tight bud.

She shook her head. The many delicious sensations that Brant was creating inside her threatened to consume her and made any kind of speech impossible.

But when he pushed her blouse up to take the tight nub into his mouth, it felt as if an electric charge coursed through her. Her stomach tightened with an empty ache as he continued to tease the small bud, and a swirling heat began to pool at the juncture of her thighs.

So intense were the unfamiliar feelings, so breath-taking, she pushed against his shoulders. "Please... stop."

He raised his head and stared at her for several long moments, then cursing, rolled to the other side of the bed to sit up. "Annie, I—" He stopped to bury his head in his hands. "I never meant for things to go that far."

She suddenly felt as if she'd been dipped in ice water. Of course he hadn't meant it. A man like Brant was used to a woman with more finesse, more experience, not one who bolted at the first stirrings of desire. His back was to her, but she could just imagine the disgust in his expressive blue eyes.

Taking a deep breath, she tried to ignore the burning pain of disappointment as she rose from the bed. "Don't worry about it. I know I'm not the type that men fantasize about."

She gathered her jeans and shirt, then started to walk into the bathroom to change. But Brant's hand suddenly circled her upper arm and turned her to face him. How had he managed to get to his feet and round the bed so fast?

"Where the hell did you get that idea?" he asked, his frown formidable.

"I may wear glasses, but I'm not blind. When I look in the mirror, I can see that my hair looks like limp straw when it's down, and that my features are...ordinary." Shrugging one shoulder, she met his gaze head-on. "There's nothing about me that could be considered re-markable in any way."

Her eyes widened at the pithy phrase Brant blurted

out. "Sweetpea, I don't know which mirror you've been looking into, but it's the wrong damn one."

"What do you mean?" she asked,

"Your hair looks and feels like spun silk," he said, reaching out to stroke the blond strands. Smiling, he cupped her chin with his hand, then gently chafed her lower lip with the pad of his thumb. "Your eyes are a beautiful shade of emerald, your lips are perfectly shaped." He grinned. "And they felt pretty damn remarkable both times I've kissed you."

Her heart skipped a beat as she gazed up at him. "They did?"

Nodding, he stared at her for what seemed an eternity, then quickly stepped back. "Now, get changed so we can get out of here. Otherwise, I might forget that I'm supposed to be playing the part of a trustworthy gelding, instead of a man who would like nothing more than to get you back in that bed and kiss you again." His smile curled her toes and caused a heaviness to pull at her lower stomach. "And more."

As they left the outskirts of Denver, Brant set the cruise control, then glanced over at Annie. She was busy sorting through all the shopping bags from their trip to the mall and the western-wear store.

When she held up a bag from the Sleek and Sassy Lady Lingerie Boutique, and started rummaging through it, he swallowed hard, fixed his eyes on the road ahead and kept them there. That was the one store he hadn't gone into with Annie. He hadn't dared. Just the thought of her choice of underthings still made him break out in a sweat and had him imagining all sorts of scenarios. And every one of them ended with him removing scraps of silk and lace.

Brant gripped the wheel and clenched his teeth. He'd made a damn fool of himself last night when her garter belt and panties—if they could be called panties—fell at his feet. Then he'd made an even bigger fool of himself this morning when he'd let his hormones override his good sense. But Annie's lips were the sweetest, sexiest he'd ever had the pleasure of kissing. And, he decided, could quickly become an addiction if he wasn't careful.

He concentrated on breathing in and out for several seconds. Ten years ago he'd made a vow to steer clear of women like Annie. He had nothing in common with them. Something deep in his gut kept telling him that Annie was different, that she wasn't the same type of woman as Daphne. And what disturbed him the most was, he found himself hoping his instincts were on target—that she was nothing like Daphne.

"How are the new contacts?" he asked in an effort to take his mind off the direction his thoughts had strayed. After Annie had finished shopping, she'd asked him to take her to one of the vision-care chain stores. "Are you getting used to them?"

"Actually, I think I like them very much," she said, sounding happy. "Thank you for mentioning them."

A warm feeling spread throughout his chest. It felt good to make her happy. Too good.

Clearing his throat, Brant searched for something else to say. "Did you get everything you'll be needing for the next week?"

Placing the sacks at her feet, she sighed. "I forgot to buy something to sleep in."

"I'll stop in Cheyenne," he said, trying not to think about what her choice of sleepwear looked like.

She remained silent for a moment. "You've spent so much on me already, I really hate for you to spend more."

He chuckled. "It's not a problem, sweetpea."

"That's what you keep saying." She paused. "Do you have some old T-shirts? I could sleep in one of them."

Brant decided it had to have been a miracle that kept him from steering the truck off into the ditch at Annie's suggestion. His heart pounded and his stomach muscles tightened at the thought of her sleeping in one of his shirts. For some strange reason, he liked the idea more than just a little bit.

"Uh, fine by me. But are you sure you don't want me to stop in Cheyenne?"

She nodded. "I'm sure. That way you won't have to spend more money."

He was getting tired of her worrying about him spending money. "Annie, this is the last time we're going to talk about this. I can more than afford to buy as many clothes as you want."

"Well, I still intend to pay you back after I return home," she said stubbornly.

"No, you won't."

"Yes, I will."

"Like hell." He pulled the truck onto the shoulder of the interstate, killed the engine, then turned to glare at her. "Let's get this settled once and for all. You're not going to pay me back. I bought the clothes for you, you're going to wear them and that's it."

"But—"

"No buts about it, lady."

She stared back at him for a moment before finally giving in with a sigh. "Okay, whatever you say."

"I'm glad we have that settled," he said, leaning over to plant a quick kiss on her perfect lips. "Now, let's get home. I'd like you to see the Lonetree before it gets dark."

As he pulled back onto the interstate, it bothered him that Annie thought he couldn't afford what they'd bought. Didn't she think he was successful at what he did? Did she think that just because he preferred jeans and boots, his standard of living was below hers?

Hell, he didn't flaunt the fact that his bank account was well into the six-figure column. Truth be told, he didn't even care. He worked hard, led a fairly simple life, and wouldn't have it any other way.

Concentrating on the road ahead, Brant tried to ignore the disappointment settling in his chest and the tight knot forming in his stomach. Had his gut instinct been wrong? Was Annie really as materialistic as Daphne had turned out to be?

Annie had no idea why Brant was so adamant about her not reimbursing him, or why he'd gotten so upset.

She only wanted to make sure he knew she wasn't trying to take advantage of his generosity.

Deciding his attitude must have something to do with male pride, she gazed out the truck window at the snow-covered scenery and mentally calculated how much they'd spent in the various stores. He might think he'd convinced her to drop the idea of paying him back, but he was in for a big surprise. She'd been raised by Carlotta Whittmeyer, the most stubborn, headstrong woman in southern Illinois. And this was one of the few areas where she and her granddaughter were just alike. Brant Wakefield might think he'd won this one, but he hadn't. He would get his money back, whether he liked it or not.

Her decision made, Annie settled back to enjoy the view. The mountains were, in a word, breathtaking. "It's beautiful out here, Brant."

"You've never seen the Rockies?" he asked, sounding shocked.

She shook her head. "Not really. My mother and father brought me out here on a camping trip when I was very small, but I don't remember anything about it." An ache settled in her chest at the thought of her parents and how much they'd missed together as a family. "After they died, my grandmother wouldn't allow me to travel very often, and never anywhere that she thought would pose a danger."

Brant reached over and clasped her hand. "I'm sorry, sweetpea. I remember you said they'd been killed." He tenderly traced his thumb over the back of her hand. "I lost my mom right after she had Colt, then Dad died ten years later."

"How old were you?" she asked, gently squeezing his hand. His callused palm against hers felt reassuring, and a warm secure feeling spread throughout her being.

"I was six when Mom died and almost seventeen when Dad got killed in a ranching accident." He drew her hand up to his mouth, then kissed the back of it. "But at least I had Morgan and Colt."

She'd always wanted a brother or sister. What she'd gotten was her grandmother's cranky cat, Sherlock. "The three of you are close, aren't you?"

He nodded. "Oh, we have our arguments like all brothers do, but there's nothing we wouldn't do for each other. We know that whenever one of us needs something, all we have to do is let the other two know."

"That must be nice," she said, unable to keep the wistfulness from her voice.

They fell into a companionable silence for some time before Brant turned the truck off the highway and onto another road. "We just crossed the Lonetree's eastern boundary," he said, smiling fondly.

Annie looked around. She didn't see a house. "How far is your home from the main road?"

"About six miles as the crow flies," he said, chuckling at her obviously shocked expression.

"Brant, how big is this ranch?"

"A little over a hundred and fifty thousand acres," he said, stopping the truck at the top of a rise.

Her eyes widened. "That's a lot of land."

Shrugging, he pointed to the valley below them. "There's ranch headquarters."

Annie's eyes widened. One of the biggest, most beautiful log homes she'd ever seen sat at one end of the valley, close to several barns and sheds. Smoke rose from a large stone chimney as if beckoning those who lived there to come into its warmth. The fields surrounding the place were blanketed with snow, and the approaching shadows of twilight as the sun slid behind the mountains in the distance created a scene that could have easily been featured on a Christmas card.

"My God, Brant, it's gorgeous," she said, sitting forward.

"You really like it?" he asked, sounding skeptical.

She turned to face him. "I love it. How long has your family owned the Lonetree?"

Smiling, he shifted the truck into drive and slowly drove down the snowpacked lane. "The Wakefields settled here a hundred and fifteen years ago this summer."

"Is the house that old?" It looked a lot larger and more modern than what someone would have built in the nineteenth century.

He laughed. "Somewhere in there I'm sure the old cabin still exists. But each generation has added more to it."

He turned onto a driveway with a square arch over it. The sign hanging from the wooden structure had Lonetree Ranch painted in the center and symbols on either side that Annie assumed to be ranch brands.

"See the section on this side of the porch?" he asked. "Morgan had that added two years ago."

"There wasn't already enough room for the three of you?" Annie asked incredulously.

"Morgan wanted a room for the pool table and big-screen TV," Brant answered, parking the truck at the side of the house. "There's even enough room for three recliners and a big couch, too."

"Oh, the loungers are certainly a must," she said, laughing.

He reached down to release the latch on his shoulder belt, then did the same with hers. Tugging her over to the center of the bench seat, he wrapped his arms around her. "Hey, lady, when you have a busted leg, those things are darned nice."

Her smile faded. "You've had a broken leg?"

"I've broken one leg and torn up the ACL on the other knee," he said as he threaded his fingers in her hair.

"ACL?"

"Anterior cruciate ligament," he explained with a smile.

"Was that from fighting bulls?" she asked breathlessly.

"The torn ACL was. The broken leg was from falling off a hay wagon when I was thirteen."

"Who took care of you?" she said, touching his lean cheek with her hand.

"My brothers when they weren't busy with chores," he answered, his hand cupping the back of her head. "Most of the time, I took care of myself."

"You should have had someone with you all the time," she said, her heart aching at the thought of him being hurt and left alone to fend for himself while his brothers tended the ranch. She told herself she'd feel that way about anyone who'd been injured. But she suspected the feeling was more intense because she knew that Brant had been the one in pain.

His intense blue gaze caught hers and held it as he stared down at her. "Would you take care of me if I got hurt, sweetpea?"

Without a moment's hesitation she nodded. But before she had a chance to think about her hasty agreement, Brant groaned and pulled her head forward. Settling his mouth on hers, he hungrily tasted her lips, tugging gently on her lower lip with his teeth.

A tingling sensation started in her limbs and quickly spread to every part of her body. Drugging in its intensity, the feeling quickly settled in the pit of her stomach to form a rapidly tightening coil.

As wave after wave of excitement coursed through her, Annie lifted her arms to wrap them around his neck. Tangling her fingers in the thick black hair brushing his collar, she held him close and took pleasure in once again being kissed by the sexiest man she'd ever known. But when Brant slipped his tongue between her lips to stroke the inner recesses of her mouth, the coil in her belly tightened to a heated ache and an emptiness deep inside caused her to shift restlessly.

Wanting more of his touch, she reached up to take his hand from the back of her head and placed it on her breast. Had she been able to think straight, she would have been appalled at her wanton actions. But rational thought was beyond her capabilities. All she wanted was to feel his hands on her again.

"Ah, sweetpea." He gently kneaded the sensitive mound through the fabric of her cotton shirt. "You feel so damn good."

The sound of a truck pulling to a halt beside them, then seconds later the rap of knuckles on the driver's window, sent a chill up Annie's spine. Before she could jerk away from Brant, he tightened his arm around her as he slowly moved his hand down to her waist.

"Excuse me, sweetpea, but I have a brother to strangle." Turning, he opened the window. "What the hell do you want, Morgan?"

"Sorry to break up the fun, but I need your help," a deep voice said. From her vantage point, Annie couldn't see Brant's brother, but he sounded as if he might be in pain.

She heard Brant groan as he moved to get out of the truck. "How did you jerk your shoulder out of joint this time?" he asked. "You know I hate when I'm the one who has to pop it back in place."

Annie looked around Brant at the man standing next to the truck, holding his limp left arm close to his side. Morgan Wakefield was every bit as good-looking as both of his brothers and had the same intense blue eyes. But strain lines bracketed his mouth and she could tell that he was hurting.

"I went over to check on the Shackley place and fell

through a rotten board on the porch step," Morgan said, backing up for Brant to get out of the truck. "I hit my shoulder on one of the support posts." He muttered a curse. "And believe me, you don't hate having to do this nearly as much as I hate having to have it done."

"Shouldn't he see a doctor?" Annie asked, scrambling out of the truck behind Brant.

Both men shook their heads. "Big brother, here, dislocated his shoulder a few years back, but instead of having surgery to fix the problem, he just lets it slip out of joint on a regular basis." Brant snorted. "And Colt and I get the pleasure of popping it back in for him."

"Quit your moaning and let's get this over with," Morgan said through gritted teeth. "It's not out of joint completely this time."

"House or barn?" Brant asked.

"Barn," Morgan said, turning to walk toward one of the well-kept structures several yards away.

Brant placed his hands on her shoulders. "It might be best if you stay here, sweetpea. This isn't something you're likely to want to see or hear." He grimaced. "Hell, it's not something I want to witness." Pressing a quick kiss to her lips, Brant turned and followed Morgan.

Annie watched the two brothers disappear into the barn. All three of the Wakefield men were tall, had the same impossibly wide shoulders and narrow hips, and were extraordinarily handsome. But there was something about Brant that was different. Maybe it was his easygoing manner, his engaging smile.

As she stood pondering what she found so enchanting in Brant that his brothers might lack, a loud shout, followed by rapid, unintelligible phrases came from the barn. Seconds later, Brant sauntered out of the big double doors and walked over to where she stood by his black truck.

"Is your brother all right?" she asked, alarmed that Brant would leave Morgan in such obvious pain.

"Yeah, he'll be okay." Brant opened the truck and handed her the shopping bags, while he grabbed his duffel bag. "It's best we go inside and let Morgan get the cussing out of his system." Chuckling, Brant shook his head. "If we don't, your tender sensibilities are going to end up being offended—real quick."

When Annie heard a very clear, extremely graphic word come from the barn, she grinned. "I think you might be right about going into the house."

He frowned and hurried her up the porch steps. "That was just the warm-up. In another second or two he's going to cut loose with the really creative stuff." Brant seemed to take a deep breath as he reached for the doorknob. "It's probably not as fancy as what you're used to, but welcome to the Lonetree Ranch, sweetpea."

Chapter 6

Brant held the door for Annie to precede him into the house. He wondered if she'd like the rustic, western decor of the Lonetree ranch house, or if she'd be like Daphne and start making suggestions about how much better it would look with this piece of furniture or that work of art.

"Brant, your home is beautiful," Annie said, wandering from the foyer into the great room. He heard her suck in a sharp breath at the fire blazing in the big stone fireplace. "I love this. It's perfect for the room."

When she turned to face him, he caught the first glimpse of her expression and he could tell that she meant every word she'd said. "You don't find it a little too rustic?" he asked cautiously.

"Not at all." Her eyes bright with enthusiasm, she reached out to run her fingers over the colorful Native American throw on the brown leather couch. "It couldn't be more appropriate."

Why her opinion of his home should matter, Brant didn't have a clue. But Annie's appreciation for the Lonetree ranch house caused warmth to fill his chest and the tension that he hadn't even realized gripped his shoulders to ease.

Shrugging out of his jacket, he helped her out of hers, then plucked the hat from her head. "Make yourself at home while I go hang these on the pegs by the door."

When he walked back into the room, Annie had dropped the shopping bags on the floor and was seated on the couch, running her hand along the blue slate top of the coffee table. "This is a very unusual piece of furniture," she said, smiling up at him. "I really like it. Who thought of placing a slab of stone on top of a tree stump?"

"I think my mom and dad came up with that idea in self-defense." He laughed when she arched a perfectly shaped eyebrow. "When Morgan and I were young, we had these trucks that we used to love running along the top of Mom's coffee table. They really tore up the finish, not to mention got us in a heap of trouble. By the time Mom got pregnant with Colt, she'd made Dad refinish the table twice. I guess they figured with three kids in the house they'd go broke buying new stain and varnish, so they put their heads together and this is what they came up with."

"That's a wonderful story," Annie said, sounding wistful. "I wish I had memories like that."

"Your grandmother didn't allow you to play like a normal kid?"

Shaking her head, she smiled sadly. "I had a playroom upstairs and wasn't allowed to have my toys in any other part of the house."

"Why?"

"I think Grandmother had the idea that I would scratch her antiques or clutter up the rest of the house with them."

Brant stared at her for several seconds before pulling her up from the couch and into his arms. He'd never known what it was like not to be allowed to be a kid, not to feel as if the house he lived in was home. He'd always had a close family, and after their parents died, he and his brothers had grown even closer.

But Annie had never had that. She'd gone to live with her grandmother after her parents' deaths. From what he could gather about the old woman, she'd never made Annie feel as if she had a home.

"I'm sorry, sweetpea," he said, stroking her silky hair. "It must have been lonely, playing in that room all by yourself."

She surprised him when she shook her head. "It really wasn't all that bad, actually." Her smile lit his soul. "I was much happier in my playroom than I was in the mausoleum Grandmother wanted to call a house."

He chuckled. "That bad, huh?"

"Oh, yes." Her smile faded and she shuddered against

him. "All the furniture was dark and dreary." She turned
her head to look around the great room, before she
turned back to gaze up at him. "It's nothing like this.
Your home feels warm and friendly. Like a family lives
here. My grandmother's home has always been more
like a Victorian museum."

Brant didn't know what to say. But the thought of
Annie as a lonely little girl, discouraged from feeling
that her grandmother's house was her home, made his
stomach churn. A protective feeling swept through him
that damn near took his breath, not to mention scared
the hell out of him.

Annie wasn't his type. She was books and art,
charity fund-raisers and plays. He was rodeo and
ranching, smoky honky-tonks and country music.

But their differences didn't seem to matter to his
libido when she wrapped her arms around his waist and
rested her head against his chest. Holding her close
was playing hell with his vow to keep his distance, but
he could no more step away from her than a buffalo
could roost in a tree. Something about Annie made him
want to make it up to her for her lousy childhood, had
him wanting to keep her from ever being lonely again.

"Brant, don't you think the lady might like to see her
room and freshen up before supper?" Morgan asked,
breaking into Brant's disturbing thoughts. "Although,
come to think of it, she doesn't look nearly as hungry
as you do."

Glancing up, Brant saw his brother standing in the
doorway leading into the kitchen, his left arm in the

sling they kept for the times when his shoulder popped out of joint. Morgan wore a smug smile that set Brant's teeth on edge. If he could have reached his brother, he would have throttled him right then and there.

"Annie, I don't think I introduced you to my older brother, Morgan," Brant said, releasing her. He reached down to gather the shopping bags she'd set on the floor, along with his duffel bag. "He's also known as the smart-mouth Wakefield." Heading for the stairs, Brant added, "Morgan, this is my friend, Annie Devereaux. She'll be staying here until we take off for Anaheim."

"Nice to meet you, Annie," Morgan said, nodding his head.

"It's nice to meet you, too," Annie said, smiling.

Brant stood back and let her precede him up the log-planked stairs to the second floor, then followed her. The irritating sound of Morgan's deep chuckle had Brant casting a murderous glare over his shoulder. "I'll see you in the office after supper."

Morgan laughed out loud. "I'll be looking forward to it, little brother."

Two hours later, Brant found Morgan sitting behind the desk in the study, his boots propped on the edge of the polished walnut surface. He used the long-neck bottle of beer he held to motion for Brant to pick up one just like it on the other side of the desk.

"So what's the word on the Shackley heir?" Brant asked, taking the bottle and sinking into one of the leather armchairs. "Have the lawyers found her yet?"

Morgan frowned. "Yes, and no."

Brant took a long draw on his bottle. "You want to explain that one?"

"Yes, they found Tug's daughter." Morgan shook his head. "In a cemetery."

"Then what happens to Tug's ranch?" Brant asked, sitting forward. "Does that mean we'll be able to buy it? Or will the law firm put it up for auction?"

"Neither."

Brant blew out a frustrated breath. There were times when getting details out of Morgan was like trying to sweet-talk a donkey into going somewhere he didn't want to go. "I assume there's a reason the ranch won't go up for sale?"

Morgan nodded. "The woman had a daughter."

"So she doesn't want to sell?"

"They don't know because they can't find her." Morgan leaned his head back against the high back of the leather desk chair. "All they know for sure is that she's somewhere between Seattle and San Diego."

Whistling low, Brant shook his head. "That covers a lot of territory."

"Yeah, and in the meantime, I'm stuck with keeping an eye on the place." Morgan took a swig of his beer. "Enough about my trying to buy out our dead neighbor's property. How did Colt do in Saint Louis?"

Brant shrugged. "He made his first two rides, but he lost the rope about three seconds into his final ride and I had to save his butt again. He ended up in third place, overall."

"So he managed to keep from getting hurt this time?" Morgan asked.

"Not exactly." Brant set his empty beer bottle on the desk. "He did a header dismount off his first bull and suffered another concussion."

Grinning, Morgan shook his head. "Well, it's a good thing he landed on his head. Otherwise he might have really hurt himself."

"Yeah, but his brains are going to be mush," Brant said, laughing.

"I didn't know he had any to begin with," Morgan said dryly. When they stopped laughing, Morgan asked, "By the way, where is our baby brother?"

"He went home with Mitch Simpson. He's going with Mitch to buy Kaylee's birthday present." At Morgan's lifted eyebrow, Brant held up his hands. "Don't ask me. He keeps saying she's nothing but a kid."

Morgan shook his head. "Kids grow up."

Nodding, Brant rested the ankle of one leg on the knee of the other. "She already has." He shook his head. "Kaylee's grown into a really nice-looking young woman."

Morgan eyed him for several long seconds, then asked what Brant had been waiting for. "Speaking of nice-looking ladies, what's the story with the cute little blonde upstairs?"

The fact that Morgan found Annie attractive had Brant feeling both pleased and irritated at the same time. And he wasn't sure why.

"She needed a place to stay for a week."

"Is that it?" Morgan asked, looking skeptical.

"She's in a little trouble," Brant admitted. Filling his brother in on how he'd met Annie and why she was on the run, he finished with, "You wouldn't have left her to deal with that pasty-faced little bean counter, either."

Morgan shook his head. "Nope." He looked thoughtful for a moment. "But from what I saw earlier, there's more to the story than you're telling."

"No way," Brant protested. "She's from the same type of background as Daphne. And we both know what a disaster that turned out to be. I'm just trying to help her out of a bind, that's all."

"Anything you say, brother."

"Really."

"Sure."

Morgan's knowing grin had Brant wishing he had another chance to jerk on his brother's sore shoulder. Rising to his feet, he headed for the door. He called Morgan a name as he walked out into the hall that had his brother laughing so hard he'd probably fall out of his chair. At that moment, nothing would have made Brant happier.

He might be attracted to Annie, but that's as far as Brant intended for it to go. She was from a different world than his, and he'd been shown in the past that those worlds tended to collide.

Brant decided not to dwell on it as he climbed the stairs, entered his room and headed for the shower in his private bathroom. In a week, he'd turn Annie over to her grandmother's care and get on with his life.

But long after he stretched out on the bed, he lay staring at the ceiling, thinking about the kisses he'd shared with Annie and the fact that she was lying just down the hall in one of his T-shirts. She kissed with a shy passion that was quickly becoming an addiction for him. What would it be like to hold Annie's sweet body to his? To take his shirt off her and feel himself sinking into her softness, to bring her to the brink, then take her into a realm where their backgrounds didn't matter? Would she make love with the same innocent enthusiasm as she did when she kissed him?

His lower body hardened to an almost painful state as his hormones kicked into overdrive, along with his overactive imagination. Curses hot enough to peel paint rolled off his tongue as he kicked off the blankets and headed back into the bathroom. Turning on the cold-water tap, he stepped beneath the icy spray.

His teeth chattering like a set of out-of-control castanets, Brant decided that one of two things would happen by the time he took Annie to her home in Illinois. He'd come down with a really nasty cold, or he'd end up being a raving maniac with a perpetual arousal.

He glanced down at his stubborn body. Or with his luck, he'd end up in a constant state of arousal, as well as coughing his head off from double pneumonia.

Annie yawned for the third time as she stood looking out the window in the great room at the mountains in the distance. She'd spent a sleepless night wondering if she might not be running from the wrong man. Brant represented everything in life she'd been taught to avoid. He thrived on taking risks and tempting fate every time he stepped into a rodeo or bull-riding arena.

But whether she'd been cautioned to avoid his type or not, she'd felt more exhilarated, more alive in the past three days than she'd ever felt in her life. And whether it was wise or not, she found herself more than just a little attracted to him. That's why she'd tossed and turned throughout the night. She'd analyzed it over and over and came to the same conclusion each time. She was falling for him.

Sighing heavily, she traced her finger along the window facing. Each time he kissed her, she found herself not only wanting his lips on hers, she wanted to feel his warm masculine skin pressed against her, wanted to explore his body and have him explore hers.

She shifted from one foot to the other. There was no sense in denying it. She wanted Brant.

What would it be like having him hold her against his big, hard body? How would it feel to have him make love to her?

"What are you thinking about, sweetpea?" he asked, walking up behind her.

It was all Annie could do to keep a nervous giggle from erupting as she turned to face him. If he only knew the direction her thoughts had taken, he'd be shocked right down to the soles of his cowboy boots.

"Nothing really," she said, smiling. "I was just enjoying the beautiful view."

Glancing over the top of her head, he nodded. "I've always liked looking at the Shirley Mountains from that window." He looked back down at her and his charming grin curled her toes inside her new boots. "How would you like to go play in the snow?"

"I've never done that," she said, returning his smile. "It sounds like it might be fun."

"Never?"

She shook her head. "No. We don't get that many deep snows in southern Illinois, and if we did get snowfall deep enough, my grandmother was always afraid I'd get sick if I went out to play."

He put his arms around her waist and drew her close. "Well, you're not a little girl anymore, Annie," he said gently. "You can do whatever you want now."

Annie had to blink back the tears that threatened to spill down her cheeks as she stared up at him. Brant was the first person since her parents' deaths to encourage her to do what made her happy, to be herself.

"Thank you," she said, rising on tiptoe to place a kiss on his firm lips.

He looked confused. "For what?"

"For letting me be me."

"I like watching you be you," he said, lowering his head to cover her mouth with his.

As soon as his firm lips touched hers, Annie felt the familiar tingling begin to thread its way through every part of her body as it made its way to the pit of her stomach. Heat quickly followed and caused an empty ache to pool at the apex of her thighs. When his tongue coaxed her to open for him, her eagerness for him to deepen the kiss stole her breath. She wanted to feel him taste her again, wanted him to stroke the tender recesses of her mouth.

Brant moved his hands from her waist to pull her hips into the cradle of his, and the evidence of his strong arousal pressed to her lower belly caused her knees to feel as if they would no longer support her. Putting her arms around his neck, she clung to him with an abandon that shocked her. She'd never before been the passionate type. But in the circle of Brant's arms she seemed to transform from a shy, unassuming woman into a wanton who knew exactly what she needed.

The thought brought her up short and had her pushing against his shoulders to break the kiss. "I…I don't know what came over me," she said, wondering if that husky tone really belonged to her.

"Sweetpea, don't ever apologize for kissing like that," Brant said, his breathing harsh. Seeming to understand that she needed time to come to terms with this new sexual side of herself, he loosened his hold and put a bit of space between them. He cleared his throat. "So what do you say? Wanna go play in the snow?"

She took a deep breath, then gazed up into his vivid blue eyes. "Yes," she said, managing a smile. "Are we going to build a snowman or have a snowball fight?"

He laughed. "We can do those things after we get back."

"Where are we going?"

"You'll see," he said, pressing his lips to her forehead. Stepping back, he took her hand in his and led her to the stairs, then patted her bottom to urge her up the steps. "Go get the mittens and sunglasses you bought in Denver yesterday, while I get our coats and hats."

Brant watched Annie until she disappeared in the loft above, then turned to find Morgan standing right behind him. "What are you grinning at?" he asked, irritated at his brother's smug expression.

"You and that little lady are just friends, huh?" Morgan asked, rocking back on his heels.

"Yes."

Morgan threw back his head and laughed like a hyena. "Keep telling yourself that if you want to, but I think we both know better."

Brant was used to his brother's teasing. But this time, Morgan's sly observations were hitting a little too close for comfort. He was starting to feel things for Annie that were way across the line of a mere friendship.

"You think you're pretty damn smart, don't you?" Brant asked, his back teeth clenched so tightly he felt as if they were welded together.

"Smart enough to see what the score is on this one," Morgan said, strolling into the foyer. He chuckled. "You'd better start deciding which one of us you want to be the best man, me or Colt."

"I think you hit your head, along with your shoulder yesterday," Brant growled, following his brother.

"Just let me know in time to get a haircut," Morgan

said, giving Brant an irritating grin as he disappeared through the office door.

"Don't hold your breath," Brant muttered, lifting the lid on a chest beneath the pegs where he'd hung his and Annie's coats and hats the evening before.

"Were you talking to me?" Annie asked, descending the stairs.

Brant removed two Native American blankets and placed them on top of the chest, then turned to watch her cross the great room. "Nah, Morgan was being a smart-mouth again."

She smiled. "It must be nice to have a sibling to joke with."

He snorted. "Yeah, there are times when it's so much fun, I can hardly stand it," he said, holding her coat while she slipped her arms into the sleeves. Shrugging into his own jacket, he put on his hat, then took a sock cap from one of the other pegs and pulled it on top of her head. "We'll be gone for a couple of hours and I want you staying warm." He smiled at her. "Did you remember the sunglasses?"

"Right here," she said, holding up a pair of wire-rimmed frames with dark lenses. "I assume these are to keep from being blinded by the glare from the snow?"

"Yep." He put on his own pair of shades, grabbed the blankets, then took her hand in his. "As soon as we get Dancer, we'll be ready to go."

"Dancer?"

"My horse."

Annie stopped dead in her tracks. "We're riding a horse?"

"Is that a problem?"

"I've never ridden one," she said, nibbling on her lower lip.

Brant grinned. "You've never played in the snow either, but that's not stopping you, is it?"

He loved watching the sparkle of excitement fill her pretty, green eyes. "No, it's not," she said decisively. She put her sunglasses on, then flashed him a smile that sent his blood pressure up a few dozen points. "This is going to be a day filled with firsts for me. And I can't wait."

Ten minutes later, Brant placed one of the blankets on Dancer, then turned to Annie. "Ready?"

"I—" She stopped to give the gelding an apprehensive look. "Yes, but how do I get up there?"

"Just like this," he said, placing his hands around her small waist. Lifting her, he sat her astride the horse's broad back.

"Oh my God, I can't believe I'm doing this," she said, clutching the other blanket so hard he figured she'd squeeze the bright colors right out of it.

"Just relax," he said, grabbing the reins and a handful of mane to launch himself up behind her. "Now spread the blanket over your legs so you stay warm."

She did as he said, then asked, "Is there anything else I'm supposed to do?"

"Just enjoy the ride," he said, wrapping an arm around her waist to pull her to him.

But when her delightful little bottom came into contact with his groin as she settled herself against him, it was all Brant could do to keep from groaning out loud. Swallowing hard, he nudged Dancer into a slow walk out of the barn and across the ranch yard.

"I'm actually riding a horse," Annie said, laughing delightedly.

"You sure are, sweetpea." He pressed a kiss to the side of her head. "Are you comfortable?"

She wiggled her bottom back against him a little more, then nodded. "Now I am."

Brant felt as if his heart might pound a hole right through his rib cage. Annie's small body touching his from knees to shoulders was sending his hormones racing through him at an alarming rate and gathering in the region just below his belt. His palms turned sweaty inside his leather gloves. Damn! They hadn't even made it to the lane yet and he was already hard as hell.

He'd purposely decided to ride Dancer bareback because heat from the horse's body would help keep them warm. But he hadn't given a thought to what the friction from Annie's body would do to his. As the gelding plodded along the snowplowed lane, Annie's backside rubbed against his groin and had him clenching his teeth with vise-grip force.

They remained silent as they rode down the lane, then started down another road. The air was crisp and cold, but the sun shone brightly, sparkling like diamonds on the surface of the snow covering the landscape.

"Brant, this is absolutely breathtaking," Annie said, turning to look over her shoulder at him.

"You should see it in the spring when everything is new and green," he said, managing a smile. "Wildflowers cover the fields and everywhere you look you can see a mama with a new baby."

"I'd love to see this countryside in spring," Annie said, sounding sincere.

A warmth filled his chest at the thought of having Annie with him to watch the seasons change. But he ignored it. He knew better than to count on her staying around to see the flowers bloom, or the lanky little pronghorn and mule deer jumping and frisking around the valleys while their mamas grazed on the new growth. In a week she'd be going back to Illinois and her cultured way of life. And he'd stay right where he was, because that's where he belonged. The same as she'd be where she belonged.

As they rode along a ridge about three miles south of the Lonetree's headquarters, Brant pointed to the valley below. "What do you think of this?"

He heard Annie catch her breath. "Please make the horse stop."

With a slight pull of the reins, Dancer came to a halt. "What's wrong?"

She shook her head. "Nothing. I want to take a better look." She took off her sunglasses as she gazed down at the land below the low rise of the ridge. "I love the way pine trees ring the meadow on three sides and the stream winds from one end to the other." Turning to face him, she smiled. "This would be a wonderful place for a home."

Brant felt his chest tighten with feelings he'd rather not analyze as he gazed into her expressive green eyes. "That's exactly what I intend to do."

"Really?"

Grinning, he nodded. "I'm going to build the house and barns over there," he said, pointing to the east end of the valley. "And I'll have horses grazing over on the west side."

"That's the perfect place for it," she said, nodding. "But it has to be a certain kind of house."

His heart sank. Here it came. This was where she'd tell him about some modern-style brick-and-block structure that would look better on a golf course somewhere out East than in a hidden valley in Wyoming.

"What kind of home do you think would be best here?" he asked.

"It would definitely have to be a log home," she said, surprising him. "But different from the Lonetree ranch house. It would need lots of windows facing the west end of the valley, so you could see the sunset each evening." She paused thoughtfully. "The master bedroom should be on the second floor of that side, with glass doors leading out onto a balcony, too. That way you could sit outside in the summer and watch the sun as it slips behind the mountains."

Brant swallowed hard and the tightening in his chest turned to a warmth that invaded every cell in his body. Her description was exactly what he'd always envisioned. "You know, sweetpea, you're pretty damn amazing."

"Me?" She looked incredulous.

"Yes, you." Laughing, he hugged her close, and lowered his head to press a quick kiss to her soft, pink lips. "You've just managed to describe in less than five minutes what I've been planning for the last two years."

The realization that Annie wouldn't be sharing the house with him caused a pang of regret to twist his gut. But Brant pushed the feeling aside as he held her close and they gazed out across the valley that would one day be his home. She was in his arms now and that's all that mattered.

Chapter 7

Two mornings after their ride up to his valley, Brant came downstairs feeling as if he'd been on a two-day bender. His head ached from lack of sleep, his insides burned and he felt as if he was about to jump out of his own skin.

He wanted Annie. It was as simple as that. And just as complicated.

He'd spent the last three nights tossing and turning, going over all the reasons why he shouldn't become involved with her—why kissing her, making love to her, would spell disaster. But his stubborn body wasn't listening to anything his head had to say. He'd taken more ice-cold showers since meeting Annie than he'd ever taken in his entire life. And after the initial shock wore off, nothing had changed. He still wanted her with a fierceness that scared the hell out of him.

For the past few days they'd played in the snow together like a couple of kids, he'd shown her around the Lonetree and taught her to ride a horse. And with each passing day, he watched a little more of the cautious, conservative Annie disappear, to be replaced by a confident, adventurous woman. A sexy as hell woman that he was finding it hard not to kiss, not to touch.

His body tightened and he gritted his teeth as he tried to get himself under control. They came from two different worlds, and past experience had taught him that her enjoyment of the western lifestyle was nothing more than a passing fancy. By the time he delivered her into her grandmother's care, she'd be ready to return to all that was familiar to her. She'd be tired of jeans and boots, of riding horses and looking at hidden valleys where a log house would someday stand.

He wandered into the kitchen expecting to find her sitting at the table having breakfast, but she wasn't there. He'd checked before coming downstairs and she wasn't in her room. Where could she be?

Walking through the great room, he headed for the foyer to see if her jacket was still hung on the pegs beside the front door. But glancing into the office, he stopped just past the doorway, then stepped back to take a better look. Annie sat in the desk chair, her attention fixed on the computer screen sitting on the stand to the left of the desk.

"Hey there, sweetpea," Brant said as he entered the room. "I wondered where you were."

Her smile made his knees weak and his pulse race. "I asked Morgan if I could use the computer to do an Internet search," she said, keying an address into the browser.

Rounding the desk, Brant stood behind her and glanced at the screen. "What are you looking for?"

"I'm searching the archives of the newspapers in Fresno, California," she answered. "When I first met Patrick, he mentioned that he'd lived and worked in the Fresno area before moving to Illinois."

"What exactly are you looking for?" he asked. "Police reports?"

She nodded. "Uh-huh."

Annie looked so cute sitting there with her spun-gold hair tucked behind her ears, nibbling on her lower lip as she read what was on the screen. Brant wanted to pick her up and kiss her until they both needed oxygen. No matter how much he talked to himself and recounted all the reasons he should steer clear of her, he couldn't seem to keep his hands off her. Unable to resist, he lifted her hair to place a kiss at the nape of her neck.

"Is there anything I can do to help?" he murmured against her satiny skin.

He felt a tiny shiver course through her a moment before she turned to smile up at him. "As a matter of fact, there is something that you can do."

"Name it, sweetpea." At that moment, if she'd asked him to go jump in the lake, he'd have found an ax, chopped a hole in the ice and dived in.

"Would you mind checking on your brother?" she asked, her smile turning to a look of concern. "He seemed really—" she paused as if to think of a word to describe Morgan "—I don't know. Sad?"

Brant glanced at the calendar on the desk and cursed his own shortsightedness. How could he have forgotten? "Today would have been Emily's thirty-first birthday."

"Emily?"

He nodded. "She was Morgan's fiancée."

"What happened?"

"She was killed a week before their wedding."

"Oh, how awful," Annie said, rising from the chair to wrap her arms around his shoulders. "You all must have loved her very much. How long has it been?"

"It will be five years this July." He took a deep breath against the tightening in his chest and hugged Annie close. They'd all cared for Emily and felt her loss deeply. But Brant hated seeing how much Morgan still suffered, how he still grieved her passing. "This date is always tough on Morgan because he proposed on her birthday and they set the date of their wedding that same night."

"Why don't you spend the day with him, Brant." Annie touched his cheek with her soft hand. "Maybe you could help him get his mind off his loss."

"You won't mind spending most of the day on your own?" he asked, feeling torn between wanting to help his brother and wanting to be with her.

She shook her head. "I'll be fine. I'm going to be

busy looking through Internet files anyway." She rose on tiptoe to kiss his chin. "Besides, Morgan needs you right now."

"Did anybody ever tell you how special you are?" Brant asked, lowering his mouth to hers for a quick kiss.

Her lips beneath his caused an instant charge of electric current to streak through him and heat to surge through his veins. His lower body tightened instantly and he slid his hands from her waist to her hips. Drawing her close, he let her feel what she did to him, how she made him want her.

When her lips parted on a soft gasp, he took advantage of her reaction and slowly slipped inside to stroke the inner recesses of her mouth. Teasing, coaxing, he reveled in the sweet taste of her, the shy way she touched his tongue with hers.

She tangled her fingers in the hair brushing the collar of his chambray shirt, then slipped beneath to trace the column of his neck. The feel of her nails skimming across his skin caused his blood pressure to skyrocket and sent a surge of desire straight to the part of his anatomy that was already straining insistently against the fly of his jeans.

Brant broke the kiss and tried desperately to remember all the reasons why becoming involved with Annie would be a mistake. He couldn't think of a single one.

"Brant?" The sound of her passion-filled voice saying his name sent another wave of longing to every cell in his body.

Gazing down at the heightened color on her porcelain cheeks, he smiled. "You're about to kill me, Annie."

"Me?" She looked skeptical.

"Yes, you." He placed a kiss on the end of her cute little nose. "If you'll remember, I told you that I wasn't a gelding. That I'm a man with a man's desires. And right now, you're making me more aware of that fact than I've ever been in my life."

The blush on her cheeks deepened to almost the same shade of pink as her blouse, but the spark of desire in her green eyes brightened. He didn't think he'd ever seen a prettier sight. "I've never been the type of woman—"

He placed his finger to her lips and shook his head. "Sweetpea, I don't want to hear you say that about yourself again. The evidence that you *are* that type of woman is pressed up against you right now."

At Brant's heated look and candid statement, Annie's stomach did a backflip. Moistening her suddenly dry lips, she tried to think of something to say.

"Don't do that," he said, briefly closing his eyes.

"What?"

"Lick your lips," he said at the same time his body stirred against hers. He gazed at her. "It doesn't help my frame of mind right now."

Her eyes widened and her cheeks felt as if they were on fire. Averting her eyes to the front of his shirt, she murmured, "I…um, sorry."

Chuckling, Brant stepped back and she watched him take several deep breaths. "Sweetpea, don't be sorry. Just don't do it again when I'm in this kind of shape."

He reached out to place his forefinger under her chin. Lifting her head until their gazes met, he smiled. "Otherwise, I might not be able to keep my promise."

"Your promise?"

He nodded. "I told you that you could trust me. But this gallantry stuff is taking its toll." Leaning down to whisper in her ear, he added, "There's nothing that I'd like more right now than to take you upstairs to my bed and make love to you for the rest of the day and night."

Before Annie could find her voice, he kissed her on the forehead and walked out of the office without a backward glance. Collapsing in the chair behind her, she stared off into space as she came to terms with what he'd said.

He wanted her. Brant Wakefield actually wanted her the way a man wants a woman.

She'd known he liked her, enjoyed showing her around the ranch and seemed to like kissing her. But he wanted to make love to her? That was going to take some getting used to. She'd never had a man tell her that she created *that* kind of passion in him.

Nibbling on her lower lip, she turned back to the computer but sat staring at the blinking cursor for a good ten minutes after Brant left the room. There was no doubt in her mind now that she'd fallen in love with him. He was the kindest, most generous man she'd ever met, and from the moment they met he'd made her feel protected and cherished. But could he love her in return?

He'd said he wanted her, but that wasn't the same as

loving her. And although she was far from experienced in relationships between men and women, she had enough knowledge about the opposite sex to know that love wasn't a prerequisite for sleeping together.

A shiver ran the length of her spine. Beyond a few passionless kisses and a handful of clumsy hugs, Patrick had never shown that she excited him in any way. She shook her head. He'd shown more enthusiasm for her grandmother's bank accounts than he had for her. And other than a few dates in college, Annie didn't have a clue about passion and desire.

Taking a deep steadying breath, she decided it would be best to forget about what Brant had said and concentrate on searching the archives of the Fresno-area newspapers. It was much easier on her peace of mind to look for something to incriminate Patrick than to think about what was happening between herself and Brant.

Late that afternoon, Annie tucked her denim skirt around her feet as she curled up in one corner of the couch in front of the fireplace in the great room. Shuffling through the papers in her hands, she smiled. She'd found more than enough in Patrick's background to convince her grandmother to notify the authorities and start an investigation.

"What have you got there, sweetpea?" Brant asked, entering the room from the kitchen.

Glancing up, she watched his easy gait as he walked over to her. His jeans were worn and soft-looking, and they encased his long, muscular legs like a second skin. She swallowed hard and looked back down at the papers she held.

"I found—" When he sat down next to her on the big leather couch, he rested his arm along the back, then tangled his fingers in her hair. She had to clear her throat before she could finish. "I found out that Patrick was arrested for embezzlement seven years ago, then convicted and sentenced to five years in prison."

"Let me see." Brant reached for the printouts. His hand touched hers and a tiny little charge of electricity snaked up her arm.

"What he'd done wasn't discovered until after the elderly woman died and her children were dividing up the estate," Annie said, pointing to a passage on the page he held. "Since it was considered a white-collar crime, he served his sentence in a minimum-security facility."

"But, with your suspicions, this should be enough to start an investigation," Brant said, giving her a smile that curled her toes.

"Or at the very least, convince my grandmother to have her accounts audited," Annie said, nodding.

"You did good, sweetpea. Real good." He took the papers and laid them on the coffee table, then turned to pull her to him. "Why didn't you think of this before?"

The feel of his strong arms around her made thinking difficult. "I…I'm not sure why I didn't think to do an Internet search when I first suspected he was embezzling from Grandmother, but after you mentioned our going to Anaheim, I remembered that Patrick had come from California."

"And a leopard doesn't change its spots, does it?" Brant asked, grinning.

Smiling back, she shook her head. "I always thought it odd that he never wanted to talk about living there. Almost everyone wants to tell you where they came from and about their past accomplishments. But every time I asked, he'd change the subject."

Brant laughed. "It's my bet old pasty-face came right out of the California penal system just before he moved to your hometown."

She nodded. "I'm sure he probably did."

They sat staring at the fire for several long minutes before Annie broke the silence. "How's Morgan?"

"He'll be okay," Brant said, his arms tightening around her. "I talked him into riding down to Laramie with one of Colt's friends this evening. Jake Weston wants to look at a horse some guy has for sale down that way and Morgan has a good eye for horseflesh. Then, if I know Jake, he'll talk Morgan into stopping by Buffalo Gals in Bear Creek for a few beers on their way back." Brant chuckled. "By the time Morgan gets home tonight, all he'll want to do is go to bed and sleep."

"He'll get drunk?"

Smiling, Brant shook his head. "Not really. If Morgan drinks more than three beers, all he wants to do is sleep." Brant nuzzled the side of her neck, sending a shiver up her spine. "Just be glad his room is on the opposite end of the house."

"Wh-why?" she asked breathlessly.

"Because most of the night he'll be snoring so loud it'll sound like a freight train is barreling through."

She laughed. "Louder than you, huh?"

"I don't snore," he said, shaking his head.

"Yes, you do."

"Nope."

Before she could argue with him further, Brant ran his fingers up and down her ribs, sending her into a fit of laughter. "St-stop," she gasped.

"What will you give me to stop?" he asked, continuing to tickle her.

"A-anything," she said, squirming to put distance between them.

"How about a hug?"

"Y-yes."

His fingers immediately stilled and it was then that Annie realized her squirming had landed her flat on her back on the couch. Stretching out beside her, Brant took her into his arms and stared down at her for what seemed an eternity before he spoke. "Sweetpea, I've spent a miserable day."

"You have?" The simple act of breathing suddenly took great effort and she wondered fleetingly whether it was from being tickled or from the proximity of the man holding her to his body.

He nodded. "I kept reminding myself of all the reasons why I should keep my hands off you."

She wondered if she'd ever get used to his outspokenness. "And did you reach any conclusions?" she asked, slightly shocked that she'd voiced the question. She really wasn't sure she wanted to know.

Shaking his head, he brushed her mouth with his. "All I was able to decide was that I want you like I've never wanted any other woman."

Every cell in her being tingled to life at Brant's admission. "I—I don't know what to say," she stammered.

"Tell me to leave you alone, Annie," he said, kissing her forehead, her cheeks. "Tell me to get the hell away from you and keep my hands to myself."

Heaven help her, but that was the very last thing she wanted. Shoring up her courage, she shook her head. "I can't do that, Brant."

Groaning, he buried his head in her hair. "Why, Annie? Why can't you tell me to leave you alone?"

"Because…" She took a deep breath. "Because I like it when you kiss me, when you touch me."

She felt his big body shudder against her before he raised his head to gaze down at her. "That's the problem, sweetpea. I like it, too. In fact, I like it so much, I don't think I can continue to be a gentleman and walk away the next time I kiss you."

His incredibly blue eyes pinned her with their intensity and she could see the turbulence in their depths, the war he was waging with himself. He wanted her, but if she told him that wasn't what she wanted, he would back off, no matter how difficult it was for him.

Closing her eyes for a moment to gather her courage, she opened them to meet his gaze head-on. "Kiss me, Brant."

"Dammit, Annie, didn't you hear what I said?" he asked, his arms tightening around her. "If I kiss you, I won't be able to walk away this time. I'll keep on kissing you until one thing leads to another and I make love to you."

"I don't want you to walk away," she said, reaching up to place her hand at the back of his head. Drawing his head down, she touched her lips to his. "I want you to stay right here and kiss me, touch me…" She paused, then feeling as if she were jumping off a cliff, she finished, "…make love to me."

A groan rumbled up from deep in his chest a moment before his mouth came down on hers. At the first contact of his lips, Annie's eyes drifted shut and she felt as if lightning skipped over every nerve in her body. A warmth like she'd never known began to flow though her and she wrapped her arms around his broad shoulders as he traced her mouth with his strong tongue.

When he pressed forward to enter her mouth, he ran his hand down her side to tug her blouse from the waistband of her denim skirt. The feel of his palm at her waist, the contrast of a calloused masculine hand as it skimmed over smooth feminine skin sent her temperature soaring and a shimmer of excitement snaking down her spine. But when his hand cupped the underside of her breast, Annie moaned and clutched his shoulders.

Breaking the kiss, Brant chafed her nipple through the lace of her bra as he nibbled his way to the sensitive hollow behind her ear. "Does that feel good, sweetpea?"

"Y-yes."

He raised his head to gaze down at her. "Are you sure you want to make love with me, Annie?"

She nodded. "I've never been more sure of anything in my life, Brant."

He pulled his hand from beneath her blouse, then touching her cheek with his index finger, he drew it down to trace her lower lip. He stared at her for what seemed an eternity and the heat in his dark blue eyes took her breath.

Slowly rising from the couch, he held his hand out to her. "Let's go upstairs, sweetpea."

When Annie trustingly placed her hand in his, Brant felt as if he'd been handed a rare gift. Pulling her up to stand beside him, his heart pounded against his rib cage and his body tightened with need. They were about to take a step that would change everything between them.

"Are you really sure about this, Annie?" he asked again. The last thing he wanted was her having regrets in the morning about what they would share tonight.

To his immense relief, she nodded. "There's not a doubt in my mind, Brant."

Relieved beyond words to hear that she wanted him as much as he wanted her, he led her over to the staircase, wrapped his arm around her waist and together they climbed the stairs and walked down the hall to his room. Closing the door behind them, Brant switched on the bedside lamp.

"Brant?"

He turned to face her and the shy smile curving her

perfect lips sent his blood pressure up several points. "What, sweetpea?"

"There's…um, something I think you should know." She nervously nibbled on her lower lip as she gazed up at him.

"And what would that be?" he asked, pulling her into his arms. He lowered his head to bury his face in the silky strands of her herbal-scented hair. "If you're worried about protection. Don't. I'll take care of everything."

"Oh, I hadn't thought of that," she said, wrapping her arms around his waist. "Thank you, but that's not what I need to tell you."

A tingle of apprehension streaked up his spine. "What exactly do you need to tell me, Annie?"

She kissed the skin at the exposed vee of his shirt, sending a wave of heat straight to his loins. "I might not be very good at this. And you may even have to tell me what to do at times."

He swallowed hard as he tried to get his suddenly dry throat to work.

But before he could vocalize his thoughts, she confirmed his suspicion. "I've never done this before," she whispered.

Chapter 8

Brant suddenly felt as if he'd run headfirst into a brick wall. He pulled back to gaze at her. "Never?"

She shook her head.

Swallowing hard, he released her, took a step back, then another. He ran a shaky hand over the sudden tension gripping his neck and took a deep breath. "You're a virgin."

"That's usually the case when someone has never made love," she said, nodding.

"And you want me to be the first man you make love with?"

"Yes," she said, sounding about as certain as anyone he'd ever heard.

"Why, Annie?" He blew out the air trapped in his lungs as he tried to focus on all the reasons he should send her to her room, while he jumped into an ice-cold shower and stayed there until he spit ice cubes. "Why me? Why now?"

She closed the distance between them. "Because you're kind, giving, and the sexiest man I've ever met." Reaching out, she took his hand in hers. "And you've made me feel more like a real woman in the last few days than I've ever felt in my life."

The touch of her soft skin on his callused palm, the look of pure desire in her expressive green eyes and the smile curving her sensuous lips caused blood to surge through his veins with a force that made him light-headed. He closed his eyes in an effort to think clearly. But the feel of her fingers skimming over his knuckles, the pads of her fingertips as they traced a slow line up to the erratic pulse at his wrist, was playing hell with his reasoning.

"That's not all," she said, her sweet voice flowing over him like a warm caress.

He opened his eyes. "There…" He had to stop to clear the rust from his throat. "There's more?"

Nodding, she gave him a smile that sent his good intentions right out the window. "I want to be close to you in every way a woman can be close to a man. I want to be part of you, and you part of me."

Groaning, Brant pulled her back into his arms and held her close. "Dammit, woman, you aren't going to make this easy, are you?" He took a deep shuddering breath, then stared down at her. "You have no idea how much I want to hold you in my arms and bury myself deep inside you. But if I do that, I'll be taking something from you that you can never get back."

"I know."

"And I'd rather die than have you regret one minute—"

She placed her index finger to his mouth, stopping the rest of his argument. "The only regret I'll have is if we don't make love, Brant."

He kissed her finger. "But, sweetpea, you need to understand. I can't make any promises—"

"I'm not asking for any," she said, interrupting him. "It's my choice." Her smile made his mouth go dry. "I want you to be the first man to touch me."

And I'd damn well better be the only man to touch you.

The thought stopped him short. But as he gazed into Annie's luminous green eyes, Brant knew in his soul it was true. He did want to be the only man to hold her, touch her, make love to her. He swallowed hard and ignored the disturbing realization. If he thought too much about it, he was afraid he'd discover something about himself he wasn't yet ready to face.

He closed his eyes again and tried to fight what he was beginning to realize was a losing battle. With Annie's arms wrapped around his waist, her head nestled trustingly against his chest, there was no way in hell he could be noble and send her to her room. He was going to make love to her.

"Sweetpea, I…" Brant forgot what he was about to say as a sudden thought sent a chill straight through him. "I don't want to hurt you."

Stepping back, she reached up to unfasten the first snap on his chambray shirt. "Brant, I know there's going to be some discomfort." She moved down to the second snap. "But I trust you. I know you'll be gentle."

The feel of her fingers on his skin as she released the snap closures on his shirt had Brant clenching his back teeth so hard, he was sure they'd crack under the pressure. He took one deep breath, then another as he fought to control the sudden surge of need flowing through his veins. Annie was putting her faith and trust in him to make her first time as easy as possible. And he'd walk through hell and back to see that her confidence in him wasn't misplaced.

"I promise you that I'll do everything I can to make this easy for you, sweetpea," he said, taking her hands in his. He kissed her fingertips. "But you're going to have to help me."

"How?"

"You're going to have to stop touching me for just a few minutes," he said, trying to force his lungs to take in some much-needed air. He grinned at her puzzled expression. "Otherwise, I'm going to set the house on fire."

She smiled back at him. "That wouldn't be a good idea. It's freezing outside."

He groaned and shook his head. "I've already been frozen enough in the last few days to last me a lifetime." Seeing the question in her expressive gaze, he chuckled.

"I've been taking cold showers ever since we rented that motel room in Denver."

"Really?" She looked surprised.

He brushed a strand of silky blond hair from her smooth cheek. "You have no idea how sexy you are, do you, sweetpea?"

"I…I've never thought of myself that way," she said, her sweet voice breathless.

Brant unbuttoned the top button of her red calico blouse, then smiling, lowered his head to kiss the exposed skin along her collarbone as he eased the second button through its opening. "Believe me, you've got more sex appeal in your little finger than most women have in their whole body." He smiled when she shivered beneath his lips.

Raising his head, he held her gaze as he worked the next couple of buttons through their holes. He let the backs of his fingers brush the smooth skin of her abdomen, and by the time he reached the waistband of her denim skirt, he wasn't sure which one of them was breathing harder. When he pulled the tail of her blouse loose and parted the garment, his heart slammed against his chest at the sight of her red, lacy see-through bra.

"Is this one of the items you bought in that lingerie place in the mall in Denver?" he asked, his voice cracking like a teenager's.

"Yes," she said, treating him to a smile that spiked his blood pressure by a good fifty points. "I buy all of my underthings from the Sleek and Sassy Lady Lingerie Boutiques."

Brant ran his finger along the edge of one lacy cup. "I think I love that store," he said, blowing out a pent-up breath.

"I've heard a lot of men like looking at their catalogs," she said, her throaty laughter sending a streak of longing straight to his groin.

He pushed her blouse from her shoulders and down her arms. "The real thing is a whole lot better than seeing it in a catalog."

Tossing the cotton shirt on the trunk at the end of his bed, he reached behind her to unhook the back closure, then pull the tiny straps from her arms. The sight of her full perfect breasts caused his body to throb and his hands to shake slightly when he reached up to fill his palms with her creamy softness.

"You're beautiful, Annie."

At the feel of hard male calluses cupping her smooth feminine skin, Annie felt as if she'd melt into a puddle at his big, booted feet. But when he chafed her nipples with the pads of his thumbs, ribbons of heated excitement threaded their way from every part of her to gather into a swirling coil in the pit of her stomach. Reaching out, she grasped Brant's biceps to steady herself.

"Does that feel good, sweetpea?"

His smile, the desire in his deep blue gaze and the sound of his voice rough with passion spread heat throughout her entire body. Catching her lower lip between her teeth, she tried desperately to keep a moan from escaping.

"Don't hide it, Annie," he said, leaning forward to

whisper close to her ear. "Let me hear you when it feels good."

If she could have formed words, Annie would have told him that she was pretty sure proper ladies weren't supposed to moan. But when he lowered his head and took one taut bud into his mouth, she felt more like a real woman and less like a proper lady with each passing second. The tip of his tongue flicking her sensitized flesh, the moist heat of his mouth and his gentle sucking tightened the coil in her belly and made stifling the sound of her growing desire impossible.

When Brant raised his head, his slow, sexy smile made her knees wobble. "That's it, sweetpea. Let me know I'm bringing you pleasure."

"It's not fair," she said raggedly. "I want to touch you, too."

She reached up to take hold of the lapels of his shirt, then gave one quick jerk. Every snap on the blue chambray popped open, revealing Brant's well-developed chest and stomach.

"You're gorgeous," she said, placing her palms on the rise of his pectoral muscles.

He chuckled. "I've been called a lot of things. But gorgeous is a first."

Exploring the hard sinew, she traced her index finger around his flat nipples. The flesh puckered, and at his low groan, she glanced up. "Does that feel as good for me to touch you as it does for you to touch me?"

"Sweetpea, if it felt any better I doubt that I could stand it," he said, quickly shrugging out of his shirt.

He pulled her into his arms and the feel of his bare skin against hers, the beating of his heart keeping time with her own, tightened the coil in her stomach and sent tiny charges of electricity skipping over every nerve ending in her body. As his lips nibbled the hollow behind her ear and the side of her neck, Annie wrapped her arms around him. Splaying her hands across his broad back, she clung to him as wave after wave of heated sensation swept through her.

As he held her to him, Annie felt his hands slip between them to release the button at the waistband of her skirt, then slide the zipper down. Stepping back, he smiled encouragingly as he gave a little tug and the denim fell to her feet. When his gaze drifted down her body, she heard his sharp intake of breath, saw his body shudder at the sight of her red garter belt and matching red thong.

She watched him close his eyes and breathe deeply for several long seconds before he spoke. "Annie, I swear you're going to give me a heart attack with your choice of underwear." His voice sounded deeper than it had only moments before.

"You don't like what I'm wearing?" she teased.

His eyes popped open and the hunger she saw in the deep blue depths took her breath. "I love what you have on, sweetpea," he said, grinning. He ran his index finger along one of the garters. "But I think I'm going to love taking these little wisps of lace off you even more."

Annie barely managed to stand still as Brant unhooked the garters from the tops of her hose, then slowly pulled the nylons down her legs, caressing her thighs, her calves and the arch of her foot as he went. Straightening, he ran his hands beneath the elastic band of her garter belt and in one quick motion swept it from her body.

Pulling her to him, he nuzzled the side of her neck as he ran his hands down her back to cup her bottom and draw her closer. Shivers of need raced through her when he hooked his thumbs in the tiny waistband at the back of her thong, then pulled it down to fall at her feet.

He stepped away from her then, and the appreciation in his fiery gaze made her heart skip a beat. "You're beautiful, Annie," he said, his voice so reverent there wasn't a doubt in her mind that he meant it.

Nibbling on her lower lip, Annie gathered her courage, and reached out to trace her finger along the line of dark hair arrowing down from his navel to disappear below his belt buckle. "I like the way you look in jeans, Brant. But I'd like to see you out of them."

His stomach quivered as she worked the leather belt strap through the metal buckle, then popped the snap at his waistband. "May I?" she asked, glancing up at him.

"Aw, hell, sweetpea, I'll be disappointed if you don't," he said, grinning.

She smiled back, then taking the tab between her thumb and index finger, eased the zipper down. Her hand brushed the hard ridge of his arousal straining at his white cotton briefs and a shiver of feminine power coursed through her. But when she started to push his jeans from his lean hips, Brant caught her hands in his.

"I think I'd better take care of the rest of this," he said, sounding as out of breath as she felt.

Annie stood mesmerized as Brant removed his boots, jeans and briefs. She'd never seen a nude man, unless she counted the statues and nude artwork in museums. But the simple act of watching Brant disrobe had a far different effect on her than any work of art. Her heart was racing and the room suddenly seemed to be devoid of oxygen.

He removed something from the pocket of his jeans and placed it under one of the pillows, then turned to face her. Annie's heart skipped several beats and her eyes widened. Brant was, in a word, gorgeous. His body was far from average and looked as if it had been sculpted with an artist's eye for detail. His shoulders were wide, his chest and stomach muscles well defined, his hips and flanks lean. Long muscular legs carried him toward her, but the sight of his impressive arousal caused her heart to stop completely, then take off at a gallop. She didn't have any prior experience to draw from, but something told her that Brant was above average in more than one way.

Her gaze flew to his. He was looking at her as if she was the most desirable woman on earth. "It's all right, sweetpea," he said, catching her hands in his. "I promise we'll fit just fine."

Brant led Annie to the side of the bed, then pulling back the comforter and sheet, picked her up to gently place her on the soft flannel sheets. Stretching out beside her, he gathered her into his arms. He loved the feel of her small body against his, the contrast of soft curvy female to hard angular male.

But the feel of her warmth pressed to him quickly had Brant grinding his teeth and praying for the strength to take things slow. He'd never been so turned on in his life, and they'd barely gotten their clothes off.

Propping himself on one elbow, he leaned over to stare down at her. "Sweetpea, we're going to take this slow and easy," he said, feeling the need to reassure her.

But apparently Annie meant what she'd said when she told him that she trusted him, because she wrapped her arms around his neck, pulled his head down to hers and planted a kiss on him that made him feel as if he just might go up in a blaze of glory. Her perfect lips on his, the shy way she deepened the kiss, sent a wave of longing straight through him and had his body throbbing with the need to brand her as his.

When she finally let him up for air, he shook his head. "Damn, woman, you're about to kill me." He pressed his lips to the slope of her breasts, then nibbling his way to the hardened tip, he added, "And I'm loving every minute of it."

He felt her slender fingers thread through his hair and hold him to her as he teased the tight bud. "Brant...I think...you're the one...killing me."

Brant grinned and raised his head. "Want me to stop, sweetpea?"

She gave him a shy smile, then closed her eyes. "No."

Kissing her sweet lips, he ran his hand over her ribs to her trim waist. "Your skin is so smooth. Just like a piece of fine satin." He felt her shiver against him when he continued the exploration over the curve of her hip and down her outer thigh. "Annie?"

"Mmm?"

"Look at me."

When her eyelids fluttered open, he held her gaze as he moved his hand to brush the inner part of her thigh. "I want you to promise me something."

"At this point...I'll promise you...anything," she said, her hands tightening on his shoulders as he drew closer to her feminine secrets.

"Tell me what feels good," he said, touching her at the juncture of her thighs.

Parting her, Brant found her moist heat, stroked the tiny pleasure point with the pad of his thumb. "I... please..." Her voice trailed off into a soft moan.

He watched her close her eyes and a blush of desire begin to color her porcelain cheeks. "Please what?"

"Please...do something," she whispered, moving restlessly against him.

"What do you want me to do?" he asked, continuing to tease her.

Her eyes flew open and she met his gaze head-on. "Make love...to me, Brant. Now."

Her throaty demand sent blood surging through his veins, but when he dipped his finger into her honeyed warmth to test her, Brant was the one having to take several deep breaths to slow his own libido. Her complete readiness for him almost sent him over the edge. She wanted him as badly as he wanted her.

"Just a minute, sweetpea," he said, retrieving a foil packet from beneath the pillow with a shaky hand.

After arranging their protection, Brant gathered her into his arms and kissed her as he parted her legs with his knee. When he broke the kiss, their gazes locked and he moved to cover her small body with his. Neither one of them spoke as he found her and moved himself into the tight warmth of her luscious body.

His body urged him to plunge forward, to bury himself deep inside her, but he held back. Annie was new to making love, and her body needed time to adjust to the invasion of his.

The strain of holding himself back caused Brant's muscles to quiver and burn as he carefully eased forward. Watchful for any sign of discomfort, he stopped when he reached the barrier of her virginity.

"Annie," was all he could manage to say a moment before he covered her mouth with his, and kissing her, pushed past the veil to make her his own.

Brant felt her soft gasp against his lips, her nails scoring his shoulders as he merged them into one. Being inside of Annie was heaven and hell rolled into one. The thought that he'd caused her any kind of pain just about tore him apart, yet his body was urging him to complete their union, to race toward the summit of mind-shattering completion. But Annie wasn't ready for that and he'd die before he hurt her any more than he'd already done.

Holding his body perfectly still, he raised his head and brushed a strand of silky blond hair from her forehead. "I'm sor—"

"Brant, it's all right," she said, smiling and placing her finger to his lips to stop his apology. Even as she spoke, he felt her body relaxing around his, accepting him as part of her.

When she arched into him, Brant had to concentrate on the control he was trying so hard to maintain. Annie was telling him without words that she was ready for the next step in their lovemaking, that she wanted him to take her to a place only lovers go. He answered her movement as he slowly, carefully began to move inside her.

He watched the passion once again color her cheeks, felt her body fully accept his. His muscles burned with the need to quicken the pace, to race to the satisfaction that awaited him. But he fought it. Brant was determined to bring Annie to the brink with him, to make sure she too found release from the sizzling tension surrounding them.

Easing his hand between them, he gently stroked her and reveled in the urgent need widening her pretty, green eyes, the tightening of her body around his. He sensed that she was close, and leaning forward, whispered against her lips, "Let go, sweetpea. I'll take care of you."

He watched Annie tightly close her eyes, then heard her moan his name as she gave in to the storm of pleasure raging within her. Tiny feminine muscles clutched at him and he felt himself being drawn into the tempest with her. But only after he was sure her passion was spent did he submit to his own hungry need.

Groaning her name, Brant wrapped both arms around her and held her close as he thrust into her one final time. A charge of electric current seemed to course through him a moment before his body stiffened, then spasmed as he found his own release.

Annie held Brant close as his big body shuddered, then sagged on top of her. She loved the feel of his weight pressing her into the mattress, loved the way his harsh breathing felt against the sensitive skin of her neck as he recovered from their lovemaking.

She squeezed her eyes shut and caught her lower lip between her teeth. She might as well face facts. She loved everything about Brant. And the fact that their time together was fast approaching an end was almost more than she could bear. Tomorrow they would leave for Anaheim, then two days later go to her home in Illinois.

"Are you all right?" he asked. His lips moving against her skin sent shivers of renewed excitement up her spine.

"I'm wonderful," she said, hugging him tighter.

He propped himself on one forearm to gaze down at her, and the concern on his handsome face took her breath. "Are you sure, sweetpea?"

Smiling, she nodded. "That was the most incredible experience of my life."

He stared at her for several long seconds before his charming grin broke through. "I promise that next time it will be even better."

Her heart skipped a beat and her stomach fluttered. "Next time?"

"Oh, yeah, sweetpea." He moved to her side, gathered her into his arms and pulled the sheet and comforter over them. "But not tonight."

"Why not?" She immediately felt her cheeks heat with embarrassment at the disappointment she detected in her own voice.

Brant cupped her breast with one large hand and kissed her shoulder. "I hated having to hurt you in order to make love to you, sweetpea. And I don't intend for it to happen again."

"It wasn't—"

"I don't want you getting sore," he said, shaking his head.

Annie felt his lower body stir against her. "But—"

He took a deep breath and hugged her close. "We'll wait."

She'd started to tell him that it hadn't been *that* uncomfortable. But the gentleness of his tone, the protective way he held her, took her breath. Brant was trying to do what he thought was best for *her,* not what he really wanted to do. She'd never felt more cherished in her entire life.

Long after his soft snores signaled that he'd fallen asleep, Annie lay within Brant's warm embrace, staring at the ceiling. In a few days, she'd be back home presenting her grandmother with evidence that Patrick Elsworth was a crook and hopefully convince the woman to have her accounts audited.

So why did the prospect of completing what she'd set out to do leave her feeling so…empty?

Turning her head to gaze at Brant's handsome features relaxed in sleep, Annie wondered if he would try to stay in contact with her after he took her to her grandmother's. Or would he leave her behind and never look back?

A lump formed in her throat and tears filled her eyes. She knew exactly why she felt the way she did. Returning to Illinois meant that she might never again be with the only man she'd ever loved.

Chapter 9

Brant paid the cabdriver, then turned to take Annie by the elbow to guide her toward the personnel entrance of the arena in Anaheim. He'd purposely avoided thinking about this day. But now that it was here, there was no way to avoid it.

After the last round of the PBR event ended this evening, he and Annie would board a plane to Saint Louis, then rent a car and drive to her home in southern Illinois. The first thing tomorrow morning, she'd be back to her life of books, art and charity functions, and he'd return to the Lonetree and the unpretentious life he loved.

It's the way things were meant to be. The way they

had to be. But if that was the case, why did his gut clench into a tight knot every time he thought about it?

When they entered the building and walked down a long corridor into an open area, they sidestepped a man wearing headphones as he danced across the floor. "I know that different people have their own ways of preparing for these things," Annie said, looking doubtful. "But break dancing?"

Putting his disturbing thoughts aside, Brant laughed. "That's Gil Daniels, the barrelman. He's practicing."

"I remember seeing him in Saint Louis, but we weren't introduced," she said as Gil did a couple of backspins, then moonwalked his way to the other side of the staging area. "By the way, what does he do besides dance and hide in the barrel when the bull gets too close?"

"A barrelman distracts the bull occasionally, but mostly he entertains the crowd between rides and while the bulls are loaded into the chutes," Brant answered, steering her down the corridor leading to the VIP area.

"It doesn't seem fair that you don't have a barrel to jump into when the bull chases you," she said, sounding concerned.

"Don't worry about me," he said, chuckling. "I'm pretty quick on my feet."

Looking down at the sexiest woman he'd ever known, his smile faded. How was he ever going to be able to let her go?

Night before last, he'd made love to her for the first time. But due to a flight delay yesterday, they'd had to rush straight from the airport to the arena in order to make it to last night's round of bull riding. Then, by the time they got checked into the hotel, Annie had been so tired, she'd fallen asleep almost as soon as her head hit the pillow.

But Brant couldn't bear the thought of not holding her one more time, making love to her.

"Annie?"

"What?"

"I have something to ask you," he said, making a snap decision.

He stopped, set his duffel bag down and took her into his arms. God, how he loved touching her, holding her soft little body to his.

"Would you mind—"

"Tell him to stay on his toes today, Annie," Colt said as he and his best friend, Mitch Simpson, along with a crowd of other riders and their families, walked toward them. Both men stopped, gave Brant a knowing grin and a thumbs-up. "I've got a rematch with Kamikaze this evening."

"Try landing on your feet instead of your head and I won't have to worry about saving your sorry behind," Brant retorted, irritated by the interruption.

Both men laughed as Mitch stuck out his hand to Annie. Brant reluctantly loosened his hold on her but kept his arm around her shoulders and held her to his side.

"I don't think we've been introduced. I'm Mitch Simpson. I think you sat with my kid sister in Saint Louis."

Annie placed her hand in Mitch's, and Brant clenched his back teeth together so hard he figured it would take a crowbar to pry them apart. Mitch had a reputation with the ladies, rivaled only by Colt's, and Brant was having a hell of a time resisting the urge to belt the man.

"I'm Annie Devereaux," she said, smiling. "I enjoyed talking with Kaylee. But I didn't see her last night. Will she be here today?"

"No," Mitch said, continuing to hold Annie's hand. "She stayed home to coddle that new mare I bought her for her birthday."

"Tell her I'm sorry I didn't get to see her," Annie said.

When Brant sent a dark scowl Mitch's way, the red-haired cowboy finally dropped Annie's hand, but the grin he sent Brant's way was anything but repentant. "Kaylee said the two of you had a good time. She's going to be sorry she missed you, too."

"Yeah, can you believe that?" Colt asked, grinning. "She'd rather spend time with that buckskin nag than watch me ride."

Brant studied Colt. Was that a hint of disappointment he heard in his brother's voice?

"Kaylee's got more sense than to waste her time watching the likes of you," Mitch teased. "She's seen you ride enough to know what's going to happen."

"What's wrong with the way I ride?" Colt asked with mock indignation.

"It's not your ride," Mitch said, laughing. "It's your

dismount. You always land on your head and they end up carrying you out of the arena, toes up."

"Do not," Colt said stubbornly.

"Do, too," Mitch insisted.

The two men tipped their Resistols to Annie and continued the good-natured ribbing as they walked on toward the VIP area where the buffet tables had been set up.

Turning his attention back to Annie, Brant wrapped his arms around her again. "Now, let's get back to what I wanted to ask you."

She smiled at him and he felt warm all the way to the darkest corners of his soul. "Ask away, cowboy."

"I've already checked us out of the hotel, but would you mind if I got another room somewhere and changed our flight to sometime tomorrow?" he asked, his request spilling out in a rush.

Her smile faded and for several long, wordless seconds, she stared at him. "Are you asking me to spend one more night with you, Brant?" she finally asked softly.

"Yes."

Placing her hand to his cheek, she nodded. "I'd like that." She nibbled on her lower lip for a moment before she added, "I want to spend one more night with you holding me, making love to me." She looked thoughtful for a moment before smiling shyly. "Besides, you made me a promise you haven't kept."

"I did?" With the sweet sound of her voice wrapping around him, the feel of her body close to his, he could barely remember his own name.

Rising on tiptoe, she whispered close to his ear, "You promised that when we made love again, it would be even more incredible than the first time." She kissed his chin, then smiled. "But we haven't made love again. So you owe me, cowboy."

His heart slammed against his ribs and his body immediately jerked to life. Here they stood in the middle of a crowd and he was getting harder than hell just thinking about holding her, loving her.

Brant grinned. "Sweetpea, I'm a man of my word. I'll change our airline reservations right after we grab a bite to eat."

After dining with the bull riders and other PBR personnel in the VIP room, Annie stood behind the bucking shoots, waiting for Brant to return from changing into his bullfighting garb. As she watched the men preparing the dirt floor in the arena, she thought about how eagerly she'd accepted Brant's invitation to delay their trip home by another day.

Carlotta Whittmeyer's very dutiful, prim-and-proper granddaughter, Anastasia, would never dream of telling a man that she'd like to spend the night making love with him. But a week ago, Anastasia had taken a chance, walked along a ledge and changed her life forever. And with the encouragement of a kind, caring, sexy cowboy, she'd become Annie—a woman who was beginning to learn the joy of experiencing life, not just watching it pass her by.

Smiling, Annie glanced down at her clothes. Even

they were different. Anastasia preferred loose-fitting skirts and blouses in neutral, nondescript colors. She'd never dream of wearing a bright red, tapered shirt, form-fitting jeans and western boots. But Annie found that she really liked them. She liked the colors, the way they felt, and the way Brant looked at her when she wore them. Reaching up, she grinned as she touched the wide brim of her black Resistol. She even liked wearing a western hat.

Unfortunately, her grandmother would never embrace the change in her. Sighing, Annie stared at the brightly colored, padded barrel waiting to be rolled out into the arena. Carlotta would expect Annie to be the same unadventurous creature who wore baggy clothes and lived life through the pages of a book.

But she could never be that person again. Nor could she dutifully follow her grandmother's directives. Annie was her own person now. And no matter what happened between herself and Brant, she would always be grateful to him for encouraging her to break free of that restrictive, narrow existence.

Lost in thoughts of how much she'd changed in the past week, it took a moment for the sound of a familiar male voice to catch her attention. But when it did, Annie froze. Afraid to move, she cast her gaze around to see where Patrick was. He had to be close. His voice was too clear, too loud, not to be more than a few feet away.

When she finally located him, her heart hammered in her chest. No more than ten feet to her left, Patrick stood with his back to her, talking to a group of cowboys. It appeared he was showing her picture to them and questioning them about seeing her.

Panic rose in her throat and she desperately looked around for somewhere to hide. Glancing to her right, she abandoned that direction immediately. There was no way she'd climb into an enclosure with one bull, let alone a pen filled with the large, mean-looking beasts. She'd rather take her chances with Patrick Elsworth than do that.

Think, Annie. Where was she going to go?

Her desperate gaze suddenly zeroed in on the barrel in front of her. It was big enough, and chances were, no one would think to look for her there.

Slowly, so as not to draw attention to herself, Annie eased up to the side of the specially made barrel, hoisted herself up and slipped inside. Holding her breath, she waited to see if Patrick had noticed.

But as the seconds ticked by, Annie began to relax. She'd wait a few more minutes, then climb out of the barrel and find Brant.

Just as she decided that Patrick had probably moved on and it was safe to leave her hiding place, she felt the barrel tilt precariously, then land on its side nearly knocking the breath from her. Feeling herself being rolled forward, she wondered what on earth was going on.

Then she realized exactly what was happening. Once the grounds crew finished preparing the dirt floor, the barrel would be moved into place. She was about to be rolled into the arena.

"Hey, stop! I'm in here!"

Unfolding her arm from where she had wrapped it around her waist in the close confines, Annie stretched it toward the opening to catch the attention of whoever was moving the barrel. Unable to see anything as she tumbled over and over, she blindly felt around until her fingers came into contact with a man's hand.

"What the hell?" the man shouted. The barrel was suddenly jerked upright and a very shocked-looking clown with an exaggerated greasepaint smile peered down at her through the opening. "Lady, what do you think you're doin' in there?"

"Please, keep your voice down," Annie pleaded. If Patrick was still in the vicinity, she didn't want the man giving her away. "I need you to find Brant Wakefield."

The man looked exasperated. "You need me to do what?"

Why did some men have to be so obtuse? She closed her eyes to the dizziness swirling within her from being rolled over and over, and tried to focus on being patient.

"Please, it's very important." When the man continued to stare down at her, anger cleared the last traces of her disorientation. "I'm not going to get out of your stupid barrel until you find Brant Wakefield. Is that clear enough for you?"

Brant looked at the crowd of people milling around the staging area. Where the hell was Annie? Fifteen minutes ago she'd been standing by the chutes watching the grounds crew level the dirt on the arena floor. Now she was nowhere in sight.

Seeing his brother walking toward him, Brant asked, "Have you seen Annie?"

Colt shook his head. "The last time I saw her was in the VIP room with you." He grinned. "Come to think of it, I haven't seen Mitch, either." At Brant's succinct curse, Colt's expression sobered. "Hey, I was just kidding. You know Mitch wouldn't beat your time with a woman."

"I know," Brant said, distracted.

Looking concerned, Colt asked, "Is something wrong?"

"I'm not sure," Brant said, continuing to scan the crowd.

"If you need help, you know all you have to do is say the word," Colt said seriously.

Brant nodded. "Thanks, Colt. I'll do that."

He watched his brother's relaxed stride carry him toward the back of the chutes where the rest of the riders were gathering. The one thing Brant had never doubted about his brothers was their loyalty, or their willingness to be there for him when the chips were down.

"Hey, Brant," Gil Daniels called. He hurried over to where Brant stood. "I need your help with somethin'."

"Not now, Gil," Brant said, dismissing the man.

"This can't wait."

"It'll have to," Brant said impatiently. "I need to find someone."

When he started to walk away, Gil caught him by the arm. "You *need* to come with me."

Brant glared at the man. "I can't take the time right now, Gil. I've got to—"

"And I don't have time to wait for that little blonde you were with earlier to decide to get out of my barrel if you don't," Gil retorted.

"Annie's in the barrel?" Brant asked incredulously.

Gil shrugged and turned toward the barrel by the gate leading into the arena. "Hey, she didn't tell me her name and I didn't ask. All I know is she said she wouldn't get out of the damn thing until I found you."

Hurrying over to the barrel, Brant looked inside to find Annie gazing up at him. "What the hell are you doing in there?"

"Patrick's here."

"Are you sure?" he asked, looking around.

She nodded. "He was talking to some of the riders and showing them my picture."

He looked around. Elsworth was nowhere in sight. "He's gone now." Reaching his hand inside the opening, he helped Annie stand up, then lifted her from the barrel. "Sweetpea, you just about gave me a heart attack when Gil said you were inside this thing."

"She was about two seconds from being rolled out into the arena," Gil grumbled as he once again tipped the barrel on its side and rolled it through the gate.

Brant watched Annie nervously nibble on her lower lip. "It was the only place I could find to hide without Patrick seeing me." She shuddered. "He was so close."

Pulling her into his arms, Brant held her tightly. What the hell was he going to do to keep her safe?

There were forty-five bull riders counting on him to be there to save their butts when they dismounted their rides. But the woman in his arms needed him to keep her safe from a far greater threat.

When he saw the event coordinator walking toward them, Brant breathed a sigh of relief. "Sarah, I need your help."

The tall, slender blond grinned. "If it involves another shopping trip, it will have to wait until tomorrow."

"Not this time," he said, shaking his head. Without going into a lot of detail, Brant explained that Annie was trying to avoid Elsworth. "Can you keep Annie with you until the last round is over?"

"Of course." Sarah motioned for Annie to follow her. "Come on, Annie. The guy you're trying to avoid won't be allowed behind the chutes. And if he does manage to find a way back there, we'll have forty-five cowboys with enough adrenaline running through their veins to take out a platoon of marines waiting for him."

"Stay with Sarah," Brant said, kissing Annie on the forehead. "I'll see you after the last ride."

"Please be careful."

"You can count on it, sweetpea." He grinned, and lowering his voice so only she would hear, he added, "We have a date tonight."

He watched Annie follow Sarah, then hearing his name come across the loudspeaker, Brant turned to jog into the arena. He had no intention of letting a ton of pissed-off beef, a pasty-faced little weasel named

Elsworth, or anything else stop him from spending the night with the most exciting woman he'd ever known.

Brant crouched in the ready position, waiting for the gateman to pull the rope and release the last ride of the night. In a split second, a rider astride two thousand pounds of bovine fury would explode from the chute and into the arena. Eight seconds after that, he'd make sure the cowboy made it to safety and his job would be done until next weekend.

When the gate swung wide, Brant waited a moment then ran in front of the bull. Circling close, he successfully turned it and kept the animal from carrying the rider too far out into the arena and a safe getaway.

But four seconds into the ride, the cowboy lost his grasp on the bull rope and fell to the ground dangerously near the bull's heavy hooves. When the rider failed to move, Brant knew immediately that the man had been knocked unconscious from hitting the ground headfirst. Without hesitation, he fell on top of the cowboy, covering the defenseless man with his own body, protecting him from the pounding Brant knew the bull was famous for giving to fallen riders. He'd never lost a rider yet, and he wasn't about to start now.

Knowing that the other two bullfighters would be right there turning the bull away from him and the unconscious cowboy, Brant held his breath and hoped he didn't get too roughed up. He had only one night left with Annie and he damn well didn't intend to spend it in the hospital. Or worse yet, be too banged up to hold her, love her one last time.

When a blunted horn connected with his ribs, the air rushed from his lungs and pain knifed through his torso, but Brant continued to cover the fallen man. He was confident the protective vest and padding he always wore under his bullfighting garb would keep him from serious injury, but he was going to be sore as hell before this was over with.

Then just as suddenly as the pummeling began, it ended. The other two fighters had distracted the bull, it ran through the gate leading to the pens behind the chutes, and the sports-medicine team came rushing into the arena to tend to the unconscious man.

"Are you all right, Brant?" one of the physical trainers asked, stopping beside him.

"I'm fine," he said, slowly rising to his feet. He brushed away the dirt the bull's hooves had kicked in his face. "I've got a couple of bruised ribs, but nothing's broken."

"Are you sure?"

"Yep." Brant gritted his teeth against the soreness already seeping into his side as he bent down to pick up his battered hat. "I've had enough cracked and broken bones to know the difference between hurting and being hurt."

Nodding, the man turned to help the others as they stabilized the now-conscious cowboy's neck with a foam collar and lifted him to a backboard.

Brant waited until they'd carried the man from the arena and the overall winner of the event was being announced, before he made his way behind the chutes to find Annie. But before he located her, he saw Patrick Elsworth coming toward him.

"I've been looking for you, Wakefield. I almost didn't recognize you with your makeup on."

"Funny, I haven't been looking for you," Brant said with a shrug. He'd like nothing more than to bury his fist in the pasty-faced little weasel's nose. Then a sudden thought hit him. Elsworth had used his name. "How did you find out my name?"

Elsworth looked quite pleased with himself. "I bribed the desk clerk in Saint Louis and found out who you were and that you're part of this dog and pony show. After that I did an Internet search to find out where the PBR would be next." He shook his little-weasel head. "But that's not important. Where is she?"

Brant didn't even consider pleading ignorance and asking who "she" was. "Annie's where you can't get your hands on her," he said through clenched teeth. "Now, get out of my way before I lose what's left of my temper and kick your skinny little butt."

"Annie?" Elsworth laughed. "Carlotta's going to love that. She'll give you a tongue-lashing you won't soon forget for calling her precious granddaughter anything but Anastasia."

Knowing the man would follow him if he tried to find Annie, Brant started toward the dressing room. Just as he figured would be the case, Elsworth fell into step beside him.

"You know the old lady is the one with the money."

"Do tell," Brant said. He needed to keep the little weasel moving away from the chute area where Annie was.

Elsworth nodded. "I don't know what Anastasia has told you, but she's just waiting for the old woman to kick the bucket. That's the only reason she puts up with her grandmother's edicts."

Brant wasn't sure who Elsworth was describing. It certainly wasn't Annie. But he wasn't going to argue with him as long as they were moving away from her.

Spotting Colt and Mitch a few feet ahead of him, Brant quickened his pace. When he walked up beside them, he asked, "Colt, do you remember what we talked about earlier?"

His brother looked first at Brant then at the man standing next to him. "Yep."

"I need that favor now," Brant said, quickening his pace.

Grinning, Colt closed the gap left by Brant and put an arm around Elsworth's shoulders. "I think Mitch and I can take over from here."

"Think you can give me about fifteen minutes head start?" Brant asked, breaking into a jog.

"Sure thing, bro," Colt answered, laughing when Elsworth tried unsuccessfully to elbow him in the ribs and connected with his riding vest. "Take more time if you need it."

"Thanks," Brant called over his shoulder.

"What do you think you're—" was all he heard the weasel say as Colt and Mitch hustled Elsworth away.

By the time he entered the dressing room, Brant was out of his shirt and had his protective vest unfastened. Changing in record time, he removed his makeup, packed his duffel bag, then went in search of Annie. He had to get them out of the arena and on the road to their hotel before Colt and Mitch finished detaining Elsworth.

He'd told her that he wouldn't let Elsworth get anywhere near her. And Brant intended to keep that promise or die trying.

Chapter 10

Annie impatiently waited for Brant to fit the hotel key card into the electronic door lock, then close the door behind them. As soon as he secured the dead bolt and turned on the light, she threw her arms around him. "Brant, I was never more frightened in my life," she said, her insides still shaking.

He grunted as if he was in pain. "You're safe now, sweetpea. Elsworth has no idea where we are."

When Brant had joined her behind the bucking chutes at the arena, he'd thanked Sarah for helping to keep her out of Patrick's sight, then hurried Annie to a cab. During the short ride to the hotel he'd explained about his run-in with Patrick. But that wasn't what had her near tears and shaking like a leaf.

"I'm not concerned about Patrick," she said, cupping Brant's lean cheeks with her hands. "I thought my heart would stop when that bull tried to gore you. Are you all right?"

"I'm a little sore," he admitted. "And tomorrow I won't feel like moving too fast, but I'll be fine."

"Are you sure?"

He nodded. "I've been in a lot worse wrecks than that little skirmish tonight."

She watched him place his hat on the shelf in the closet, then slowly remove his jacket. "Did the doctor look at you after you left the arena?" she demanded.

"Sweetpea, I'm fine. Really." He turned to face her. "I've got a couple of bruises, but that's it. Promise."

Blinking back the threatening tears, she hung her jacket beside his. "Brant, I've never seen anything as heroic as you throwing yourself on top of that downed rider. That was incredible."

"Nope." He reached for her, and wrapping her in his strong embrace, touched his lips to her forehead in a featherlight kiss. "*You're* incredible."

It was so like him to minimize his role in saving the cowboy's life. The more she got to know Brant, the more she admired his humble courage.

Annie reached up to unsnap his chambray shirt. When her fingers brushed his firm, warm skin, he closed his eyes and smiled.

"Does that feel good?" she asked.

"If it felt any better, I'd think I'd died and gone to heaven," he said, opening his eyes. His grin held such promise, it took her breath. "But I don't want to be selfish. Let's make you feel good, too."

When he reached for the buttons on her shirt, Annie barely managed to stand still as he carefully slid each round disk through its buttonhole. His fingers lingered on the sensitive skin of her abdomen, his touch sending shivers through every part of her.

By the time Brant tugged her shirt from the waistband of her jeans, her heart raced wildly. He pushed the garment from her shoulders, then tossed it to the side and reached for the front clasp of her Chantilly lace bra. "You know, sweetpea, if I didn't know you wore this type of stuff before we met, I'd swear you were trying to drive me out of my mind."

Smiling, she ran her hands over his shoulders, sliding his shirt off as her palms skimmed down his biceps. "Would you have preferred that I bought sensible cotton panties and bras when we went shopping in Denver?"

"Hell, no." He shook his head emphatically. "I'm finding I really like wispy lace and triangles with strings. I'm glad you stuck with them."

From the look in his deep blue eyes, Annie was glad she had, too. But all thought ceased when Brant unhooked her bra, and peeled it away from her breasts. Reaching out, he cupped her in his callused palms, and the feel of his rough hands on her overly sensitive skin set off tiny electric sparks of excitement skipping throughout her body. When he teased her tightening nipples with the pads of his thumbs, she closed her eyes and reveled in his gentle touch.

"That feels good," she murmured.

Opening her eyes, she quickly unbuckled his belt, and popped the snap at the top of his jeans. Her heart skipped several beats when she saw the insistent bulge straining against his fly and a tight coil began to form in the pit of her belly.

"You...um, seem to have a problem," she said, glancing up at him.

His sexy grin and heavy-lidded gaze sent heat racing through her as he lowered his head to kiss the tip of her breast. "I always get this way when I get close to you, sweetpea," he said, moving to take the other tight peak into his mouth.

Her knees suddenly felt weak and rubbery. Reaching out to wrap her arms around his waist, she felt a chill race up her spine at his groan of pain.

"You *are* hurt." Pulling away from him, Annie searched his torso. A huge, ugly bruise covered a large section of his ribs on the left side. Tears filled her eyes as she gently touched his mottled skin. "Oh, darling, it looks awful."

"It's nothing," he insisted.

"It is, too." Taking him by the hand, she led him over to the side of the bed. "Let's make you comfortable." She did her best to ignore the feel of his pulsing arousal as she lowered his zipper and shoved his jeans down to his knees. "Sit down and I'll remove your boots."

Once she'd stripped him down to his briefs, she pulled on her blouse and buttoned it, then grabbed the ice bucket. "Lie back and relax. I'll be right back with some ice." Brant started to protest, but she shook her head. "I'm not accepting no for an answer. You've taken care of me all week. It's my turn to take care of you."

Brant watched Annie remove the key card from his jacket pocket, check the diagram on the back of the door for the location of the ice machine, then hurry out into the hall. The concern he'd seen in her green eyes when she realized he was hurting had sent a warmth spreading all the way to the far reaches of his soul.

Carefully stretching out on the bed, he stared up at the room's textured ceiling. Having Annie fuss over him felt damn good. Almost as good as when he did the same with her. What would it be like to have her with him all the time, taking care of him, making him feel as if his comfort was important to her?

He cursed vehemently and gritted his back teeth against the longing that invaded every fiber of his being. There was no sense wondering about things that would never happen. All they'd have together was tonight. Tomorrow he'd take Annie to her grandmother's, drive back to Saint Louis to catch a flight home, and that would be the end of it. He and Annie came from entirely different walks of life and he'd learned the hard way the two just didn't mix.

When the door opened and Annie walked into the room with a bucket of ice and a plastic bag, Brant smiled at the determination on her sweet face. He'd let her nurse his wounds a little longer, then show her that his injury wasn't nearly as bad as it looked.

"I found a maid's cart and picked up an extra plastic bag," she said, entering the bathroom. Moments later, she walked up to the side of the bed to gently place the ice pack to his side.

He immediately felt goose bumps rise along his skin. "Damn, sweetpea! That's cold."

"Ice usually is," she said, smiling. She sat on the bed next to him. "I'm not very up on first-aid techniques. How long should we leave this on?"

"Not long." He reached up to once again work the buttons free on her blouse. "My thoughts are running in a warmer direction."

"But you're hurt," she protested.

"Take my word for it, Annie. I'm not that bad off." He finished unbuttoning the garment, then pushed it from her slender shoulders. "My ribs may be sore, but my other parts are working just fine."

He took the bag of ice and placed it on the nightstand, then sat up to take her into his arms. The feel of her breasts crushed to his chest, her beaded nipples pressing into his flesh, sent his temperature up and chased away any chill he'd experienced from the cold compress.

Reaching between them, he unfastened her jeans and slid the zipper down. "Why don't you shimmy out of these and get comfortable, sweetpea?"

As she bent to remove her boots, she nervously caught her lower lip between her teeth. A week ago, the thought of stripping in front of a man would have embarrassed her to death. But this wasn't just any man. This was Brant. The man she loved.

When she stood up to push her jeans down, the light in his eyes sent her pulse racing and chased away all traces of apprehension. Never in her wildest imaginings had she envisioned a man looking at her the way Brant was at that very moment. His blue gaze was filled with such heated desire, such hunger, that it caused her knees to wobble.

Hooking her fingers in the string waistband of her underwear, she slowly slid them from her hips and was rewarded by Brant's sharp intake of breath. "You're the sexiest, most desirable woman I've ever seen, sweetpea," he said huskily. "Come here."

Annie sat down on the bed beside Brant and when he wrapped her in his arms, the feel of his firm, masculine form pressed to her softer, feminine one caused a tingling heat to course through her. Reclining against the pillow, he pulled her down with him, then immediately covered her mouth with his.

She closed her eyes and reveled in the feel of his kiss, but when his tongue separated her lips to entice her with the taste of his passion, heat and light danced behind her closed eyes. His hands on her body, the scent of him wrapping around her, sent shafts of longing to the very core of her being.

As he lightened the caress, he nibbled kisses to the hollow at the base of her throat. "You have no idea how much I've wanted you this way again, Annie," he said, his warm breath teasing her sensitized skin.

"Brant," was all she could manage to get out as he slowly, tenderly ran his hand down her abdomen to the crisp curls hiding her feminine secrets.

Raising his head, he caught and held her gaze as he parted her, then touched her with such exquisite care it brought tears to her eyes. "I love the way you say my name, sweetpea."

Unable to remain still, she ran her palms over his chest, over the ripples of muscle covering his stomach. But when her fingers touched the waistband of his shorts, she smiled. "Aren't you a little overdressed, cowboy?"

His deep chuckle caused a fluttery feeling to tighten in the most feminine part of her. "Why don't you help me take care of that problem?"

When he lifted his hips, Annie carefully pulled the cotton briefs over his strong arousal and down his muscular thighs. Her breath caught at the sight of his overwhelming maleness. But his low groan quickly had her glancing up at him.

"It hurts to move, doesn't it?"

He shook his head. "Not that much."

But she detected the strain in his voice, saw the wince he couldn't quite hide. "Brant—"

Reaching out, he pulled her down beside him. "Sweetpea, I'm not going to lie to you. I'm sore as hell. But I'm not so bad off that I can't spend the night making love to you."

"But how can you—"

His sexy grin sent another wave of goose bumps down her arms. "There are other positions we can explore." He placed a tender kiss on her forehead. "Ones where you're in control and do most of the moving." He paused. "That is, if you don't mind."

The idea of taking charge of their lovemaking caused her stomach to flutter and the coil within her to tighten.

Feeling a bit shy, yet excited at the prospect of bringing him pleasure, she smiled. "Will you show me how to touch you?"

She watched his eyes darken with emotion as he took her hand in his and guided her to him. "Sweetpea, I thought you'd never ask," he said huskily.

When he showed her how to caress him, she reveled in the new feelings coursing through her. Never in her entire life had she felt more feminine or more powerful than she did at that very moment.

"Yeah…um, that's it." He groaned, then moved to take her into his arms.

Smiling, she placed her index finger to his lips and shook her head. "No. I'm taking care of you tonight, darling."

Annie watched him close his eyes and tighten his jaw as she explored his velvet skin, the firmness of his desire for her. The feel of him beneath her palm, the strength of his passion, fueled her own hunger, and quickly had her body yearning to give him pleasure in the most intimate way a woman can give to a man. Heat coursed through her veins and the empty ache of unfulfilled need intensified with each passing second.

"Brant…I need—"

Apparently, he understood what she couldn't put into words. "In my jeans pocket," he said, motioning to the pile of clothes beside the bed. When she retrieved the foil packet and handed it to him, he caught her hand in his and guided it back to him. "Let's do this together, sweetpea."

Helping Brant take care of their protection, she

glanced up, and the fire burning in the depths of his blue eyes took her breath. He was handing her control of their lovemaking, and with that his complete confidence and trust. Her heart swelled with more love than she'd ever dreamed possible as she moved to straddle his lean hips and guide him to her.

Annie closed her eyes and reveled in the emotions swirling through her as she took him inside, felt him fill her body with his. A completeness like nothing she'd ever known swept through her and she knew beyond a shadow of a doubt that they were sharing much more than the mere act of lovemaking. Brant was her mate, the other half of herself.

When he placed his hands at her hips, she glanced down into the face of the man she loved with every fiber of her being and lost sight of where he ended and she began. Slowly rocking against him, she felt waves of desire flow through her, and the tension they shared quickly built into something far bigger than either one of them.

Without warning, she felt herself poised on the edge, her body a tight coil of feeling. Wrapped in a haze of need, she heard Brant groan, felt him surge within her as he swept her up and took her with him into the realm of sweet pleasurable release.

Long after Annie had fallen asleep, Brant held her close. He loved the way her small body felt against his, loved the scent of her enveloping him with its sweetness. Hell, he just plain loved everything about Annie.

He sucked in a sharp breath. When had he fallen in love with her?

Closing his eyes, Brant tried to tell himself that it wasn't love, that what he felt for her was nothing more than a deep fondness. But when she snuggled against him and murmured his name, feelings so strong they invaded every cell of his being swamped him.

How could he have let himself fall in love with her? Hadn't he learned from past experience that a woman like Annie could never be happy with a daredevil cowboy like himself? What would he do when she tired of the adventure and excitement and went back to a more cultured way of life? Could he survive when that happened?

His gut twisted into a tight knot. She'd eventually get bored with his lifestyle, and try to salvage what they had between them by trying to get him to fit into her world—something he just couldn't do. Then, how would he ever survive watching Annie leave him?

Brant took several deep breaths in an effort to ease the ache tightening his chest. The answer to that question was simple. He couldn't stand to watch her feelings for him fade as she lost interest in living a simpler life.

Easing her out of his arms so he wouldn't wake her, he slowly sat up on the side of the bed and buried his head in his hands. In his heart, he knew what he had to do. Tomorrow after he took her to her grandmother's, he'd wish her a nice life, kiss her goodbye one last time, then spend the rest of his life wishing that things could have somehow been different for them.

* * *

When Brant pulled the rental car to a stop in her grandmother's driveway, Annie's heart sank. This was the last place she wanted to be.

Glancing over at the handsome cowboy behind the steering wheel, she had to blink back tears. Once she got out of the car, Brant would go back to the Lonetree. Without her.

"You weren't kidding about this place, sweetpea," he said, looking around the neatly kept three-story Victorian. "Even the outside looks like a museum."

She nodded. "Normally this type of house looks homey and welcoming from the outside." Staring at the life-size Greek statues peeking their heads above the top of the hedge maze at the side of the house, she added, "But not this one. It's about as warm and friendly as a cold, gray winter day."

"It definitely has a 'keep off the grass' look to it," he agreed, opening the driver's-side door. He walked around the front of the shiny blue sedan to help her from the car.

"Thank you for everything, Brant," she said, unsure of what else to say. "I don't know what would have happened if you hadn't—"

"Don't think about it, sweetpea," he said, placing his finger to her lips. "Everything worked out."

"Have a safe trip back," she said, turning to go inside the house before she did something stupid like throw her arms around him and beg him to let her go to the Lonetree with him. She started up the walk, but to her surprise, Brant put his arm around her shoulders and fell into step beside her.

When she glanced up at him, he smiled. "I thought I'd walk you to the door, and maybe get an invitation for a cup of coffee before I start back."

Annie returned his smile. "Of course." She'd like to offer him more than a cup of coffee. She'd like to offer him her heart. "Would you like to stay for supper?"

Climbing the steps, he checked his watch. "I'm sorry, but I won't have time, sweetpea. My flight leaves Saint Louis tonight around ten."

As she stood in front of the heavy mahogany door with the stained-glass pane, Annie took a deep breath, then pressed the doorbell. Seconds later, Carlotta Whitt-meyer opened the door with a scowl firmly in place.

"Where have you been, young lady?" she demanded. "I called the library when I arrived home, but that *child* you have working for you was anything but helpful. She said she had no idea where you were, but that Patrick had been trying to find you all last week." Carlotta stopped to look at Brant, her gaze raking him from the top of his black Resistol to his big, booted feet. "And just who is that?"

"Brant Wakefield, ma'am," he said, offering his hand.

The thin, gray-haired woman's icy glare darted to his hand, then with a sniff, she turned back to Annie. "Anastasia, I want answers. And what on earth are you wearing? You look like some kind of cowgirl in those jeans and that hat. And where are your glasses."

"It's nice to see you too, Grandmother," Annie said. "Let's go inside and I'll explain everything."

When the older woman stood aside to let them enter, Brant followed Annie through the entryway and into the…parlor? That was the only word he could think of that would fit the room. Dark antiques with heavy brocade upholstery were arranged before an intricately carved fireplace, and paintings in gilded frames hung on the flocked walls. The place gave him the creeps and made him feel as if he should be viewing it from the doorway behind a velvet rope. Following Annie over to an uncomfortable-looking settee, he could well imagine how dismal her childhood had been in this house.

Seating himself beside her, he could feel the tension in her small body, and reaching out, took her hand in his. "It's going to be fine, sweetpea."

"I take it you've been off somewhere with this… man," Carlotta said, making it sound as if he was the stuff scraped off the bottom of boots after a trip through the barnyard.

"Grandmother! Brant is the kindest, most generous man I've ever met. And he helped me when I had no one else to turn to," Annie said, giving him a look that sent warmth racing through him. Reaching into the inside pocket of her jacket, she handed the ring she'd taken from Elsworth to her grandmother. "This is yours. It's what started everything."

"Mine?" Carlotta shook her head. "I've never seen it before."

"It represents several thousand dollars of your

money," Annie said. "Money that Patrick embezzled from your accounts."

Brant listened as Annie explained what she'd discovered about Elsworth and the threats he'd made. But to his amazement, the old woman completely ignored her.

"Don't you realize the risks you took by going off with a stranger? Haven't I taught you anything?" Carlotta stopped to send him a narrow-eyed stare. "Not to mention the damage it could do to your reputation. I can't bear to think what my friends at the garden club would say if they found out you'd traipsed off somewhere with a cowboy."

Deciding he couldn't listen to the woman another second, Brant rose to his feet. "Mrs. Whittmeyer, I don't mean any disrespect, but you've got your priorities so screwed up it's pitiful. Who gives a damn what a handful of blue-haired biddies have to say? Annie was in danger from the crook you thought would be the perfect match for her, not me."

He heard the old gal suck in a sharp breath, then shake her head. "My granddaughter's name is Anastasia. And this is none of your business, Mr. Wakefield." Pointing toward the foyer, she added, "Please, don't let us keep you any longer. I'm sure you can find the door on your way out."

Annie jumped to her feet. "Grandmother, I won't stand for you talking to Brant that way!"

The woman looked thunderstruck by Annie's outburst. He'd bet this was the first time in her life that Annie had openly disagreed with the old gal.

"It's all right, Annie," he said, turning to her. He placed his hands on her cheeks and gazed down at her, trying to memorize every feature, every sweet detail of her beautiful face. "Take care of yourself, sweetpea."

The tears filling her pretty, green eyes almost brought him to his knees. "Brant—"

"I have a flight to catch." Lowering his head, he brushed her lips with his, then turned toward the door and walked out without a backward glance.

Once he was outside, Brant walked directly to the rental car and slid into the driver's seat. He had to take several deep breaths in an effort to ease the tightening in his chest before he could fit the key into the ignition and back the sedan out into the street.

The hardest thing he'd ever done was walk away from Annie. But if he hadn't left when he did, he'd have ended up sweeping her into his arms and taking her back to the Lonetree with him. And that would have been a huge mistake for both of them. No, it was better that he'd walked out when he did.

Stopping at a red light on his way out of town, Brant cringed when a bright-yellow BMW barely avoided rear-ending the car in front of it as it slid to a stop on the opposite side of the intersection. He shook his head as he watched the driver impatiently tap his fingers on the steering wheel. But as he watched the man, Brant felt every nerve in his body tense.

It was Patrick Elsworth.

Annie's statement about desperate men resorting to desperate measures suddenly came back to Brant with crystal clarity. Unless he missed his guess, Elsworth was headed for the Whittmeyer place. And if his impatience was any indication, he was about as desperate as any man Brant had ever seen.

A mixture of fear and anger burned at Brant's gut when he watched the BMW take off like a jackrabbit. No telling what the sorry excuse for a human being planned to do to Annie and her grandmother.

But Brant was going to put a stop to whatever it was before it ever got started. If Patrick Elsworth so much as laid a hand on Annie, he was a dead man. Brant would make sure of it.

Chapter 11

Brant found a place to turn around and headed back to Annie's grandmother's. Stopping once again at the red light, fear churned his insides and he gripped the steering wheel so hard he'd probably leave his fingerprints embedded in it. What if he couldn't get back to them in time?

"Turn green, dammit!"

Once the light changed, the tires squealed and the rear end of the rental car fishtailed as he forcefully pressed down on the accelerator. He thanked the good Lord above that there weren't too many cars on the road ahead of him as he raced back to Annie. He didn't make a habit of exceeding the speed limit, but he'd do whatever it took to keep her from being harmed.

He saw the BMW parked in the Whittmeyer driveway, and pulling the sedan in behind it, blocked it from being moved. He prayed that he wasn't too late as he jumped from the car and sprinted to the front door. Hoping for the element of surprise, he quietly opened the door and slipped inside.

"Yes, I took your money," he heard Elsworth say threateningly. "And you're not going to do anything about it."

Brant carefully crossed the foyer to the parlor door and waited. Anger burned at his belly and he had to force himself to wait. He didn't want to tip the man off to his presence before he was ready to make his move.

"Yes, I will," Carlotta said angrily. "I'll have you arrested."

"No, you won't," Elsworth insisted. "I have no intention of spending any more time in prison, nor do I intend to leave town. I'm staying right here in the same town with you, and I'll leave you both alone, as long as you and your granddaughter keep your mouths shut. Otherwise, you'll both end up like that old woman in Fresno."

"You killed her?" Annie asked. "How did you do it without the authorities finding out?"

"There are ways," Elsworth said, sounding smug.

"My God, Patrick, how could you do something like that?"

The tremor of fear in Annie's voice turned the anger in Brant's gut to pure fury. He'd heard enough.

"It was easy. I found that certain poisons—"

Elsworth never finished his explanation as Brant clamped a hand down on his shoulder, spun him around and planted his fist in the man's pasty face. To Brant's immense satisfaction, Elsworth went down like a chunk of lead.

"I've been wanting to do that for more than a week," he muttered, flexing his throbbing fingers on one hand while he rubbed his sore ribs with the other. Turning to the frightened females clutching each other on the settee, he asked, "Are you two all right?"

Annie eased her grandmother back against the settee a moment before throwing herself into his arms. "How did you know Patrick was here?"

Brant hugged her trembling body to his. "I passed him on my way out of town." Noticing that Elsworth was coming to, he kissed her forehead, then set her away from him. "Go call the police, while I watch this little weasel."

As Annie went to make the call, Brant stood over Elsworth. When the man sat up and rubbed his rapidly swelling jaw, Brant warned, "Don't even think about getting up or I'll knock you on your butt again. Nobody threatens the woman I love."

When the police led Patrick out to the cruiser for his free ride to the Williamson County jail, Annie closed the door behind them, walked back into the parlor and into Brant's arms. "Thank you. I don't know what would have happened if you hadn't shown up when you did."

"Don't think about it," he said, hugging her close. "A little over a week ago I made you a promise that

Elsworth would have to come through me before he laid a hand on you. And I meant it."

As he continued to hold her, Annie glanced over at her grandmother. Normally very outspoken, Carlotta had been strangely quiet during the whole ordeal.

"Grandmother, don't you have something you'd like to say to Brant?" she asked, giving her a meaningful look.

"Yes." Carlotta hesitated, then added, "Thank you for helping us out of this…situation." She slowly rose from the settee, and stepping around Annie and Brant, walked toward the foyer. "I think I'll wait in the other room while you say your goodbyes."

"Grandmother—"

"It's all right," Brant said, placing his finger to her lips. When she started to tell him there was no excuse for her grandmother's rudeness, he shook his head. "She's entitled to her opinion, sweetpea."

"Even if she's wrong?" Annie asked, snuggling into his embrace.

"Yep." His arms tightened around her. "I need to go, or I'm going to miss my flight."

Tears filled her eyes and her lungs suddenly felt as if she couldn't breathe. The thought of never seeing him again, never being held by him, was more than she could bear. "Brant, I love you."

His body stiffened against hers, then groaning, he placed his finger under her chin to tilt her face up to his. She watched him close his eyes, felt a shudder course through him before he looked down at her again. "And

I love you, sweetpea. More than you'll ever know." He took a deep breath. "That's why I'm going back to the Lonetree and you're staying here."

Annie felt as if her heart was being torn in two. Brant loved her, but he was still going to walk out and never look back. "Why, Brant?" Old insecurities began to surface. "Is it because I'm not—"

"Don't," he said, interrupting her. "You're the sexiest, most beautiful woman I've ever known." He smiled sadly. "But you're used to art exhibits and concerts, while I'd rather ride Dancer up to the ridge and look out over the beauty of the land, or go play chicken in some rodeo arena with a ton of pissed-off beef."

"But I don't enjoy art exhibits or concerts," she said, trying to make him understand how wrong his perception of her was. "I'd rather watch the wildlife babies playing in a meadow than—"

"I know you think that would be enough, sweetpea. But six months from now you'll be bored and wishing for your old life back." He sighed heavily. "You can't change who you are any more than I can be someone I'm not."

"What happened to make you feel this way, Brant?" She needed to understand.

He smiled sadly. "About ten years ago, while I was still in college, I knew a girl from Boston who thought she wanted the same kind of life I had. But it didn't take long for her to get tired of it. Then she tried to get me to dress up and play like I was having fun in her world." He shook his head. "It didn't work." Lowering his head, he kissed her with a tenderness that broke what was left of her heart. "Be happy, Annie."

Then without another word, he released her, walked through the door and out of her life.

"Is he really what you want, Anastasia?" her grandmother asked as she walked back into the room. "Do you really think you could be happy being a rancher's wife?"

Tears streaming down her face, Annie didn't even have to think twice before answering. "Grandmother, I love him with all my heart, and I've never wanted anything more in my life than to be his wife and live on that huge ranch of his in Wyoming." She covered her face with her hands as the sobs she'd held back broke free.

Carlotta surprised her by crossing the room to wrap Annie in her arms. "Let's sit down and see if we can work this out."

Once her grandmother had led her over to the settee, and settled them both on the uncomfortable couch, Annie accepted the handkerchief Carlotta offered. "I'm sure you heard him." She knew for certain the woman had been eavesdropping and had heard word for word what had been said. "He's convinced that I'd become bored and want to return to my way of life here." Meeting her grandmother's gaze, Annie shook her head. "But he couldn't be more wrong. I've never felt more exhilarated, more alive, than when I was with him on his ranch, or watching him do his job saving bull riders."

Carlotta sighed heavily, then patted Annie's hand.

"You're your parents' child." She dabbed at her own eyes with a lace-edged hankie. "I think I've always known that. But I was so afraid I'd lose you like I lost your mother." Smiling sadly, she said, "Can you forgive me for making your life miserable all these years?"

"Oh, Grandmother, I wasn't miserable," Annie said, putting her arms around the older woman.

"Yes, you were," Carlotta insisted. "We both knew it." She shook her head. "But I thought if I exposed you to all the things I found enjoyable, you wouldn't take the risks your mother took. Now, after seeing you with that young man, I know I was wrong." Patting Annie's cheek, Carlotta smiled. "I've never seen you look more like your mother than when I opened that door this afternoon to find you standing there with that cowboy by your side. There was a radiance about you, a spark of life in your eyes that I hadn't seen since you came here to live with me."

"But you were so…" Annie's voice trailed off as she searched for just the right word.

"You might as well say it," Carlotta urged with a self-deprecating grin. "I was rude."

Annie couldn't keep from smiling back. "Yes, you were."

Carlotta shrugged. "I've been a fool."

"I wouldn't go that far, Grandmother."

"I would." Carlotta took a deep breath. "I was too obtuse to see Patrick for what he really was. But your young man—"

"His name is Brant, Grandmother."

"Brant saw, and as far as I'm concerned, he's proven himself." Carlotta reached out to take Annie's hand in hers. "He may take risks with his own safety, but he would never take risks where you're concerned."

Annie shook her head. "It's probably not an issue now. He made it pretty clear he doesn't think we have a future together."

"Then prove him wrong." For the first time in her life, Annie watched a genuine grin light up her grandmother's wrinkled face. "Show him just how persistent and stubborn a Whittmeyer woman can be."

Grinning back, Annie asked, "You think a Whittmeyer woman with the last name of Devereaux can pull it off?"

Carlotta laughed out loud, the unfamiliar sound seeming to brighten the room with its rarity. "You were raised by the best. There's not a doubt in my mind that you can bring that young man to his senses." Rising from the settee, she motioned for Annie to follow her. "Come into the kitchen and help me put on a pot of tea. We have a strategy to plan."

Brant stood behind the chutes at the PBR event in Albuquerque, doing what he'd done every second of every day for the past month—thinking about Annie. Hell, he couldn't even look up into the crowd and see a blond-haired woman without having his heart pound against his ribs and his stomach feel like the bottom had dropped out of it. And it had happened again just a few minutes ago. On his way from the dressing room to the arena, he'd seen a little blond walking along with Mitch's sister, Kaylee. They'd been quite a distance ahead of him, but he'd damn near broken his neck trying to run across the smooth surface of the staging area on cleats in an effort to catch up to them.

He glanced over at Colt and Mitch as they went through their stretching ritual in preparation for their rides. And he would have caught them too, if those two boneheads hadn't stopped him to ask advice about the bulls they'd drawn.

Taking a deep breath, Brant shook his head. It was just as well. It would have turned out to be one of Kaylee's friends from college, or the new girlfriend of one of the riders.

When the last of the bull riders had been announced, Brant walked into the arena with the other two bull-fighters working the event with him. The surge of adrenaline he always felt when he stepped out into an arena helped to clear his head and he focused on getting through the next few hours. Once he did that, he was going to admit defeat, travel back to Illinois, and wear out the knees on his jeans if he had to, crawling at Annie's feet, begging her to give him another chance.

For the first fifteen minutes of the round, Brant found himself wondering why he was even there and couldn't wait for the night to be over. It seemed that every rider so far had drawn a "union bull"—when the horn blew, the animal quit working and trotted docilely out of the arena and back to his holding pen.

But after those first few rides, all hell broke loose.

Starting with the bull Mitch had drawn, every one of them blew out of the chutes like a cyclone. Then, once the rider had been bucked off or had dismounted, the bull turned around and went after the cowboy with blood in his eyes. It kept Brant on his toes and his thinking about Annie to a minimum.

His adrenaline was at peak level by the time Colt's name was called, and Brant knew immediately that something was wrong when his brother tried to dismount. Thanking the good Lord for building him a little taller than most bullfighters, Brant ran forward, leaned over the back of the raging, spinning animal and worked to free Colt's hand from where it had hung up in the bull rope. It took a couple of tries, but using every bit of his six-foot-one-inch frame, Brant finally managed to slip Colt's hand free.

As Colt ran to the safety of the chutes, Brant started to push away from the angry animal, but the bull had reversed his spin and was already turned before Brant could get his feet back under him. Watching the bull lower his head, Brant knew there was no escaping the inevitable. He was going airborne.

Five minutes after being tossed around like a rag doll, Brant found himself lying on a training-room examining table, answering questions about where he hurt and how bad. "I told you, I'm all right," he said for the third time. "Now, give me the go-ahead and let me get back out there to do my job."

"You know the drill," the physical trainer, Ben

Wallace, said calmly. "Anytime you lose conscious-
ness, you have to be checked out thoroughly."

"Hell, I didn't much more than close my eyes," Brant
argued, starting to sit up. "I was out all of thirty seconds,
a minute, tops."

"Brant, stop arguing with the man and let him do *his*
job."

Brant's heart stopped, then pounded hard against his
ribs at the sound of the familiar female voice. Was he
hallucinating? Had he suffered a worse concussion than
what he'd thought?

Raising up on one elbow, he looked around, his gaze
zeroing in on the woman standing just inside the
training-room door. She was wearing a black Resistol,
jeans, a hot-pink western shirt and a pair of fairly new-
looking boots.

Damn, she looked good. Real good.

"Annie. That was you with Kaylee, wasn't it?" he
asked, suddenly feeling awkward.

He wasn't real thrilled with the idea of having her
see him like this—laid out on an examining table, his
face smeared with a mixture of greasepaint, dirt and
God only knew what else. It wasn't exactly the way he
wanted to look when he pleaded his case to her.

"You saw us?" she asked, walking over to stand
beside him.

"Yeah, for about three seconds, before I was waylaid
by the two boneheads," he said sourly.

"Kaylee gave Colt and Mitch strict orders to delay

you if you came out of the dressing room before we could get to our seats," she said, nodding.

"You mean, they knew you were here and didn't tell me?" he asked, irritation beginning to burn his gut. The next time he saw his younger brother, Brant was going to throttle him.

She shook her head. "It's not important whether anyone knew and didn't tell you. I'm not here to play games. I have something to say, and you're going to listen, cowboy."

Brant had never seen Annie look more determined. Sitting up on the side of the examining table, he started to put his feet on the floor, but she blocked him by moving to stand between his knees.

"I don't think this is the best time, sweetpea."

"I think it is." She turned to the physical trainer and smiled. "I think this nice man will agree that your injuries are too serious for him to let you leave until after you've listened to me."

"That's right," Ben said, grinning.

Brant glared at the man. "Do me a favor, Ben. Don't help."

Chuckling, Ben headed for the door. "I think I'll go watch the rest of the bull riding."

Once the man left the room, Annie turned her attention back to Brant. "You know I'm pretty darned tired of people telling me what they think is *best* for me." She poked his brightly flowered shirt with her finger. "I'm perfectly capable of making my own decisions."

"I've never tried to—"

"Oh, yes you have," she said, cutting him off. "You decided that you knew what was best for me a month ago when you walked out of my grandmother's house." Reaching over to pick up a towel from a utility cart, she wiped at the streak of dirt along his jaw. "You said you knew that I would get bored and eventually want to go back to my former way of life." She stopped scrubbing his face to give him a pointed look. "Like I'd want to go back to living in a mausoleum."

She seemed to be gaining steam, and he didn't think he'd ever seen her look more beautiful. God, how he loved her.

"Annie, there's something I'd like to tell you."

"I'm not finished yet," she said, shaking her head. "I've never felt more alive in my life than when I was with you at the Lonetree, or watching you risk your life to save bull riders. And I'm not willing to go back to that dismal existence I led before I met you."

"You're not?"

It was all Brant could do to keep from grabbing her and kissing her senseless right then and there. Instead, he gripped the edge of the padded table with his hands to keep from doing just that. He was enjoying this new, more assertive side of Annie and he wanted to hear the rest of what she had to say.

"No. I'm not ever going back to living the way I did before." She turned her cleaning efforts toward his forehead. "A little over a month ago, I met and fell in love with a wonderful man, who has this misguided belief that a woman from Illinois couldn't possibly be happy with a man from Wyoming." Finished with cleaning his face, she tossed the towel on the bed beside him, then gave him a look that sent his blood pressure skyward. "But I'm not going to give up on us without a fight. I'm going to follow this cowboy around like a buckle groupie—"

"Bunny," Brant corrected, grinning. Unable to hold himself in check any longer, he reached out to pull her into his arms. "They're called buckle bunnies, sweetpea."

"All right, I'll be a buckle bunny and follow him everywhere he goes, if that's what it takes for him to come to his senses." She stopped to nibble on her lower lip before she added in a more timid tone, "And if he really loved me, he'd stop me now and ask me to marry him, before I make a complete fool of myself."

"Oh, he loves you, sweetpea," Brant said. "Don't ever doubt that. But you were doing such a fine job of reading him the riot act, which he deserves, he didn't want to interrupt."

Lowering his head, he covered her mouth with his and kissed her with every bit of the love he'd felt since first seeing her shivering on that balcony in Saint Louis. When he finally broke the kiss, her lips clung to his as if she couldn't get enough of him, either.

"God, I've missed you, sweetpea," he said, kissing her forehead, her cheeks, her perfect little nose. "Can you ever forgive me for being such a damn fool?"

"Yes," she said, sounding as breathless as he felt. "But don't let it happen again."

He threw back his head and laughed. "I take that to mean you won't let me get away with it, even if I did come up with another lamebrained notion."

"That's right, cowboy," she said, her smile touching his soul.

Gazing down at her, Brant's amusement faded. "I promise you that I'll never, as long as I live, make another fool mistake like that again." He reached up with a shaky hand to cup her satin-smooth cheek. "You're the most exciting, most beautiful woman in the world, and I won't risk losing you again. I love you more than life itself, Annie. Will you marry me and make the Lonetree your home?"

"Oh, Brant, yes, I'll marry you," she said, throwing her arms around his neck. Tears filled her eyes as she shook her head. "But I don't think the Lonetree ranch house is the place for us."

His heart stalled for a split second, then settled back down. He'd be happy anywhere, as long as Annie was by his side. "Where do you want to live, sweetpea?"

"I want us to build that big log home in your valley," she said, her radiant smile causing his body to tighten. "I want us to watch the wildlife babies playing at the edge of the meadow when their mothers bring them down to the creek for a drink. And every summer evening I want to sit on the balcony with you and watch the sun as it slips behind the mountains." Gazing up at him, her voice softened. "Then, when I have babies with Wakefield-blue eyes, I want to raise them there."

Feeling as if she'd turned every one of his dreams

into reality, Brant gave her a quick kiss. "Sweetpea, it will be my pleasure to do all those things. But it's not my valley anymore."

"It's not?" She looked and sounded so disappointed, he felt like a heel for teasing her.

"It's our valley," he said, holding her close. "Our own little part of the Lonetree Ranch."

"I love you, Brant," she said, her voice filled with emotion.

"And I love you, Annie."

She snuggled against him. "I feel like we're about to start an incredible adventure."

"We are, sweetpea." Releasing her, Brant jumped down from the examining table, took her hand in his and headed for the door. "Are you ready to begin?"

Smiling at him, she nodded. And, as he led her from the training room, Brant knew in his heart they were embarking on the most incredible, most fulfilling adventure of their lives.

* * * * *

LONETREE RANCHERS: MORGAN

A special thank-you to the Professional Bull Riders

Chapter 1

"What the hell do you think you're doing in here?"

In the process of building a fire in the big stone fireplace, Samantha Peterson jumped and spun around at the sound of the man's angry voice and the old wooden door slamming back against the wall. The biggest cowboy she'd ever seen stood like a tree rooted in the middle of the threshold. Lightning flashed outside behind him and every story she'd ever heard about the bogeyman flooded her mind.

His eyes were hidden by the wide brim of his black cowboy hat pulled down low on his forehead, but if the grim set of his mouth was any indication, he was not only the biggest cowboy she'd ever seen, he was also the angriest. He took a step forward at the same time a gust of wind whipped his long black coat around his legs. That's when Samantha noticed he held a rifle in one big gloved hand.

"I…I'm…ooh—" Samantha bent forward slightly, squeezed her eyes shut and groaned from the sudden tightness gripping her stomach.

"Good God, you're pregnant!" He sounded shocked.

Anger coursed through her. He'd scared the bejeebers out of her and all he had to say was, "You're pregnant?"

"Thank you for informing me…of that fact," she said through clenched teeth. "I doubt that I'd…have noticed otherwise."

"Are you all right?"

His voice sounded too close for comfort, but that was the least of Samantha's concerns. She had a feeling this wasn't one of the Braxton-Hicks contractions that she'd been experiencing for the past couple of weeks. It felt too different to be false labor. This felt like it might be the real thing. But that wasn't possible, was it? She still had three weeks before she reached her due date.

"No, I'm not all right," she said as the tight feeling decreased. Ready to give the man a piece of her mind, she straightened to her full height. "You scared the living daylights…"

Her voice trailed off as she looked up—way up—at the man standing next to her. The sheer size of him sent a shiver of apprehension slithering up her spine and had her stepping away from him. The top of her head barely reached his chin. At five foot six, she wasn't an Amazon by any means, but she wasn't short, either. But this man was at least ten inches taller and appeared to be extremely muscular.

"Look, I'm sorry I yelled," he said, his deep baritone sending another tremor through her that had nothing whatsoever to do with fear. "I expected to find one of the local teenage boys getting ready to throw one of his Saturday night beer busts."

"As you can see, I'm not a teenage boy." Samantha moved away a couple of extra steps. She needed to put more distance between them, in case a fast getaway was in order. At least, as fast as her advanced pregnancy would allow. "And I can assure you, I'm not getting ready to throw a drinking party."

His mouth curved up in a smile and he used his thumb to push the wide brim of his cowboy hat up, revealing the most startling blue eyes she'd ever seen. "Let's start over." He extended his big hand. "I'm Morgan Wakefield."

When she cautiously placed her hand in his, his fingers closed around hers and a warm tingle raced through her. As he stared at her expectantly, she had trouble finding her voice. "I'm, uh, Samantha Peterson," she finally managed as she tugged her hand from his.

"Nice to meet you, Mrs. Peterson."

"That's *Ms.* Peterson," Samantha corrected. "I'm not married."

His gaze traveled to her swollen stomach, then back

to her face before he gave her a short nod. Had that been a hint of disapproval she'd detected in his expression just before he gave her a bland smile?

If so, that was just too darned bad. It was none of his business whether she was married or not.

As they continued to stare wordlessly at each other, the sound of dripping water drew their attention to the corner of the room. Hurrying into the kitchen, Samantha rummaged through the cabinets until she found a large pot.

When she returned to the living room, she shoved it under the steady stream of water pouring from the ceiling. "That's just great. Not even the roof on this place is in decent repair."

She watched Morgan Wakefield's eyes narrow. "Why do you care if the roof leaks or not?" he asked slowly.

"I was hoping it would at least keep me dry tonight," she said, gazing at the rain water collecting in the pot.

"You're staying? Here? Tonight?"

"Yes. Yes. And yes," she said, smiling at his incredulous look. "I inherited it from my grandfather."

"You're Tug Shackley's granddaughter?"

Samantha nodded and walked over to the wide stone hearth to slowly lower herself to a sitting position. Another contraction was building, and making sure to keep her breathing deep and even, she focused on relaxing every muscle in her body.

When it passed, she looked up to find that Morgan had propped his rifle against the armchair and stood with his hands on his narrow hips. He was watching her as if he didn't quite know what to think. "Are you sure you're all right?"

"Yes. I'll be fine just as soon as I have my baby," she said, reminding herself to stay calm, even though the baby was coming earlier than expected. "Do you happen to know where the nearest hospital is?"

If the widening of his vivid blue eyes was any indication, it had been the last thing he'd expected her to ask. "Oh hell, lady. You're not—"

"Yes, I am." She almost laughed at the horrified expression that crossed his handsome face. "Now, if you'll answer my question concerning the location of the nearest hospital, I'll get in my car and go have my baby."

He removed his hat and ran an agitated hand through his shiny sable-black hair. "You can't drive yourself to the hospital."

"And why not, Mr. Wakefield?" she asked, staring up at him.

Not only was he one of the biggest men she'd ever met, he was one of the best-looking. He had a small white scar above his right eyebrow and his lean cheeks sported a day's growth of beard, but it only added to his rugged appeal.

"The name's Morgan," he said, jamming his hat back on his head. "And it's not safe for you to be driving in your condition. What if the pain caused you to run off the road?"

Samantha awkwardly pushed herself to her feet.

"That's a chance I'll have to take. Now, if you'll excuse me, we'll have to get acquainted some other time. Right now, I have to go deliver my baby."

He stubbornly shook his head. "Where's your car parked?"

"In the garage, or shed, or whatever you want to call that dilapidated thing behind the house." She collected her shoulder bag from the mantel. "Why?"

"The nearest hospital is over sixty miles from here, in Laramie." He held out his hand. "Give me your keys and I'll drive you down there."

"That's not necessary," she said, shaking her head. "I'm perfectly capable of—"

Arguing with Morgan, she was unprepared for the contraction that wrapped around her belly and seemed to squeeze the breath out of her. When she dropped her purse and bent double, he caught her by the shoulders and supported her until the feeling eased.

"You can't even stand up when the pain hits." He picked up her purse and held it out to her. "Now, give me your keys and I'll go get your car."

As much as she hated to admit it, he was right. Digging in her purse, she handed him the keys to her twenty-year-old Ford. "You might have trouble starting it. It's kind of tricky sometimes. I think it might need a tune-up."

"Don't worry. I think I can handle starting a car," Morgan said dryly. Taking the keys from her, he turned toward the door, but stopped abruptly when she started to follow. "There's no sense in both of us getting drenched. Stay inside until I get the car pulled up closer to the porch, then I'll help you down the steps."

"I think I can navigate a set of steps by myself," she argued.

"They aren't in the best repair and I don't think you want to deal with a broken leg, in addition to having a baby."

He left the house before she could argue the point further and sprinted across the yard. He'd waited for this day for almost eighteen months. Tug's heir had finally been found. Unfortunately, she had the idea that she was going to take up residence in the place. And at the moment, she for damned sure wasn't in any shape to listen to his arguments about why she should sell it to him, instead of carrying out her plan of moving in.

He almost laughed as he folded his tall frame into the driver's seat of the compact car. Women. Where did they get these empty-headed ideas anyway? She'd have to be blind not to see that it would take more money than it was worth to fix up this dump.

Inserting the key into the ignition, he turned it and the dull clicking sound that followed sent a chill racing up his spine. He glanced at the dashboard. There wasn't one of the indicator lights lit. He closed his eyes in frustration and barely resisted the urge to pound on the dash with his fist. The battery was as dead as poor old Tug.

When he climbed out of the bucket seat and raised the hood, he rattled off a string of cuss words that would have done a sailor proud. The battery terminals were so covered with corrosion he wouldn't be surprised to see that it had eaten through the cables. He looked around for something to knock some of the oxidation loose, but abandoned that idea immediately. Even if he got rid of most of the crud without breaking the contacts, there was no way to charge the damned thing. He slammed the hood back down with force.

Desperation clawed at his insides as the gravity of the situation settled over him. The only way to get help would involve him riding his horse back to the Lonetree through a pouring rain to get his truck. That would take at least thirty minutes going across country. Then it would take another forty-five minutes to drive the road between the two ranches.

Morgan shook his head as he stared at the sheet of rain just outside the shed's double doors. Riding through a downpour didn't bother him. Hell, he'd done that more times than he cared to count. But the creek between his ranch and this one always flooded when it rained this hard, and it would be impossible to cross now. He could use the road, but that would take a couple of hours to get back to her, and he didn't like the idea of leaving a pregnant woman—a woman in labor, no less—by herself. And he'd bet his right arm that she wouldn't be any crazier about his leaving her alone than he was.

For the first time since meeting Samantha Peterson, he allowed himself to think about his first impression of her. Her golden-brown hair framed a face that could easily grace the cover of a glamour magazine. But her eyes were what had damned near knocked him to his knees when he'd first seen her standing by the fireplace. Whiskey-brown with flecks of gold, they'd made him think of hot sultry nights and long hours of passionate sex.

Morgan sucked in a sharp breath. Now where the hell had that come from?

He cussed a blue streak. It had been quite a while since he'd enjoyed the warmth of a woman's body and the long dry spell was beginning to take its toll. What he needed was a trip to Buffalo Gals Saloon down in Bear Creek for a night of good old-fashioned hell-raising. He was sure to find a willing little filly down there to help him scratch his itch and forget how lonely the long Wyoming winter had been.

Shaking his head, he turned his attention back to the matters at hand. Now was not the time to lament how sorry his sex life was. What he and Samantha Peterson were facing right now was a lot more important.

A sinking feeling settled over him as he reviewed the options to their present dilemma. He might as well accept the inevitable and start preparing for what had to be done. Within the next few hours, he was going to have to add the delivery of a baby to his arsenal of emergency medical skills. Unless, of course, by some miracle someone else showed up. And the chances of that happening were slim to none.

Sighing heavily, he turned back to her car, opened the trunk and rummaged around until he found what he was looking for. Gathering pillows, sheets, blankets and towels, he ran back to the house.

By the time he walked through the door, Samantha sat on the hearth with her gaze transfixed on the faded picture hanging on the opposite wall. She looked as if she was in some kind of daze and he wondered if she might be going into shock.

But as he mentally reviewed what he knew about treating shock victims, she took a deep breath, slowly blew it out, then looked at him expectantly. "Are we ready to go?" she asked, rising to her feet as if nothing had happened.

Relieved that she seemed to be all right, he shook his head and tried to think of a way to break the news as gently as he could. He sighed heavily. Some things just couldn't be sugar-coated.

"The battery's dead. I'm afraid we're stuck here for a while."

Her pretty amber eyes widened considerably as she looked around the room. "But I have to go to the hospital. There's no doctor here. What if…I mean the baby is early. There might be a need for—"

Walking over to her, Morgan placed his hands on her shoulders. The last thing he needed right now was for her to go into a blind panic. "Take a deep breath and listen to me, Samantha. You're not alone. I'm here."

"Are you a doctor?" Her expressive eyes begged him to say that he was.

At the moment, Morgan would have given every-thing he owned for a medical degree. "No, I'm not," he answered truthfully. "But we'll get through this. You've got my word on that." He just hoped liked hell he could live up to the promise.

"What about your car, or truck, or whatever you came in?" she asked hopefully. "Can't we use that?"

He ran his hand over the back of his neck in an effort to ease some of the mounting tension and shook his head. "I rode my horse. Getting back to the Lonetree, then driving back here in my truck, would take hours."

"Your horse," she repeated, looking more apprehensive by the second.

"I tied it in the barn when I arrived," he said, hoping she didn't get hysterical.

She brightened suddenly, as if she had the answer to the immediate problem. "What about a cell phone? Everyone has a cell phone these days. You can't go to a movie or out to dinner without hearing one ring."

"I have one, but certain areas of this region are dead zones," he explained. "This is one of them. Even if I'd bothered to bring it with me, it would be useless without a signal."

She opened her mouth to say something, but instead of words she let loose with a low moan. The hair on the back of his neck stood straight up and his gut twisted into a tight knot. When she began to fold, Morgan pulled her to him and supported her weight while the pain held her in its grip.

Sweat popped out on his forehead and upper lip. This was going to be hard as hell to deal with. He didn't like seeing anything in pain, and definitely not a woman. He'd rather climb a barbed wire fence buck naked than to see a female in pain.

How was he going to handle Samantha going through hours of labor and not be able to do a damned thing but watch? And what if things didn't go like they were supposed to?

He swallowed around the lump forming in his throat. He knew all too well what could happen if something went wrong. At the age of seven he'd lost his own mother because of complications during the birth of his youngest brother, Colt. And she'd been in the hospital.

The pain ebbed and the woman he held took a deep breath. "I've got to maintain my focus," she said, sounding determined. "It will make all of this much easier if I can do that."

Morgan wasn't sure if she was trying to convince him or herself. But at the moment, it didn't matter. His biggest concern was to get her off her feet, make sure she was as comfortable as possible, then start gathering some of the supplies he'd need.

"Why don't you sit by the fire while I get the couch pulled over here for you to lie down?" he asked, helping her lower herself to the raised stone hearth.

"You, um, haven't by any chance done this before, have you?" she asked. Her hopeful tone caused the knot in his gut to tighten.

He refrained from answering as he pulled the drop cloth from the dingy green couch, threw it onto a chair and shoved the heavy piece of furniture closer to the warmth of the fire. He'd delivered hundreds, maybe thousands, of babies in his lifetime. But none of them had been human. And somehow, he didn't think Samantha Peterson would be all that impressed with his expertise as a bovine obstetrician. With any luck she wouldn't ask him again, and he wouldn't have to tell her.

"Well, have you?" she persisted.

Morgan almost groaned out loud. Why couldn't she just drop it and accept the inevitable? He was the best— the only—source of help she was going to get.

"Yes, and no." He unfolded one of the sheets he'd retrieved from her car and arranged it over the sagging piece of furniture, along with a couple of pillows. "If you count the calves and colts I've delivered, yes, I've done this before." He helped her up from the hearth and over to the couch. "If not, then no, I haven't."

She sat down suddenly and went into that trancelike state that she'd been in when he'd come in from trying to start the car. Fascinated, he watched her take deep, rhythmic breaths and lightly massage her swollen belly as she stared at the brim of his hat. Her porcelain cheeks colored a deep rose, but her determination to ride out the pain was evident in the set of her stubborn little chin and her unwavering concentration.

When she came out of the daze, she looked up at him and continued talking as if nothing had happened. It was the damnedest thing he'd ever witnessed.

"There's a book on pregnancy in my handbag. I think it has emergency delivery instructions and a list of things you'll need." She nervously caught her lower lip between her teeth before she continued, "I hope you're a quick study."

If there was one thing Morgan admired, and a surefire way of judging what a person was made of, it was watching how they handled themselves in a tense situation. And he'd have to give credit where it was due. The little lady settling herself back against the pillows on the sagging green couch had her share of grit.

He could tell by the shadows in her pretty whiskey-colored eyes that she was scared witless. But the firm set of her perfectly shaped mouth indicated that she wasn't going to panic. Whatever came their way, she was going to deal with it.

Giving her the most reassuring smile he was capable of under the circumstances, Morgan handed her the over-sized purse. "You find that book. I'll take care of the rest."

She pulled the book from the depths of the bag, then, shoving it into his hands, went back into another one of her trances. While she took deep, even breaths and stared off into space, he quickly scanned the index of the book she'd given him for instructions on an emergency, at-home delivery.

Turning to the page the index had indicated, he read the first entry. Calling 9-1-1 was out of the question. He skipped down to the second directive—if possible call for help.

Well hell, that was a no-brainer. If he could call someone else to assist, he'd call 9-1-1.

When his gaze dropped to the third instruction, he

swallowed hard and glanced at her as she came back from wherever she went in her mind to escape the pain.

"What?" she asked when he continued to stare at her.

He cleared his throat. There was no easy way of breaking news like this to a woman he'd known for— he checked his watch—a little less than an hour.

"It says you need to strip from the waist down," he finally answered, making sure to keep his voice even and his gaze steady.

"Is that necessary right now?" she asked just as calmly. He wasn't sure, but it looked as if her already flushed cheeks turned a deeper shade of crimson.

Shrugging, Morgan handed her the book and walked into the kitchen to find another pot. He needed to get some water boiling in order to sterilize a few things he would have to use during the delivery. And she needed to come to grips with the way things had to be.

When he walked back into the living room on his way to set a couple of pots outside to collect rainwater for boiling, he noticed that she'd used one of the blankets he'd brought in from the car to drape over her lap. Glancing to the end of the couch, he saw that her jeans were neatly folded on the arm, while her tennis shoes and socks sat on the floor beside it. She didn't look his way and he didn't comment on the fact that she'd obviously done as the book had indicated.

"Would you feel better lying down?" he asked when he returned from placing the pots on the porch steps.

She shook her head. "Not yet."

Sweat beaded her forehead as she handed him the book

and, once again, focused her energy on riding the current wave of pain. Standing there watching her, Morgan had never felt more useless in his entire life. He wanted to help her, but he didn't have a clue how to go about it.

Needing to do something, anything, he turned to the woodbox by the fireplace, removed several logs, then carefully stacked them on the dying fire in the grate. Even though it was early May, and fairly warm, there was a damp chill to the room, and he figured he would need all the light he could get when the time came for the baby's grand entrance. Besides, he needed something to keep himself busy in order to take his mind off what Samantha was going through.

The dry wood caught immediately and the fire blazed high, chasing away the approaching shadows of late afternoon. He shrugged out of his duster and tossing it toward the chair where he'd thrown the drop cloth, went in search of some other source of light. Fortunately, he found two kerosene lamps in the pantry with full reservoirs. He returned to the living room, placed them on the mantel and lit the wicks with some stick matches he'd found in the kitchen, then sat on the hearth and picked up the book. Running his finger down the list of preparations, he glanced up. Where the hell was he going to find two pieces of sturdy string to tie off the cord?

He scanned the room, then zeroed in on Samantha's tennis shoes sitting where she'd placed them by the end of the couch. Her shoe laces would have to do. He checked the book again. It didn't say anything about sterilizing what he used to tie the cord, but he figured it couldn't hurt. Just to be on the safe side, he'd toss them in the boiling water along with his pocket knife. Even if the hot water caused them to shrink, they should still be long enough for what he needed.

He laid the book within easy reach, then stood up and unfastened the cuffs of his chambray shirt. Rolling the long sleeves to the middle of his forearms, he waited for Samantha to relax her intense focus.

"The book says we need to start timing your contractions in order to tell how you're progressing. Let me know when you feel another one coming on."

She nodded. "They're coming closer together."

They were getting stronger, too. That much he could tell from the tiny strain lines bracketing her mouth. On impulse he reached out and took her hand in his. Giving it a gentle squeeze, he tried to reassure her. "You're going to do just fine, Samantha."

She squeezed back. "Remind me of that in a few hours."

"Will do," he said, nodding. He had no idea why the trust she was placing in him caused his chest to swell, but it did. Deciding that he could analyze what it meant later, he released her hand and started for the door. "I'll be right back. I'm going to go get the rainwater I've been collecting so that I can put it on the fire to boil."

"Morgan?"

The sound of his name on her soft voice sent a tingle up his spine. He swallowed hard and turned back to face her. "What, Samantha?"

"Thank you for being so calm. It really helps." The look she gave him clearly stated that she was counting on him to get her through whatever happened.

At a loss for words, he nodded and walked out to the porch to get the pots of water. Samantha had no way of knowing that his insides were churning like a damned cement mixer from thoughts of all the things that could go wrong, as they had with his mother.

Morgan took a deep breath, then slowly released it. And if it was the last thing he ever did, he had no intention of letting her find out.

Chapter 2

Four hours later, Morgan sat on the hearth in front of Samantha where she perched on the edge of the couch. For the last hour he'd watched her alternate between sitting forward and leaning back against the pillows in her effort to get comfortable. She had his hand in a death grip as she rode the current wave of pain and it surprised him how strong she was. It felt more like a lumberjack had a hold of his hand than a woman, and her nails digging into his palm felt as if she might draw blood. But if it helped her get through this, he'd gladly let her rip the skin clean off.

As he watched her stare off into space and pant her way through the contraction, his admiration for her grew by leaps and bounds. She was in tremendous pain, but her determination to stay on top of it, to ride it out, was amazing.

He was sure she was in what the book called "active labor" because of the duration of her contractions and the time between them. He glanced at his watch. They still had the "transitional labor" to go through and, if the book was right, they probably had another couple of hours before they got to the actual delivery. He just hoped he could last that long. With every contraction Samantha had, his gut twisted tighter and he felt a little more helpless than he had only moments before.

When she blew out a deep breath, signaling that the contraction had ended, he asked, "Is there anything else I can do? The book says that you might have some back pain? Do you need your back rubbed?"

"Would you mind?" she asked, releasing his hand. She winced. "My back is killing me."

Removing his Resistol, Morgan sailed it like a Frisbee to land on the chair with his duster, took a deep breath and eased over to sit next to her on the ugly green couch. He slipped his hand beneath her pink T-shirt to lightly kneed the muscles of her lower back, and valiantly tried to ignore the fact that her skin felt like satin beneath his callused palm. Now was not the time for him to remember how much he missed the way a woman's softness felt.

"Is it helping?" he asked.

"A little." She suddenly took a deep breath and once again focused on riding out another wave of pain.

Morgan continued to rub her back with his right hand as he glanced at the watch on his left wrist. This contraction had come a lot faster than the last one. He watched the second hand sweep around once, then halfway around again before Samantha blew out a deep breath, signaling it was over.

"Stop touching me," she said sharply. "You're making it worse."

"Okay," he said, removing his hand from beneath her shirt. He knew for certain that he hadn't rubbed her back *that* hard.

Frowning, Morgan moved back to the hearth and picked up the book. Unless he missed his guess, they were moving on to the next step.

Yep. Sure as shootin', Samantha had all the signs of a woman in "transitional labor." She'd suddenly become as irritable as a bear with a sore paw, didn't want to be touched, and the most telling of the symptoms was the duration of the last contraction.

He wiped the sweat from his forehead and watched her struggle to stay focused as the next wave of pain hit her. Her face was flushed, her golden-brown hair hung in damp tendrils from perspiration and the lines of strain around her mouth had deepened.

He'd never felt more useless.

When she blew out a deep breath, he laid the book aside and wiped her face with a cool damp washcloth. Her gaze met his, and it was damned near his undoing when tears filled her pretty amber eyes.

"I don't think...I can't do this, Morgan."

Making sure the book was within easy reach, Morgan took her hands in his. "You're doing just fine, Samantha." The instructions had indicated that he should encourage her and help her stay focused. He wasn't sure how the hell to go about that, but he'd do it or die trying. "You're in the home stretch, sweetheart. It won't be much longer."

He watched her eyes cloud with pain, felt her hands tighten on his in a death grip. She started to say something, but a moan came out instead.

It tore him apart to see her hurting and not be able to do anything to help. "Look at me, Samantha."

Her breathing ragged, she shook her head. "This is…too hard," she said, her voice cracking.

"Come on, Samantha, look at me," he said more firmly.

When she finally did as he commanded, Morgan nodded. "That's it, sweetheart. Stay focused and squeeze my hands as hard as you can. Concentrate on transferring the pain to me."

He wasn't sure if the book supported his way of taking her mind off the contraction, but he didn't care. All that mattered was that it seemed to be working. Samantha held his gaze and damned near cut off the circulation to his fingers as she tightened her hands on his.

What seemed like an eternity, but couldn't have been more than a couple of minutes later, she suddenly released his hands to lay back against the couch. "I need to push."

The hair on the back of Morgan's neck shot straight up

and his stomach did a back-flip. "Are you sure?" he asked, flexing his fingers in an effort to return the circulation.

Nodding, she scrunched her eyes shut, grabbed her knees with her hands and pushed with all her might.

Morgan wanted to run like hell. Instead, he grabbed the book, quickly read what he needed to do, then prayed like he'd never prayed before.

He could do this. Along with his dad and brothers, he'd played baby doctor to the herds of Lonetree cattle for as long as he could remember. Surely he could deliver one little human baby.

Placing the book within easy reach, he washed his hands in one of the pots of water that he'd boiled earlier, then fished his sterilized pocket knife and Samantha's shoelaces from the other. Fortunately, the water had cooled enough that it wasn't scalding, but it was still damned hot. His mind on what was about to take place, he barely noticed.

To Morgan, the next thirty minutes seemed to pass in a fast-forward blur. Samantha worked hard to push her baby out into the world as he uttered words he hoped were encouraging. Then, just after midnight, a little baby boy with dark brown hair slid out into his waiting hands, opened his mouth and started yowling at the top of his tiny lungs.

A lump the size of his fist formed in Morgan's throat as he stared down at the child he'd helped to enter the world. Awed by the miracle he'd participated in, he couldn't have strung two words together if his life depended on it.

"Is my baby all right?" Samantha asked, sounding stronger than he would have thought possible after what she'd been through.

Relieved that things had turned out the way they should, Morgan tied off the cord in two places, cut it between the ties, then wrapped the baby in fluffy towels. His hands shaking slightly, he placed the infant in her waiting arms.

Clearing his throat, he finally managed, "I'm not a doctor, but he looks normal to me." He grinned. "If his squalling is any indication, I'd say he's mad as hell about this whole birthing business though."

"He's beautiful." He watched tears fill Samantha's eyes as she glanced up at him. "I can't thank you enough for helping us, Morgan."

"You did all the work." Finishing the last of what the instructions indicated should be done, he washed up and rolled his sleeves back down to fasten them at his wrists. "Have you picked out a name for him?"

The smile she gave him made Morgan feel as if the sun had broken through on a gray, cloudy day. "As a matter of fact, I think I have," she said softly. "How does Timothy *Morgan* Peterson sound?"

Two days later, Samantha sat on the side of her hospital bed, staring at the discharge papers the nurse had handed her only moments ago. Now what? Where were she and the baby supposed to go? And how were they supposed to get there?

She didn't have her car. And even if she did, it

wouldn't run. The morning after Timmy had been born, Morgan rode his horse back to his ranch, then drove over to her grandfather's place in his truck to take her and the baby to the hospital.

She sighed as she looked at her son sleeping peacefully in the bassinet. She could call a cab. But where would she have it take her and Timmy? She certainly couldn't afford the fare for a sixty mile trip back to her newly inherited ranch. She shook her head. Make that her newly inherited dump.

"Do you need help getting dressed?" the nurse asked, strolling back into the room with a complimentary bag of sample baby products. She picked up Timmy from the tiny bed to wrap him in a soft, baby blue receiving blanket. "By the way, I caught your husband in the hall and told him you two were ready to leave."

Dumbfounded, Samantha blinked. "My husband?" The woman had to have confused her with another new mother. "I'm not—"

"I sent him to bring his truck around to the front entrance," the woman said as if Samantha hadn't spoken. "Once you're dressed, I'll get a wheelchair and you and this little darling can be on your way."

"But I still have to go down to the business office to make arrangements to pay the bill. And I'm not—"

"Don't worry, Samantha. It's taken care of," Morgan said, walking through the doorway as if he owned the place. He handed her a shopping bag. "All you have to do is put these clothes on and we can get out of here."

"I'll get the wheelchair," the nurse said, her shoes making a whispering sound against the tiled floor as she quickly left the room.

Samantha stared at the man who had been her rock throughout the birth of her child. He was without a doubt one of the best-looking men she'd ever seen. And apparently one of the most arrogant.

"What do you mean it's taken care of?" she demanded. She wasn't sure what he'd done, but she had a feeling she wasn't going to like it when she found out.

"We'll talk about it on the drive home."

"I think we'd better discuss this right now," she said flatly. She wasn't going anywhere until he told her what was going on.

Completely ignoring her protest, he took the shopping bag from her stiff fingers, opened it and pulled out a cream-colored T-shirt and denim jumper. "I wasn't sure about the size, so I had a clerk pick out everything. She said these were 'one size fits most'—whatever that means." He looked a little unsure as he shoved them into her hands and turned to leave. "Go ahead and get dressed so we can get out of here. I'll be waiting with the truck when the nurse brings you out the front entrance."

"Morgan, I want to know what—"

"I don't want to argue with you, Samantha," he interrupted. "It's not good for you, and I really don't have time for it. I'd like to get back to the Lonetree by lunchtime. So get dressed and I'll meet you out front."

Before she could demand answers, he grabbed the

small overnight case she'd brought with her to the hospital, turned and left the room, leaving her to stare after him. She needed to get back to her grandfather's ranch—make that hers now—to see about her car. And with very little money, she really didn't have any other options of getting there.

She sighed heavily, then removing the tags from the jumper and T-shirt, slipped the pieces of lightweight cardboard into her purse. She wasn't a charity case. As soon as she could, she'd pay Morgan back for the clothes.

Hurriedly changing from the hospital gown, she hardened her resolve to find out what he meant about the hospital bill being taken care of. They had a good sixty-mile drive ahead of them, and if he'd done what she suspected, they were going to have a long talk on the way. A *really* long talk.

Fifteen minutes later, when the nurse guided the wheelchair through the double glass doors of the hospital's front entrance, Morgan was leaning against the fender of his shiny silver-gray truck, his arms folded across his chest, boots crossed at the ankles. His denim jacket emphasized the width of his shoulders and his well-worn jeans hugged his muscular thighs like a second skin. She gulped. He looked like every woman's fantasy—rugged, handsome and thoroughly masculine.

When he saw her, he smiled as he straightened to his full height and opened the passenger door of the shiny pickup. A tiny shiver coursed through her when his hand brushed her breast as he reached to take Timmy.

"You three make a nice little family," the nurse said, watching Morgan cradle the baby with one arm, while he helped Samantha up onto the bench seat with the other. "Have a safe trip home."

"Thanks. We'll do that," he said, handing the baby to Samantha. He closed the door of the truck before she could correct the nurse about them being a family.

"Why didn't you tell her we aren't together?" Samantha demanded when he slid into the driver's seat and turned the key in the ignition.

"It just seemed faster and a whole hell of a lot easier than explaining the situation," he answered, shrugging one shoulder.

She fastened the seat belt over the car seat she'd had him get from her car the day before when he'd brought her and the baby to the hospital to be checked over. "You don't approve of my having a child without a husband, do you?"

"I can't say that I do, or don't," he said, putting the truck into gear. He steered it out onto the street, then glancing at her, added, "Samantha, I don't know the circumstances." His expression turned grim. "But the baby's father should have been here to help you through this."

She watched the easy way Morgan handled the big truck as he navigated the traffic. He was a man in complete control, and one who could be counted on in any situation. Unlike Timmy's father.

Her chest tightened at the thought of the man who'd fathered a child he cared nothing about. How could she have been so wrong about Chad?

When they first started living together, they'd both worked at achieving the true give and take of a successful relationship. But six months later, Samantha suddenly realized that things had changed between them. She'd been the one doing all of the giving and he'd been the one doing the taking. Then one day she'd come home from work to find that he'd moved to L.A. to pursue his dream of becoming a musician. That's when she realized how shallow and uncaring Chad really was. He hadn't even bothered to face her to tell her things were over between them. He'd left a rather impersonal note stuck to the front of the refrigerator, saying that he'd had fun, but that it was time for him to move on.

"There's really not that much to tell," she found herself saying. Why Morgan's opinion mattered, she had no idea. But for some reason she wanted him to know that the choice to handle everything on her own, hadn't been hers. "We weren't married, and I didn't find out I was pregnant until after he and I had parted company."

She watched Morgan's hands tighten on the steering wheel, and she knew what he was thinking before he even asked, "He doesn't know about the baby?"

"Oh, I told him," she said, trying to keep her voice even. She would not allow herself to dwell on how hurt she'd been by Chad's decision. "I didn't ask him for any kind of help when I told him. I just thought he should know he'd fathered a baby, and that he might want to be part of Timmy's life. But he wasn't interested in knowing his child now, or in the future. He offered to sign away all legal rights to Timmy, and I accepted. End of story."

"Why would he do a dumb-ass thing like that?" Morgan asked bluntly. He shot her a scowl that stated quite clearly what he thought of Chad, and she knew beyond a shadow of doubt that it would be the last thing he'd do in the same situation.

Gazing down at her sleeping son, Samantha blinked back the threatening tears. "I suspect he thought it would insure that I'd never ask for any kind of financial help from him."

Morgan snorted. "I think a man who shirks his responsibilities and denies his child should be shot."

Samantha swallowed around the lump in her throat. "I think Timmy and I are better off this way."

"How do you figure that?" Morgan asked, clearly unable to comprehend her reasoning.

"Chad turned out to be very selfish and self-centered," she answered, gently touching her son's soft cheek. She took a deep breath to chase away the sadness she always felt when she thought of all that Timmy would miss by not having a father. "Why would I want a man like that helping me raise my son? It's not the kind of example I want set before Timmy. Besides, he deserves a father who loves him unconditionally, not one who simply views him as a monthly support check."

Morgan was silent for several long moments before he nodded. "I couldn't agree more. But when a man gets a woman pregnant, whether he ever sees the child or not, he has an obligation to help her."

Reaching the outskirts of Laramie, he set the cruise control, then stretched his right arm out along the back of the seat. His fingers brushed her hair and she felt warmed all the way to her toes.

Startled by her reaction, Samantha scooted over to lean against the door. "I have a question," she said, determined to regain her equilibrium.

He glanced her way and smiled. "And that would be?"

His easy expression caused her pulse to skip a beat. She took a deep breath to chase away her accompanying breathlessness. "When you walked into my room back at the hospital, you said everything had been taken care of at the business office. What did you mean?"

"Just that," he said, staring at the road ahead. "The bill is paid."

Samantha felt her stomach start to churn. "Would you like to tell me who paid it?"

"I did."

Anger swept through her. "Why?"

"Call it a baby gift," he said, his smile so darned charming that she had to fight the warmth filling her chest.

She shook her head as she tried desperately to hang on to her anger. "A baby gift is a high chair, a blanket, a set of bibs. It's *not* paying a hospital bill."

His smiled faded and a muscle began to work along his lean jaw. "Look, Samantha. I've got the money, and I don't mind helping out."

"I don't need your help," she said stubbornly. "I'm not a charity case."

He shook his head. "I never said you were."

"How much was the bill?" Reaching into her purse, she removed a pad of paper and a pen. "I'll reimburse you as soon as I find a job."

"No, you won't."

"Yes, I will."

"Dammit, woman." He looked exasperated. "I said no."

"You're used to people doing what you tell them to do, aren't you?" she asked, already knowing the answer.

He shrugged, but remained silent.

"Well, let me treat you to a reality check, cowboy." She stuffed the paper and pen back into her handbag. "I've been on my own since I was eighteen. I make my own decisions and I pay my own way."

As she glared at Morgan, the baby suddenly opened his eyes, waved his little fists in protest and wailed at the top of his lungs. Their raised voices had startled him.

"Why don't we put this argument on hold until we get home?" Morgan asked, steering the truck off the main road.

Samantha quieted the baby, then looking around at the scenery, she frowned. Nothing looked familiar and she knew for certain they hadn't traveled this road when Morgan had taken her and Timmy to the hospital the day before.

"Where are we going?" she asked, noticing the neatly fenced pastures on either side of the road.

"I'm taking you to the Lonetree," he said, as if that explained everything.

"Do you need to pick up something before you take me to my place?" she asked cautiously.

"No."

A knot of suspicion began to form in the pit of her stomach. "Then why are we—"

"I thought you and the baby should stay at my ranch for a few days," he said, turning onto another road.

She shook her head vehemently. "I most certainly will not be staying at your ranch."

"Don't be stubborn about this, Samantha. Your grandfather's house isn't in any shape for you and the baby to stay there." He made it sound so darned reasonable, she wanted to scream.

But as she thought about what he'd just said, some of her anger drained away. She hated to admit it, but Morgan was right. The house only had a fireplace in the living room for heat, there was no running water and no electricity. Besides all that, the roof leaked.

Frustrated beyond words, Samantha had to fight the sudden urge to cry. It just brought home how low her circumstances had become. For all intents and purposes, she was as homeless as the foster child she'd been after her mother passed away.

Slowing the truck to a stop, Morgan turned to face her. "I understand how much you value your independence, sweetheart. And I swear I'm not trying to take that away from you. But you have to be realistic about this." He reached over the car seat between them to cup her chin in his big palm, sending a wave of goose bumps shimmering over her skin. "Right now, you need help. Please, let me do the neighborly thing and lend a hand."

She caught her lower lip between her teeth to keep it from trembling. Where else was she going to go? She had a newborn to take care of, no place to live and she'd exhausted her bank account to make the move from Sacramento to Wyoming. If it was just her, she'd politely refuse Morgan's offer. But she had to think of what was best for Timmy now.

"I don't have any other choice," she finally said, blinking back tears. "And I really hate not having options."

"I know, sweetheart. I feel the same way." His understanding smile warmed her to the depths of her soul. "But you'll be on your feet and back in charge of things before you know it."

As she stared into his incredibly blue eyes, Samantha wondered if he'd ever been in a situation that he couldn't control. She doubted it. A man like Morgan was always in complete command of everything going on around him.

Resigned, she took a deep breath. "I'll need to get some things from my car."

He released her chin and turned his attention to the road ahead of them. Shifting the truck into drive, he nodded. "After I got back from taking you and the baby to the hospital yesterday, I had a couple of my ranch hands take one of the tractors and tow your car over here. One of them is a pretty fair mechanic and he's got it down at the machine shed, trying to get it running again."

Before Samantha could tell him to keep track of how much the repairs cost, they topped a hill overlooking a beautiful valley. A sprawling log ranch house, along with several neat-looking barns and outbuildings stood majestically at one end, while a large herd of black cattle grazed at the other.

"Is that your ranch?"

He nodded. "That's the main house. My brother, Brant, and his wife, Annie, have their home about three miles east of here."

"How big *is* this place?" Samantha asked incredulously.

"We've been on Lonetree land ever since we turned off the highway," he answered without blinking an eye.

"That was some time ago," she said, awed by the idea of such a large piece of property.

He nodded. "About six miles."

"Well, it certainly is beautiful," she said, marveling at the contrast between her newly inherited property and this well-kept ranch. She wondered if she'd ever be able to get hers looking as nice. If she could, she knew for certain she'd be able to find backers for the camp she wanted to open for homeless children.

Morgan didn't say anything, but she could tell by the slight curving at the corners of his mouth that her comment had pleased him.

When they drew closer, he turned the truck onto a lane that led to the house. Tall wooden posts stood on either side of the road, supporting a log spanning the width between them. As they passed beneath it, Samantha caught a fleeting glimpse of the words Lonetree Ranch carved into a wooden sign suspended from the middle of the arch.

He stopped the pickup at the side of the house, then got out and came around to help her from the passenger side. "I had Bettylou, the wife of the man working on your car, come by and make up one of the guest rooms," he said, unfastening the lap belt from the baby's carrier. He lifted it from the center of the bench seat, then using the handle, carried it in one hand as he cupped her elbow with the other to guide her up the steps of the front porch. "After I get you two settled in your room, I'll go down to the machine shed and check to see if Frank knows what's wrong with your car. I'll get your things while I'm at it."

His big hand warmed her arm through the light jacket she wore and sent a tremor up her spine. She quickly stepped away from him.

"I won't need everything from the car," she said, waiting for him to open the door. "Timmy and I won't be staying more than a couple of days."

Holding the door for her, he smiled. "We'll see."

She needed to make it clear to him, she wasn't a charity case, nor did she intend to take advantage of his generosity. Before she could respond to his obvious disbelief, they entered the foyer of the Lonetree ranch house and she forgot anything she'd been about to say. The interior of the log home was every bit as impressive as the exterior.

When Morgan led her into the great room, her breath caught. "This is absolutely gorgeous."

A huge stone fireplace with a split log mantel stood against the outside wall of the room, the rounded blue, gray and tan stones the perfect accent to the golden hue of the varnished log walls. The house had a warm, friendly feel to it, but it was the openness that Samantha fell in love with. The ceiling was vaulted and open all the way to the huge log rafters, and the rooms seemed to flow from one into another.

"Make yourself at home," Morgan said, placing the car seat with her sleeping son on the most unusual coffee table she'd ever seen.

A thick, flat piece of dark blue-gray slate rested on a pedestal base made from a section of an entire tree trunk. The bark had been left on and contrasted beautifully with the warm patina of the polished hardwood floor and the burnt sienna colored leather furniture.

"Were you going for durability?" she asked dryly.

Chuckling, Morgan shrugged. "Brant and I ruined the surface of my mom's other table so many times by running our cars and trucks over it, that Mom and Dad came up with the idea of a slate topped table before Colt was born. Then after Mom died, and Dad was faced with raising three rowdy boys by himself, I don't think he had much choice but to keep it."

"You were raised by your father?"

She noticed a fleeting shadow in his intense blue eyes a moment before he nodded. "Mom died while giving birth to our youngest brother, Colt."

Samantha gazed up at him for several long seconds. "I'm sorry, Morgan. I know what it feels like to lose your mother," she said quietly. "I was almost seventeen when mine passed away."

As they stood staring at each other, the baby suddenly let loose with a lusty cry, breaking the somber mood that had come over the two adults.

"It's time for him to nurse," she said, releasing the straps securing Timmy in the baby seat. "Is there somewhere I could—"

"I'll show you to your room," Morgan said, nodding toward the staircase behind her. The stairs, banister and railings of the loft area above were crafted from the same golden wood as the walls, and added to the rustic appeal of the house.

Samantha held the baby close and tried to concentrate on breathing as she climbed the split-log steps beside Morgan. He'd placed his arm around her waist to steady her and his touch was doing some very strange things to her insides. Tingles raced the length of her spine and a warm, protected feeling seemed to course through her.

Needing to put a little distance between them, she waited for him to lead the way across the loft and down a hall where several bedrooms were located. Her uncharacteristic reaction to him had to be due to a major postnatal hormone imbalance. That's all it could be, she decided. After giving birth two days ago, there was no way she could possibly be feeling any kind of physical awareness. Was there?

When he opened the door to a room at the end of the hall, her eyes misted over. A cradle, made up with soft-looking, baby-blue bedding sat by a beautiful four-poster bed. She couldn't remember a time since her mother's passing that anyone had been as thoughtful as Morgan had been in the past few hours. He'd made sure she and the baby had a ride home from the hospital, offered them a place to stay and had gone to the trouble of arranging for Timmy to have a warm, comfortable place to sleep.

She put her son in the cradle, then turned back to Morgan. Reaching up to place her hand at the back of his neck, she drew his head down to kiss his lean cheek. "You're the most thoughtful man I've ever met," she said, her voice shaking slightly from the emotion welling up inside of her.

Before she could draw away, Morgan pulled her into his arms, then staring down at her for no more than a split second, lowered his mouth to hers and kissed her. It wasn't anything more than his lips pressed to hers, but her knees shook and her head swam. Then, just as quickly, he released her with a muttered curse.

Looking as startled as she felt, he started backing from the room. "I…I'll get your things from the car."

Before she could remind him that she wouldn't be needing everything, he turned on his heel and left the room so fast Samantha wouldn't have been surprised to see that his boots had left skid marks on the polished hardwood floor.

She brought her fingers up to touch her tingling lips.

Why had he kissed her? But more important, why did she feel like she wanted him to kiss her again?

Turning to pick up Timmy, she decided that it would definitely be in her best interest to find somewhere else to stay as soon as her car was repaired. Although Morgan Wakefield had shown her more concern and kind consideration than anyone had in longer than she cared to remember, he also represented a temptation that she wasn't ready to deal with and wasn't sure she would ever be able to resist.

Chapter 3

His jaw clenched so tightly it would probably take an oral surgeon to pry it apart, Morgan descended the stairs and crossed the great room to the front foyer. Once he stood outside on the porch, he took in several deep breaths in hopes of clearing his head. He couldn't believe what he'd just done.

Samantha had only meant that little peck on the cheek as an expression of gratitude. There hadn't been anything sexual about the gesture.

But his body hadn't seen it that way. When she'd drawn his head down to press her soft lips to his jaw, he'd responded with a fierceness that had almost knocked him to his knees. And, like a damned fool, he'd grabbed her and kissed her like a teenager with more hormones than sense.

At least he'd come to his senses before he had the chance to take the kiss to the next level. He uttered a pithy curse. So why was he regretting that he'd kept it simple?

Grinding his back teeth, he stared at the acres of pasture stretching out in front of him. Like the grass in the fields, his body was just awakening from an extended dormant period. That's all there was to it. The winter had been a long, cold one, and it was only natural that a man would be feeling the effects of not having a woman around to help him stay warm.

He ran a frustrated hand across the back of his neck and swore a blue streak. What he needed was a night in the arms of a willing woman. Then maybe he could forget how Samantha's amber eyes reminded him of long sultry nights, of tangled sheets and soft sighs.

Unfortunately, he had a feeling that it was more than the need for sexual release that caused his reaction to her. And that's what bothered him.

Since his fiancée's death, he hadn't allowed himself to look at another woman for anything more than a few hours of harmless, consensual fun. And that only happened once or twice a year when the loneliness got so bad he thought he'd jump out of his own skin.

The all-too-familiar ache of guilt and regret settled in his chest as he thought of Emily Swensen. They should have been celebrating their sixth wedding anniversary in a couple of months. Instead, he would be making his annual trip to the cemetery down in Denver to place flowers on her grave.

Gazing down the lane, Morgan thought about the woman he'd promised to marry. Emily had been his best friend, as well as his lover. And she'd be alive today if it wasn't for him.

He took a deep shuddering breath. He'd been so sure that he knew what was best for her when he'd insisted she make that trip to Denver to visit her sister the week before they were to be married. She hadn't wanted to go, but he'd convinced her of how lonely it would be for her while he caught up on spring chores. She'd finally agreed to make the trip, but the day she left she'd had tears running down her cheeks, as if she'd known they would never see each other again.

That was the last time he'd seen her alive. Two days later, he'd received the phone call that still haunted his dreams. Emily had been killed, and her sister seriously wounded, in the cross fire between police and a couple of thugs trying to rob a jewelry store in downtown Denver.

Guilt knotted his gut, the feeling so strong it took his breath. His presumption that he knew what was best had gotten an innocent woman killed, and proven that his judgement was faulty. He'd never run the risk of making another mistake like that again.

He'd come to terms with never having a wife and family, and he'd learned to live with the loneliness, the cold, empty spot beside him in his bed. And that's the way it was going to remain.

In a few days, he'd offer Samantha quite a bit more for her grandfather's ranch than it was worth, insuring that she wouldn't have any money worries for a while. Then she and her son could move on, and he'd settle back down to his routine of running the Lonetree and making it the best privately owned ranch in the state of Wyoming.

"Hey, boss? You got a minute?"

Morgan turned toward the sound of Frank Milford's voice. He'd been so lost in his disturbing thoughts, he hadn't heard the man's approach.

"What do you need, Frank?" he asked, descending the porch steps.

"I think you'd better get Ned and Chico to haul that hunk of junk down at the machine shed to a scrap yard," the man said, wiping grease from his hands with a rag.

"It's that bad?" Morgan asked as he continued walking toward the shed.

"It ain't worth the powder and lead to blow it up with," Frank said, falling into step beside Morgan.

"What's wrong with it?"

"What ain't?" Frank asked disgustedly.

"You want to cut to the chase and give me a rundown so I'll know what it will take to fix it?" Morgan asked patiently. He was used to Frank's tendency to exaggerate.

Frank shook his head. "When I put a new battery in it and fired 'er up, there was a real wicked knock in the engine. Besides needin' spark plugs, new belts and hoses, I'd say it's getting ready to throw a rod."

"How long would it take to rebuild the motor?"

Morgan asked, knowing it would take longer than he was comfortable with.

The sooner Samantha's car was fixed, the sooner she and her son could be on their way with a nice fat check in her pocket. Then maybe he wouldn't feel as if he were outgrowing his jeans every time she looked at him with those whiskey-brown eyes of hers.

"It'll probably take a couple of weeks," Frank said. "Maybe longer." He followed Morgan into the building they used to repair and maintain the ranching equipment. "Ford doesn't make that model anymore. Hell, I'm not even sure we can still get parts for it."

A relieved feeling swept through Morgan, quickly followed by a knot twisting at his gut. He had a feeling that Samantha would be staying a lot longer than either of them had anticipated. What bothered him was how much the idea appealed to him.

Shaking his head, he decided that a psychologist would have a field day with that one. "Go ahead and make a few calls to see what you can come up with, Frank."

"You're the boss," the man said, tossing the greasy rag onto a workbench. "But if it was me, I'd cut my losses and find another set of wheels."

As Frank walked over to the phone to start calling auto parts stores down in Laramie, Morgan opened the driver's door of Samantha's car to grab the keys from the ignition. Opening the trunk, he pulled out a couple of battered pieces of luggage, and a sack filled with what looked like baby items.

Tucking the sack under his arm, he picked up a

suitcase in each hand and started for the house. Samantha wasn't going to be happy about the turn of events. For one thing, she clearly couldn't afford to have the car repaired. And for another, her stay at the Lonetree had just been extended for an indefinite period of time.

The relief he'd felt earlier increased, causing Morgan to utter a cuss word he reserved for the most serious of situations. The long, cold winter must have been longer and colder than he'd realized. He wanted a woman and baby underfoot—reminding him of the family he'd never have—about as much as he wanted to see the cattle market take a nosedive.

"Are you sure it's that serious?" Samantha asked. "When I left Sacramento, it was fine." She frowned. "Except for a clunking sound when the motor was running."

Morgan swallowed the bite of sandwich he'd been chewing and nodded. "It's not a matter of *if* the engine breaks down, it's more like *when*. It might last for another few hundred miles, or it could blow a rod before you got it backed out of the machine shed."

"I can't afford this right now." She placed her sandwich back on her plate untouched. Only moments ago, the roast beef and cheddar melt had looked delicious. But with Morgan's news about her car, Samantha's appetite deserted her.

"Don't worry about it." He took a drink of his iced tea, then shrugged. "It's taken—"

"Don't you dare," she warned.

"What?"

"You know what." She shook her head. "This is my problem and I'll solve it. You took care of the hospital bill before I could stop you. But you will *not* pay for the repairs on my car."

He gave her an exasperated look. "I've already got Frank calling auto parts stores."

"Then you can tell him to stop," she said stubbornly. "I'll just have to take my chances and hope the engine will make it until I'm able to afford to have it repaired."

"Don't be ridiculous, Samantha." His intense blue gaze caught and held hers. "What if you're out on the road with the baby and it breaks down? You can't walk miles for help with an infant, nor can you wait for someone to come along and find you." He shook his head. "This isn't a highly populated area. Out here, there are times when it's hours before another car comes by."

Her heart sank. Morgan was right. She couldn't run the risk of being out with Timmy in an unreliable car.

She took a deep breath and had to force herself to admit defeat. "All right. Have the car repaired. But only on one condition." When he cocked a dark brow, she added, "You have to let me know every penny you spend on it, so that I can reimburse you."

"I'm not worried about—"

"I am," she interrupted. She had to make him understand. "After my father left us without a backward glance, I watched my mother struggle to keep a roof over our heads and food in our mouths. It wasn't easy for her, but she did it without waiting for a man to come to the rescue. I fully intend to do the same." Rising from the table, she wrapped her sandwich and placed it in the refrigerator. "I don't ever intend to rely on anyone for what I want or need. I'll work for it and earn it, or I'll do without."

He looked as if he were about to protest, but Samantha held up her hand to stop him. "I know you mean well, but this is something I feel very strongly about. It's no secret, I've hit a low spot in my life. But it's only temporary. As soon as the doctor releases me to work, I'll get a job and pay you back." She started to leave the kitchen, but a sudden thought had her turning back. "Do you have a housekeeper or cook?"

In the middle of taking a long swig of his iced tea, he slowly placed the glass on the table and shook his head. "No. I usually take my meals down at the bunkhouse with the rest of the guys. And when I need something done to the house, my sister-in-law, Annie, takes care of it, or I pay Bettylou. Why?"

Samantha nodded. "Until my car is repaired and I find a job to pay you back, you won't be needing their help. I'll be cooking your meals and cleaning your house."

Morgan's eyes narrowed as he watched her turn and slowly walk from the room, shoulders straight, her head held high. He'd always admired those who had the grit to work and make their own way. But Samantha was taking this pride thing to the extreme. He could tell by the way she moved that she was still sore from giving birth, yet she was telling him that she was going to start cooking and cleaning for him?

"Like hell," he muttered.

Scooting his chair back from the table, he rinsed his plate and glass, then placed them in the dishwasher and headed for his study. He had the perfect solution to resolve the money issue that she seemed to think was so important.

She owned the run-down ranch that he wanted to buy. What could be more simple than him offering to buy it from her? He would end up with the land he wanted, and she'd have the cash to get on her feet and start a new, more secure life for herself and her son.

Morgan ignored the twinge in his gut at the thought of Samantha leaving as he dialed his attorney and made arrangements for the man to draw up a purchase option. Assured that the document would be delivered within the next week or two, he climbed the stairs and walked down the hall to Samantha's door. The sound of the baby crying immediately caught his attention.

"Samantha?" he called, tapping on the door.

Nothing.

Opening it a crack, he tried again. "Samantha, I'd like to talk to you—"

The sound of the shower running explained why she wasn't tending to the baby. He glanced from the closed door of the adjoining bathroom to the cradle where Timmy continued to wail at the top of his little lungs. Now what? Samantha was taking a shower and Timmy sounded as if he was gearing up for a real rip-snorter of a fit.

Morgan walked over to the tiny bed to rock it back and forth, hoping to quiet the baby until Samantha finished her shower. "Shh, little guy. Your mom will be here in just a minute."

If anything the baby cried harder.

Deciding he didn't have a choice, Morgan held his breath and gingerly picked up the infant. The only other times in his life that he'd held a baby had been when he'd helped Samantha give birth, then just a few hours ago when he'd brought her and Timmy home from the hospital. Now what was he supposed to do?

"They should issue 'how-to' manuals on this stuff," he muttered, feeling like a fish out of water.

He mentally reviewed how he'd seen Samantha hold little Timmy when he'd started crying earlier. The baby seemed to be quiet whenever she held him to her shoulder. Maybe that was his favorite position.

Morgan put the infant to his shoulder and rubbed the little guy's back like he'd seen Samantha do. Timmy instantly stopped crying and let loose with a burp that Morgan was sure rattled his tiny rib cage.

He couldn't help it, Morgan laughed out loud. "I'll bet you feel better now, don't you?" He felt something wet seep through his shirt, and glancing at his shoulder, cringed. "I guess you had a little too much for lunch, huh?"

"What's wrong?" Samantha asked as she came out

of the bathroom and hurried over to him. She took the baby, then gasped. "Oh, my. Your shirt." She placed the now quiet baby back in the cradle and grabbed a box of moist towelettes from the dresser. "I'm so sorry."

Morgan swallowed hard and shifted from one foot to the other as Samantha leaned close to wipe the spot from his shirt. Her nearness was doing a hell of a number on his insides. She smelled like lilacs and sweet woman, and her warm breath whispering over the exposed skin at the open vee of his shirt had his heart pounding so hard, he figured she could feel it beneath her fingers.

As he stared down at her, he took note of several things. Her hair was wrapped in a towel on top of her head, exposing the delicate skin of her slender neck. The long thick lashes framing her pretty eyes looked all dewy from her shower.

But the most noticeable, and most disturbing thing about her, was the way the top of her fluffy yellow robe gapped open. It gave him more than a fair view of the slope of her breasts, and the realization that she probably didn't have a stitch on beneath that robe sent blood rushing through his veins and made his jeans feel like they were way too short in the stride.

Quickly backing away from her before he did something stupid, like grab her and kiss her again, he headed for the door. "When you have time, I'd like to talk to you downstairs," he said as he stepped out into the hall. He quickly reached back to pull the door shut. "I'll be in my office."

* * *

Samantha stared at the closed door for several long seconds before she finally released the breath she hadn't been aware of holding. The earthy scents of leather, sunshine and virile male had her pulse racing and goose bumps skipping over her skin.

But it had been the feel of Morgan's pectoral muscles beneath her fingers that made her knees feel rubbery and had her catching her breath. The man was built as solid as a rock and she wondered how it would feel to be held against all that sinew, to be wrapped in arms so strong they could easily crush her, yet were gentle enough to hold a baby.

"Stop it," she chided herself.

She plopped the box of baby wipes back on the dresser, then reached up to jerk the towel from her wet hair. Her crazy postnatal hormones had to be the reason for her uncharacteristic behavior. That's all it could be. She wasn't interested in Morgan Wakefield or any other man.

Satisfied that she'd discovered the reason for her strong reaction to him, she dried her hair and traded her robe for a pink cotton, dropped-waist dress that buttoned up the front. Checking on Timmy, sleeping peacefully in the cradle, she turned on one of the baby monitors Morgan had brought in from the trunk of her car, then picking up the listening unit, walked out into the hall.

As she descended the stairs, she wondered what Morgan could possibly want to discuss with her.

She'd made it quite clear that she intended to earn her and Timmy's keep while they stayed here, and if he thought he was going to talk her out of it, he had another think coming.

Determined to set Mr. Morgan Wakefield straight, she crossed the great room and front foyer to tap on the frame of the open office door. He held a cordless phone to his ear with one shoulder as he shuffled through several papers lying on top of his desk.

"Is this a bad time?" she whispered.

Shaking his head, he motioned for her to enter the room and sit in one of the two comfortable-looking leather armchairs in front of the shiny walnut desk. "I'll check the breeding records for those two mares and get back to you on that, Brant." Morgan ended the call, then smiling, turned his attention to her. "I think I've come up with a solution to your money worries."

She settled back in one of the chairs across from him and tried not to think about how attractive he looked. Morgan had the nicest smile, and she had a feeling if he set his mind to it, he could charm the birds out of the trees. Fortunately for her, she didn't have feathers.

"You've found a job for me, other than cooking and cleaning?" she asked carefully.

His grin widened as he shook his head. "No."

His gaze held hers, causing her heart to skip a beat and making her feel like a night creature caught in the headlights of an oncoming car. She glanced to the bookshelves beyond his shoulder in order to keep from drowning in the depths of his intense blue eyes.

"What do you have in mind, if it's not a job?"

"Since discovering that your grandfather's place isn't in any shape for you to take up residence, you could sell the land," he said, making it sound extremely simple.

Smiling, she shook her head. "No. That's not an option."

His grin faded and he looked as if it had been the last thing he expected her to say. "Why not?"

"I have plans for that property."

"You do?" He looked extremely interested in what she had planned. It made her feel a little more confident.

Samantha glanced down at her hands resting in her lap as she tried to put her dream into words. "I never got to meet my grandfather because he and my mother didn't get along. He didn't approve of her choice of men, and my mother was too stubborn to admit that he'd been right about my father. To my knowledge he never even knew about me, any more than I knew that he existed." Taking a deep breath to chase away the sadness she always felt when she thought of her father, she raised her gaze to meet Morgan's. "When Daddy left us, my mother refused to come back here and admit that she'd made a mistake. Now she's gone, I haven't seen my father since I was four years old, and I have no brothers or sisters. I know it doesn't make a lot of sense, but that property is all I have that ties me to any kind of family and makes me feel like I belong."

The last thing Morgan expected was for Samantha

to have any kind of sentimental attachment to a place that she hadn't even known existed until a few weeks ago. But what was even more baffling about it was that he understood how she felt. The Lonetree was as much a part of him as the blood running through his veins.

"Are you going to try to fix up the house?" he finally managed to ask. He knew full well that she didn't have the funds to do much more than tack a piece of plastic over the holes in the roof.

Nodding, her eyes lit with enthusiasm. "I not only intend to live there, I'm going to open a summer retreat for homeless and abandoned children. I know it will take a while to get things the way I'd like, and I'll probably have to get a job to support myself while I look for financial help to get the camp started, but I'm hoping to have it ready to open next year."

"What kind of job did you have before you left California?" he asked, already anticipating her answer.

"I was a social worker for the county until government cutbacks forced the elimination of several jobs, including mine. It was my responsibility to place abandoned and orphaned children, either with relatives or in foster care." Her pretty face softened as she explained, and Morgan could tell this was something very close to her heart. "I want to continue helping children, who, for whatever reason, find themselves separated from their families. I want to make a place where they can forget, if only for a week or two, the reasons they aren't with their parents."

Morgan didn't know what to say. Her reasons for

wanting to hang on to the place were a hell of a lot more noble than what he wanted to do with the property. Helping kids beat raising bucking horses for the rodeo circuit, hands down. He suddenly felt guilty as hell at even suggesting she sell the property.

"Were you put into foster care after your mother died?" he asked, beginning to understand her desire to help children she didn't know.

He watched sadness fill her eyes as she nodded. "When my mother died, I was just like these children. I suddenly found that I no longer had a place where I belonged."

The thought that she'd been alone at such a young age with no one to turn to, tied his stomach in knots. He'd had his brothers when they lost their dad. But Samantha had been completely alone. He had to fight the urge to round the desk and take her into his arms.

"Were you placed with a good family?" he asked, needing to know that she'd had someone to take care of her.

To his relief, she nodded. "Since I was almost seventeen, I wasn't in the system much over a year. I was fortunate enough to be taken in by a very kind, older couple. They treated me like a granddaughter and I will always be grateful for that. But some children aren't as lucky as I was. Some are taken care of, but not cared for. There's a difference."

"What will you do until you get the camp started?" he asked, mentally reviewing who he knew in county government who might be able to help her get on as a case worker with social services.

"Now that I have Timmy, I'd like to find something that I could do at home, or only be away from him a minimal amount of time."

Morgan could understand her desire to be with the baby. He didn't like the idea of her being away from the little guy, either.

His heart slammed into his rib cage. Where had that come from? Why should he care? Timmy wasn't his child.

But whether the baby belonged to him or not, Morgan felt a responsibility toward Samantha and her little boy that defied logic or reason. And it scared him spitless.

Between the sudden urge to help her find a way to keep the ranch he'd wanted to buy for as long as he could remember, and the protective feelings that were building inside of him at an alarming rate, Morgan suddenly felt as if he couldn't breathe.

Rising from his chair, he grabbed his Resistol, jammed it on his head and rounded the desk. "I...uh, just remembered something I need to do," he said, knowing his excuse sounded as lame as it was. "If you want me for anything, call Frank down at the machine shed. He'll know where to find me."

She rose to follow him. "Do you mind if I look around the kitchen to see what I can make for dinner?"

He turned back to stare at her. She looked so damned pretty standing there gazing up at him that it took every ounce of willpower he possessed to keep from pulling her to him.

Slowly shaking his head, he warned, "Just don't overdo things. You got that?"

She gave him a smile that just about knocked his boots off. "Will do, boss."

"I'm not—" he took a step forward and reached out to cup her soft cheek in his palm "—your boss, sweetheart."

Her easy expression turned into one of awareness, then staunch determination. "You are until Timmy and I leave here."

He shook his head. "No—" he leaned forward to brush his lips over hers "—I'm not."

Turning, he walked from the room, out the front door and headed for the barn. If he hadn't walked away when he did, he'd have ended up taking her into his arms and kissing her until they both needed CPR.

As he entered the barn he decided checking the fence in the north pasture wasn't a bad idea. He could ride for hours with nothing more to do than try to figure out what the hell had gotten into him, and what he had to do to keep from getting in deeper than he already was.

Saddling his favorite gelding, he led the sorrel out of the barn, then swung up into the saddle. It didn't make a damned bit of sense. He'd only known Samantha for three days.

But with each passing minute, the need to help her and her tiny son became stronger. And every time he looked into her pretty amber eyes, it sure as hell felt like he was about to drown.

Chapter 4

After Morgan left, it took Samantha several minutes to bring her pulse back under control. What in the name of heaven was wrong with her? She wasn't interested in Morgan Wakefield or any other man. Between her father and Chad, she'd learned a valuable lesson. Men couldn't be counted on for anything, and only ended up letting a woman down in one way or another.

She'd had quite enough of that, thank you very much. She certainly didn't need to set herself up for more.

The best way to avoid being disappointed by a man was not to become involved with one to begin with. Period. As long as she kept that in mind, she'd be just fine.

With a determined nod, she headed for the kitchen. She'd told Morgan that she intended to cook and clean for him to pay for her and Timmy's keep. Until she gained her full strength back, she'd have to watch what she did. But as long as she didn't do anything too strenuous, and took frequent breaks, the activity would be good for her.

Setting the baby monitor on the counter, she found some paper and a pen to jot down things she'd need from the store, and started taking inventory of what Morgan had on hand. Two hours later, her grocery list filled three full sheets of paper and had her shaking her head. Besides some packages of beef in the freezer, there really wasn't a whole lot to work with.

"Samantha?"

At the unexpected sound of the female voice calling her name, Samantha jumped. Walking out of the pantry, she watched a petite blond-haired woman use the heel of her boot to shut the back door behind her, then hurry over to set two paper grocery bags on the counter.

When the woman turned to face Samantha, her smile was warm and friendly. "I'm Annie Wakefield. I'm married to Morgan's brother, Brant."

"It's nice to meet you, Annie." She smiled and motioned to the list she held. "I was just taking stock of what I could make for dinner."

Annie laughed. "I'm afraid the Wakefield men are rather limited when it comes to their diet. If it didn't moo before it went to the packing house, they don't eat it."

"I've noticed," Samantha said, grinning. "I've found several steaks and a couple of roasts in the freezer, but that's about it."

"That's why I brought over a few staples," Annie said, motioning to the bags on the counter. "While he was out riding fence, Morgan stopped by our place and mentioned that he had a guest. I know from past experience how empty that pantry is, so I gathered some things and headed this way."

Samantha nodded. "I was beginning to wonder what I was going to do with frozen beef, half a loaf of stale bread and a jar of grape jelly."

Annie frowned as she pulled items from the two sacks. "It's worse than usual. What did you have for dinner?"

Confused, Samantha shook her head. "We haven't had dinner yet."

"I meant lunch." Annie grinned. "The first thing I learned when I married Brant was that dinner is the noon meal, supper is the evening meal and the word lunch isn't part of the Wakefield vocabulary."

"I'll have to remember that," Samantha said, liking Annie Wakefield more with each passing second. "Morgan had one of the men bring a couple of sandwiches up from the bunkhouse for lun...I mean dinner, but—"

"Don't tell me he fed you one of Leon's roast beef and cheddar melts," Annie interrupted. She made a face. "They're horrible."

Samantha shook her head. "I lost my appetite after

learning my car is in need of major work. I put my sandwich in the refrigerator."

"Believe me, you don't want to go there." Wrinkling her nose, Annie opened the refrigerator door, plucked the wrapped sandwich from the shelf and tossed it in the trash. She placed a half gallon of milk, a tub of margarine and a package of cheese inside, then closed the door. "Leon means well, but he thinks everything he makes has to be smothered in hot sauce and horseradish."

Samantha shuddered at the thought of the indigestion she and Timmy would both have suffered from all that spice. "I'm glad I didn't try it. It wouldn't have been good for my baby."

Annie gave her an understanding smile. "Morgan told us what happened. Are you both doing all right? Is there anything I can do to help?"

The woman's compassion touched Samantha deeply. Before coming to Wyoming, she couldn't remember the last time anyone cared if she was all right, or if she needed help.

"We're fine," she said, blinking back tears. She'd no sooner gotten the words out than Timmy's lusty cry came through the speaker of the baby monitor. Laughing shakily, she added, "Well, we will be as soon as he nurses."

"Then you'd better not keep him waiting," Annie said, smiling back at her.

"I'll be back down as soon as he's finished," Samantha said, picking up the monitoring unit. "Thank you for being so thoughtful. I truly appreciate it."

"I have to admit to having an ulterior motive," Annie said, smiling. "I want to spend some time around your baby to see what I'm getting myself into."

"You're pregnant?"

When she nodded, Annie looked absolutely radiant. "I used one of the early home tests this morning."

"That's wonderful," Samantha said, reaching out to hug her new friend. She grinned. "When I come back downstairs, I'll bring Timmy so you get the full treatment."

"That buckskin and the bay stud would throw a nice colt," Morgan said, pointing across the feed lot to the mare chewing on a mouthful of grain.

His brother, Brant, nodded. "That's what I've been thinking. With those bloodlines, it should buck hard enough to rattle a few brains, too."

Morgan grinned. "Speaking of rattled brains, how did our little brother do this past weekend in Grand Rapids?"

"Colt rode all three of his bulls, but Mitch Simpson won the event," Brant answered. A rodeo bullfighter, Brant worked most of the Professional Bull Riders events that their younger brother competed in. "Colt ended up with a nice hefty check for his efforts, though."

"Good. Maybe he'll pay me the fifty bucks he owes me," Morgan said, turning to walk toward the house.

"What did you two bet on this time?" Brant asked, falling into step beside Morgan.

"Baseball. He said the Rockies would sweep the four-game series against the Cardinals. I said they wouldn't." Morgan grinned. "He didn't know that the Cardinals took their star pitcher off the disabled list last week. I did."

Brant laughed. "Well, you'll have to wait a couple of weeks for him to pay up. Colt went home with Mitch this weekend to help put up a fence."

"Every time we stretch fence around here, he's as scarce as hen's teeth," Morgan said, frowning.

He could understand his youngest brother's desire to help his best friend. Since Mitch and his sister Kaylee lost their parents in a car accident three years ago, Mitch had his hands full keeping the family ranch going, as well as competing at the top level of the Professional Bull Riders organization. But Colt needed to remember there was work to be done around the Lonetree, too.

"The scenery is nicer on Mitch's ranch than it is here," Brant said, his grin meaningful.

"Kaylee?" When Brant nodded, Morgan shook his head. "How long do you think it will take before the two of them wake up and smell the coffee?"

Brant shrugged. "Who knows? You know how stubborn our baby brother is."

Morgan laughed as they walked across the yard. "About as stubborn as you were when you met Annie."

"Hey, I finally came to my senses and saw the light." His smile fading, Brant asked, "Do you think Tug's granddaughter is really serious about starting a camp for foster kids? Or do you think she'll eventually give up and sell out?"

Morgan shook his head. "I don't know. She doesn't really have the money to do anything, but she's determined enough not to let that stop her."

"You know, we don't really need the land," Brant said thoughtfully.

"Nope." Morgan shrugged. "It would be nice not to have that two hundred acre chunk out of the middle of the Lonetree's western boundary, but it's been that way for the last seventy-five years."

Brant grinned. "So what's another seventy-five? Right?"

"Right," Morgan agreed, returning his brother's easy expression.

As soon as they entered the house, the unfamiliar sight of two women working side by side in his kitchen stopped Morgan short. He was used to seeing his sister-in-law, Annie, make an occasional meal for all of them during calving season or fall roundup. But seeing Samantha with a smear of flour on her chin and her cheeks flushed from the heat of the oven, reminded Morgan of everything he'd wanted, but never hoped to have—a wife, a family and a home filled with love and laughter.

He watched Brant walk up behind Annie, wrap his arms around her waist and kiss her like a soldier returning from war. Remembering the feel of Samantha's soft lips beneath his, Morgan swallowed hard. Why was he having to fight the urge to keep from doing the same thing to her?

Hells bells, what was wrong with him? He really didn't even know the woman.

As he watched Annie laughingly introduce Brant to Samantha, Morgan mentally calculated when he could take time off from the ranch for a drive down to Bear Creek. No doubt about it. He needed to make that trip to Buffalo Gals for a night of good old-fashioned hell-raising. And damned quick. Otherwise, he was going to be as crazy as a loon and climbing the walls by the end of the week.

The baby, sitting in his carrier on top of the table, suddenly let loose with a wail, gaining everyone's attention.

"He probably needs burping again," Samantha said, grabbing a towel to wipe her hands.

"I'll take care of it," Morgan said, clearly surprising Annie and Brant. He ignored their questioning looks as he gazed down at the baby. "You and I have a little experience in this area, don't we?"

Samantha grinned. "Don't forget to place the end of the receiving blanket over your shoulder."

He couldn't help it, he grinned right back. "Good idea. I've only got a couple of clean shirts left." He ignored his brother's gaping expression, carefully lifted Timmy from the carrier and held him to his shoulder. "Come on, little guy. We'll walk around a little and see if that helps." Turning back to Samantha, he warned, "Don't overdo things. If you get tired, sit down and put your feet up."

Morgan caught the questioning looks exchanged

between Brant and Annie, and he wasn't a bit surprised when his brother followed him down the hall to the great room.

"Uh, bro, you want to let me in on what's going on?" Brant asked, his smile irritating enough to make Morgan want to bite nails in two.

"There's nothing going on," Morgan answered as he gently patted Timmy's back. "Samantha and Annie are both busy, and the baby needs a little attention. I'm just helping out."

Brant snorted. "Yeah, right. To my knowledge, you've never held a baby before in your life." He pointed to Timmy. "But you sure as hell look like you know what you're doing with this one."

"If you'll remember, I had a crash course in babies a few nights ago," Morgan said, continuing to rub the baby's tiny back. When Timmy burped loudly, Morgan chuckled. "That feels better, doesn't it?"

Brant shook his head in obvious wonderment. "How did you know what to do?"

"I didn't." Morgan transferred the now content baby to the cradle of his arm. "But earlier this afternoon Samantha was busy and…" He stopped to eye his brother suspiciously. "Would *you* like to tell me why you're so interested?"

Brant hesitated before shaking his head. "Just curious."

Morgan wasn't buying it for a minute. Brant looked like the cat that swallowed the canary. "Is Annie—"

"In due time, big brother," Brant said, turning to walk back into the kitchen. "In due time."

Watching Brant saunter from the room, Morgan figured he knew what his brother was trying to keep from saying—probably under threat of bodily harm from Annie. Morgan grinned. Unless he missed his guess, he was going to be an uncle around the first part of next year, and Annie had plans of making the grand announcement during supper.

Happiness for his brother and sister-in-law filled him, followed quickly by a shaft of deep longing. Morgan had always wanted a family, but he'd have to be content with being the favorite uncle. His thinking that he knew what was best for those he cared for had already cost one life, and he couldn't take the chance of making a wrong decision for anyone else.

He gazed down at the baby in his arms. Raising a child and all the decisions it entailed was an awesome responsibility, and one that he wasn't sure he'd ever trust himself to take on. What if his judgement proved faulty a second time?

No. He never wanted to take that chance again. If he did and something happened, he'd never be able to live with himself.

"Morgan, is everything all right?" Samantha asked as she walked into the room.

"Couldn't be better," he lied.

"You look rather…grim," she said, placing her hand on his.

A jolt of electric current immediately streaked up his arm at the contact, and he suddenly felt the need to run like hell. The mother of the baby he held was far more temptation than anything he'd had to deal with in the past six years. She was soft, sensual and represented everything he couldn't trust himself to have.

"Here," he said, handing Timmy to her. "I'll be in for supper in a few minutes. I have…a couple of things I need to do before we eat."

Knowing she was staring at him like he'd grown another head, he turned and walked straight to his office. Once inside, he closed the door and walked over to stare out the window at the shadows of evening creeping over the mountains in the distance.

He wasn't at all comfortable with his attraction to Samantha Peterson. But until her car was repaired, he'd be seeing her every time he turned around.

As he watched the cattle grazing in the distance, he came to a decision. There was enough work to do around the Lonetree each day to keep him busy from daylight until well past dark. Until Samantha's car was fixed, and she and her tiny son moved on, he'd work until he dropped if need be. But he was going to keep his distance and contact with her to a bare minimum.

He had to. It was the only way he had a prayer of a chance of keeping what little scrap of sanity he had left.

"I really enjoyed the evening," Samantha said as Annie and Brant prepared to leave.

Annie hugged her. "I did, too. Remember, if you need anything at all, don't hesitate to give me a call." She stepped back and grinned. "And especially if you need someone to baby-sit Timmy."

"I'll do that," Samantha said, smiling.

After Annie's announcement at dinner that she and Brant were expecting, the couple spent the rest of the evening asking questions about pregnancy, birth and the care of an infant. Morgan had remained extremely quiet during the conversation, but not knowing him well, Samantha wasn't sure if that was unusual or not.

"I'll bring that bay stud over tomorrow to meet his new girlfriend," Brant said, putting his arm around Annie as they walked to the door.

"I'm sure Stormy Gal will be happy to see him," Morgan answered, displaying the first genuine smile Samantha had seen from him since before dinner.

Once Brant and Annie left, Samantha returned to the great room to straighten up before she took Timmy upstairs. Now that she and Morgan were alone, she felt a bit awkward. The situation seemed so…domestic.

"I enjoyed meeting your brother and sister-in-law," she said as she straightened the colorful Native American blanket on the back of the leather couch. "You have a very nice family."

"Annie's always nice," Morgan said, walking over to the fireplace to bank the fire. When he turned back to face her, he grinned. "And Brant was on his best behavior."

Samantha could tell that Morgan was very close to his family, and she had to fight the wave of envy threatening to swamp her. She'd always wanted a brother or sister—someone to be close to, someone she could share memories with.

"I'm pretty tired," she said, suddenly feeling more alone than she'd ever felt in her entire life. Being around the Wakefields reminded her of everything she'd never had—siblings who loved and cared for her. "I think Timmy and I are going to turn in now."

Making sure the baby was securely strapped in, she started to take hold of the carrier, but Morgan was suddenly at her side, his big hand wrapping around the handle. "I don't think you should be lifting this thing just yet," he said, gruffly. "It's pretty heavy, even without the baby in it, and you've overdone things today."

"Not really." Her protest would have been a lot more effective if she hadn't had to hide a huge yawn behind her hand.

"Yeah, sure," he said, easily lifting the carrier in one hand as he placed his other hand at the small of her back. "And a donkey can fly."

"You know, I think I saw one soaring over the barn when we arrived today," she said, laughing nervously. The warmth where his hand touched her back was doing strange things to her insides.

He shook his head as he guided her to the stairs. "Nice try, but I'm not buying it. You were on your feet more than you should have been today."

"Oh, really? The other night you told me you weren't a doctor."

As soon as the words were out, she felt her cheeks heat with embarrassment. Her reference to the night Timmy was born reminded her of what had taken place and that Morgan had seen most of her secrets.

But that wasn't the issue here. She wasn't about to admit that he was probably right—that she had come close to overdoing things her first day out of the hospital. "Did you receive a medical degree in the past two days that I'm not aware of?"

"Nope. But I read the rest of that book."

Her cheeks got warmer. "When?"

"After you fell asleep the night Timmy was born," he said, opening the door to her room. He waited for her to walk in ahead of him before following her. Placing the baby carrier in the middle of the double bed, he turned to leave. "Just remember to take it easier tomorrow than you did today."

Reaching out to stop him, she placed her hand on his shoulder. "Morgan?"

She needed to thank him for all that he'd done for her and the baby in the past few days. She'd told him that he was thoughtful, but she hadn't really expressed her appreciation.

When he faced her, she started to tell him how much his generosity meant to her, but the look in his incredible blue eyes took her breath. If she didn't know better, she'd think it was desire. But that was ridiculous, she thought a moment before he reached out to pull her to him.

"Samantha," was all he said as he brought his hands up to thread his fingers through her shoulder-length hair.

Fascinated by the sound of his deep baritone saying her name, she watched him slowly lower his head. Her eyes drifted shut the second their mouths met and she brought her hands up to his chest to brace herself.

Unlike this afternoon when he'd lightly brushed her lips with his, he fused their mouths together in a kiss that seared her all the way to her very soul. He traced the seam of her mouth with his tongue, asking for her acceptance, seeking her permission to explore the sensitive recesses within.

Without a thought of denying him what he sought, she parted her lips and he slipped inside to tease and taste, to explore and entice. He moved his hands to her waist to draw her more fully against him, and Samantha felt as if his big body surrounded hers. Without a thought to the insanity that seemed to have them both in its grip, she found herself leaning into his strength, melting against the solid wall of his chest.

But as his tongue stroked and encouraged her to reciprocate in kind, the sound of her son awakening to nurse helped to lift the sensual fog enveloping them.

Morgan was the first to move. Lifting his mouth from hers, he quickly stepped back to gaze down at her, his frown formidable. "Dammit, Samantha, I didn't mean for that to happen. I'm sorry."

Doing her best to gather her scattered thoughts, she straightened her shoulders and said the first thing that came to mind. "I'm not."

Dear heavens, what had gotten into her? Had she really said that?

"I mean…that is…"

Her cheeks felt as if they were on fire. What could she say after a blunt admission like that?

But what was more disconcerting than her outspokenness was the fact that she'd really meant it. She wasn't sorry. And that bothered her more than anything else.

His expression softened ever so slightly. "It doesn't matter, Samantha. I'm a thirty-four-year-old man, not a teenage boy with little or no control." He lifted his hand as if he intended to touch her cheek, then quickly dropped it to his side. "Starting tomorrow, you probably won't see me around much. Spring is one of the busiest times of the year on a ranch and there are a lot of things that need my attention. If you want or need something, call the barn or the machine shed and one of my men will see that I get the message."

Then, without a backward glance, he turned and walked from the room.

Samantha stared at the closed door. Why did she suddenly feel like she'd been abandoned again? And why on earth did the knowledge that Morgan Wakefield clearly didn't want anything to do with her make her feel like she was about to break down and cry?

She shook her head and tried to dispel the all-too-familiar feeling. She was used to men abandoning her. At the tender age of four, her father had found another woman and walked out on her and her mother as if they'd never mattered to him. Then years later, when social services contacted him after her mother's death, he'd turned his back on her again and refused to take her in.

Picking up Timmy, she sniffed back her tears. But the most devastating abandonment of all had been Chad's response to the knowledge that he was going to be a father. It was one thing for him to cast her aside, but it was an entirely different matter for him to reject their child.

But that didn't explain her reaction to Morgan's dismissal of her. They barely knew each other, and besides, she wasn't interested in him or any other man. Men weren't reliable and couldn't be counted on to be there for a woman when she needed them most.

"These feelings I'm having for Morgan have got to be hormonal," she said aloud. Turning to pick up Timmy, she shook her head. "I'll be glad when this dumb postnatal stuff is over with and I get back on track."

Chapter 5

As Morgan left the barn and slowly walked toward the house, he stared up at the starless night sky. Every night for the past month, he'd waited until Samantha had gone to bed before calling it a day. And every morning he'd hauled his sorry butt out of bed and left the house before she came downstairs. He had seen her a few times, but with the exception of Sunday dinners and a handful of visits from Brant and Annie, he'd managed to keep his distance.

But instead of lessening the itch that started the minute he first laid eyes on her, it only seemed to aggravate it. He shook his head at his foolishness. He'd even abandoned the idea of driving down to Buffalo

Gals to find a willing little filly for a night of fun and games. Something told him that he'd only end up feeling like he'd betrayed Samantha. Which was completely ridiculous. Hell, they barely knew each other.

"You're seriously screwed up, Wakefield," he muttered as he climbed the back porch steps.

Opening the door, he walked into the dimly lit kitchen and stopped short. Samantha had left the light on over the sink for him, as she always did. But instead of being upstairs in bed, she sat at the table with plans for her camp spread out, and her head pillowed on her folded arms. She was sound asleep.

He swallowed hard. She looked so damned sweet it was all he could do to keep from walking over and gathering her to him. Instead, he squatted down beside her chair to gently touch her shoulder.

"Samantha?"

"Mmm."

"Don't you think it would be more comfortable sleeping upstairs in bed?"

Her long, dark lashes fluttered a moment before she opened her eyes. The slumberous look of her amber gaze sent a shaft of longing right to his core.

He swallowed hard. This was how she'd look waking up beside him after a night of—

"I was waiting for you," she said, sitting up. She pushed her golden-brown hair back. "I need to talk to you about something."

Glancing at his watch, guilt twisted his gut that he'd kept her waiting. She'd have to get up early with

the baby tomorrow morning and it was almost midnight now.

"What did you need?" he asked, using his index
finger to brush a strand of hair from her porcelain
cheek.

"Frank said they've back-ordered that part for my car
again," she said, her voice flowing over him like a piece
of soft velvet. "And I need to drive down to Laramie in
the morning." She looked uncertain. "I wouldn't ask
unless it was really important, but would you mind if I
borrowed one of your trucks?"

Her expression told him that something was up, and
that it had her worried. "Is something wrong? Do you
or Timmy need to see a doctor?"

"No. We're both fine. Annie drove us to the clinic for
our postnatal checkups a couple of days ago," she said,
shaking her head. "But my grandfather's lawyer called
this afternoon. He said there's a problem with my inheritance and he needs to meet with me."

"Did he say what was wrong?" Morgan asked,
hoping for her sake there wasn't a lien, or someone
claiming the property for unpaid taxes.

"I asked, but all he would say was he needed to speak
with me in person so he could explain the new terms of
the will." She frowned. "He didn't mention anything about
there being any kind of stipulations on my inheritance
when he first contacted me, or when I called five weeks
ago to tell him that he could reach me here at the
Lonetree."

Morgan wasn't sure what the lawyer had found, but

he didn't like the sound of it. After old Tug had died, he'd contacted the law firm about buying the property and they'd assured him the place was free and clear, should the heir wish to sell.

"I have to make the drive down to Laramie sometime this week for fencing supplies," Morgan said, thinking aloud. "I could make arrangements to go tomorrow and take you with me. Did the lawyer give you a time to be there?"

"He said any time tomorrow morning would be fine," she answered, yawning.

"What time will Timmy wake up?" Morgan asked, rising to his feet.

She yawned again. "Early."

A warm, protective feeling that he didn't care to dwell on swept over him as he gazed down at her. "Do you think you and Timmy can be ready to leave by eight tomorrow morning?"

When she nodded, he helped her gather her camp plans, then took her hand and led her toward the stairs. At the bottom step, he kissed her forehead. "Go on upstairs and get some sleep, sweetheart. We'll deal with this in the morning."

"I don't know how long I'll be," Samantha said, staring out the windshield of Morgan's truck at the entrance to the brick building housing the law firm of Greeley, Hartwell and Buford.

"Don't worry about it," Morgan said, killing the engine and releasing his seat belt. "Timmy and I will hold down things out here, while you go in and see what the 'suit' has to say."

Samantha nodded, took a deep breath and opened the passenger door. "Keep your fingers crossed that this is something minor."

"Good luck," he said, smiling as he rested his outstretched arm along the back of the bench seat.

It was easy for Morgan to look relaxed. He wasn't the one who'd talked to Mr. Greeley yesterday. The man had been extremely evasive when she asked him if he could tell her what the terms were over the phone. He'd mumbled some kind of legalese that she assumed explained why they'd need to meet in person, and she'd finally agreed. But she didn't have a good feeling about this. Not at all.

After she spoke with the receptionist, she'd barely settled into one of the uncomfortable chairs in the waiting area than a man appeared at the open door of the hallway leading toward the back of the building. "Are you Ms. Peterson?"

"Yes."

When she rose to her feet, the balding little man gave her a nervous smile. "I'm Gerald Greeley," he said, extending his hand. "If you'll come on back to my office, I'll explain the mix-up."

Samantha's stomach suddenly felt queasy as she shook his hand and followed him down the hall. Something told her this wasn't going to be something simple, nor was he going to tell her anything she'd want to hear.

As they entered a small, nondescript office, he

motioned to a chair across from his desk. "Please have a seat."

"What's this all about, Mr. Greeley?" she asked, perching on the edge of the seat. "I thought everything was in order."

"So did we." He sighed heavily and sank into the executive chair behind the desk. "But there was a wrinkle that cropped up yesterday morning we couldn't have anticipated."

She eyed him carefully. Sweat had popped out on his forehead and he looked as if he dreaded what he had to say next.

"Why don't you just tell me and get it over with?" she asked, feeling more apprehensive by the second.

"You haven't by any chance gotten married in the past month, have you, Ms. Peterson?" the man asked, sounding hopeful.

She eyed him suspiciously. "No. Why do you ask?"

"Because to claim the land your grandfather bequeathed you, you'll have to be married, and remain that way for the next two years," he said, digging a white linen handkerchief from the inside pocket of his suit coat to wipe the sweat from his brow.

In a daze, Samantha spent the next half hour listening as Gerald Greeley explained the terms of the new will, and why the law firm had been unaware of its existence. By the time she walked out of the office and back to Morgan's truck, her stomach churned unmercifully and she felt a good cry coming on.

* * *

When Samantha opened the truck door and got in, Morgan felt as if he'd taken a fist to the gut. She was pale and looked like she might be on the verge of tears.

"Are you all right?"

She laughed, but there was no humor to it. "Not really."

He watched a tear slip from the corner of her eye, then slowly trickle down her cheek. The sight of that single droplet just about tore him apart. "Tell me what happened, sweetheart."

"I've learned that in three months the Bureau of Land Management will take possession of my grandfather's ranch," she said, sounding defeated. "And there's absolutely nothing I can do about it."

"But I thought he left everything to you." The knot in Morgan's stomach tightened painfully as he watched her impatiently swipe at a second tear.

"He had another will drawn up a few days before his death," she said, accepting the bandana handkerchief he retrieved from the hip pocket of his jeans.

"Why didn't Greeley know about it?" He hated seeing her so utterly dejected.

She shrugged one shoulder. "My grandfather used the nursing home's attorney because he knew he was dying and Mr. Greeley was out of town. After it had been witnessed and notarized, the administrator of the nursing home accidentally misfiled the will in another resident's folder." Her voice broke. "The mistake... wasn't discovered until the first part of this week... when that man passed away."

Unable to sit still any longer, Morgan got out of the truck and walked around to the passenger side. Opening the door, he reached inside and wrapped his arms around her.

Samantha immediately buried her face against his shoulder and the flood gates opened. He hated seeing any woman cry, but Samantha's heartbroken sobs were tearing him apart. He wanted to make things better, to fix things for her. But he had no idea where he'd even begin to start on this mess.

When she quieted, he continued to hold her. He enjoyed the feel of her soft body pressed to his too much to let her go.

"Sweetheart, why don't you start at the beginning," he finally said. "Maybe together we can figure out a way for you to keep the property."

"It's really very simple," she said, hiccuping. "Unless I'm married by September, the Bureau of Land Management will get my grandfather's ranch. And since I don't see that happening—"

"Married?" Morgan felt like he'd been punched in the gut for the second time in less than ten minutes.

She nodded. "The will stipulates that I have to be married at the time I claim the property, and that I have to stay married for two years after that before the deed is put in my name."

"Why in God's name would old Tug do a crazy thing like that to you?" Morgan asked, unable to comprehend the ridiculous terms of the legacy.

"He really wasn't doing it to me," she said, sniffling. "My grandfather wasn't even aware that I existed. Once my mother eloped with my father, she never came back here."

Morgan nodded. "I remember you telling me that he and your mother didn't get along. But in all that time, she never tried to get in touch with Tug?"

"Not that I'm aware of," Samantha said. She sighed heavily as she pulled away from him to open her handbag. Handing him a piece of paper, she added, "Here's the letter explaining his reasoning, although I doubt that I'll ever understand it."

When Morgan scanned the contents of the note, he shook his head in amazement. Tug Shackley's mind must have snapped before he passed on. Either that, or he was the biggest chauvinist the good Lord ever gave the gift of life. At the moment, Morgan wasn't making any bets on which one was the correct answer.

If the heir to Tug's ranch was male, there were no terms to be met, and the property could be claimed immediately. But a female heir had to be married within two years of his death, and stay that way for another two years, before she could claim her inheritance. The letter went on to state that a woman would need a husband to help her restore the ranch to its former productiveness, thus insuring her financial security. But if no heir was found, or a female heir was unmarried by the end of the time limits, the law firm had instructions to donate the land to the BLM in Tug's name.

"Now, I won't even have a connection…to my

family through the land, let alone be able to open…the camp," she said, brokenly.

"That's unacceptable." He folded the letter and gave it back to her. "We'll get married this weekend."

As if they were caught in a vacuum, time seemed to come to a complete halt.

He couldn't believe he'd just offered to marry her. But as he stood there gazing into her amber eyes, he realized it was the only thing he could do to help her keep the land that was rightfully hers.

"What did you say?" she finally asked, looking as if he'd taken leave of his senses.

"I said, we'll get married this weekend." He didn't want to dwell on how easily the words rolled off his tongue this time around.

She shook her head. "First it was my grandfather and his stupid stipulations on my inheritance, and now it's you telling me we'll get married." The dubious look in her whiskey-brown eyes left no doubt that she thought his elevator didn't go all the way to the top floor. "Is there something in the water here in Wyoming that makes men go completely insane?"

He placed his hands on her slender shoulders. "Listen to me, Samantha." When he gazed into her amber eyes, he felt as if he might drown. He wanted her. And if they were married…

He swallowed hard and did his best to ignore his wayward thoughts, as well as the sudden tightening south of his belt buckle. "You want to keep your grandfather's ranch to start that children's camp, don't you?"

"Yes, but I can't marry you to do it," she said, her voice shaky.

"Why not?"

"Well, I…that is…" Her voice trailed off and she seemed to be at a loss for words.

"Were there any loopholes?" he asked. "Any way to get around the terms of the will?"

She shook her head. "No. Mr. Greeley said he'd been over it several times, looking for some way for me to keep the land without meeting the terms. But it's quite clear. I have to be married to claim the property."

Morgan gave her shoulders a gentle squeeze. "Then what other choice do you have, Samantha?"

"I…uh, need…to think about this," she said, looking dazed. She massaged her temples with her fingertips. "This is all so bizarre. I have no job, no home and I'm about to lose the only ties I have left to my family, as well as my dream of opening the camp. But if I marry you—"

He could understand her dilemma. If he let himself think about it, he was sure he'd find it pretty unsettling, too. After what happened to Emily, he'd made a vow never to take a trip down the aisle and run the risk of being responsible for another person's well-being.

But this was different. He and Samantha wouldn't be marrying for love, and he wouldn't be responsible for making any decisions for her or little Timmy. They'd lead separate lives, and if they came together from time to time for their physical needs, then where was the harm? They'd be married and it would not only be legal, it would be perfectly moral, as well.

"Think about it on the drive home," he said as he stepped back to close the passenger door. Walking around the front of the truck, he got in and started the engine, then reached over to cup her chin in his palm. "We'll work this out, sweetheart. I promise I won't let you lose your land."

Samantha waited until she'd nursed Timmy and put him in the cradle for his afternoon nap before she took a deep breath and headed downstairs to talk to Morgan. Since their discussion in the parking lot, she'd thought of nothing else but the stipulations of her grandfather's will, and the offer Morgan had made to help her meet those terms.

Crossing the great room to the foyer, her legs shook and her insides felt as if they had turned to gelatin. As tempting as it was, she wasn't going to take him up on his offer. She'd learned the hard way not to rely on a man for anything, and she wasn't about to start now. Even if it meant giving up on her dream of starting her camp, she just couldn't do it.

When she reached his office, she took a deep breath and knocked on the frame of the open door. "Are you busy?"

"No." He smiled. "Come in and sit down."

She sank into the armchair across from his desk. "I've reached a decision."

His easy expression faded as he cocked one dark brow. "And that would be?"

"I really appreciate your offer to help me keep the land, but I can't let you put your life on hold for two years," she said, hurrying to get the words out before she changed her mind.

Rising from the chair, he walked around the desk to sit on the edge in front of her. "Samantha, I wouldn't consider it as putting my life on hold. I'd think of it more as helping you, as well as a bunch of kids who got handed a raw deal in life."

Agitated, she stood up to pace. She couldn't let him sway her. "What if you met someone? You'd be tied to me. What happens then?"

"I won't meet anyone," he said, sounding so darned sure that she turned to stare at him.

"You don't know that, Morgan."

"Yes, I do," he said calmly. He crossed his booted feet at the ankles and folded his arms over his wide chest. "You have my word that as long as we're married, I won't so much as look at another woman."

"But the marriage would be in name only," she said, making sure they had that little detail straight.

He shrugged. "That would probably make things simpler."

That hadn't been the answer she'd expected. He was a living, breathing man in his prime. He was going to remain celibate for two years? And how on earth could he be so relaxed about something as important as marriage, even if it wouldn't be a real one?

"Why are you willing to do this for me, Morgan?"

she asked, suddenly suspicious of his motives and why he was being so generous. "What's in it for you?"

"Nothing," he said, straightening to his full height. "I just want to see that you and Timmy get what's rightfully yours. And in the bargain, I'll be helping kids who really need it."

"That's it?" She was having a hard time believing that anyone would be that willing to sacrifice their freedom for someone they barely knew.

He nodded, then walked over to take her hands in his. Pulling her to him, he put his arms around her waist. "I want to help you, Samantha. And our getting married is the only way for you to keep your land and start that camp."

She caught her lower lip between her teeth to keep it from trembling. She couldn't believe it, but she was actually thinking about accepting his offer, even though it went against everything she'd vowed never to do again—rely on a man.

As if he sensed she was on the verge of going along with his suggestion, he gave her a smile that curled her toes inside her well-worn tennis shoes. Then, leaning forward, he whispered in her ear, "What do you say, Samantha? Are you going to marry me, keep your grandfather's ranch and help those kids? Or are you going to turn me down and lose it all?"

How was she supposed to think with him this close? His warm breath was teasing her neck, sending wave after wave of delicious heat skipping over every nerve in her body.

"I'm…not sure…what to do," she said, feeling extremely short of breath. His strong hands were splayed across her back, tracing the line of her spine, gently kneading her tense muscles.

"Say yes, Samantha," he commanded, kissing the sensitive hollow beneath her ear.

"But—"

He leaned back to stare down at her, his blue gaze intense. "Yes."

"Y-yes," she finally said, unable to believe she was actually agreeing to become Morgan Wakefield's wife.

Chapter 6

Morgan propped his hands on his hips as he looked around the storage area for the old trunk. It had to be here somewhere. His dad had packed all of his mother's things in it shortly after her death, and to Morgan's knowledge it hadn't moved for the past twenty-seven years.

When he spotted the corner of it, he walked over to move several boxes of Christmas ornaments that had been piled on top. Unfastening the clasp, he opened it and gazed down at the contents. The scent of jasmine drifted up from the mementos of his mother's life to flood his senses with memories of the woman who had given him life.

He'd only been seven years old when she passed away, but he could still remember the feel of her gentle touch when he'd skinned his elbow, the way she'd pressed a soft kiss to his forehead each night when she tucked him into bed, and the smell of her jasmine perfume when she hugged him close. His chest tightened. Even though Hank Wakefield had done a fine job of raising his three sons, and gone out of his way to be both mother and father to them, they'd missed a hell of a lot by not having her with them.

As Morgan dropped down on one knee to begin his search, he felt guilty. It almost felt as if he was invading his mother's privacy. But he somehow knew that she'd approve of what he had in mind and would have probably even suggested it had she been alive.

When he saw the heavy white plastic garment bag close to the bottom of the trunk, he smiled. Removing it, he carefully replaced the rest of his mother's things, then closed the lid and headed back downstairs.

"Samantha?" he called as he descended the steps.

"I'm in the kitchen."

When he walked into the room, she was putting a roast into the oven. Her porcelain cheeks were flushed from the heat and several strands of her golden-brown hair had escaped the confines of her ponytail. He didn't think he'd ever seen her look more attractive.

Handing her the white garment bag, he smiled. "I don't know what size this is, but if it fits, you could wear it on Sunday."

She stared at the bag for several seconds before she gazed up at him. "Was this your mother's?"

He nodded, suddenly unsure about his decision to offer her his mother's wedding dress for the small ceremony they had planned for Sunday afternoon. He knew for a fact that Samantha didn't have the money for a new dress and she'd flat out refused his offer to buy her one. But maybe women didn't like the idea of wearing another woman's dress for their wedding.

"I'll understand if you'd rather wear something else," he said, running his hand over the back of his neck. "I just thought—"

"No, this will be fine," she said, her voice almost a whisper. She lightly ran her fingers over the plastic, as if she touched something precious and fragile. "I would be honored to wear it, Morgan. But don't you think you should save it for after we…that is, when you meet someone else and get married for real?"

"This is most likely the only time I'll ever get married," he said, wishing his statement hadn't sounded quite so blunt.

But he wasn't about to explain his decision to remain a bachelor, or his reasons behind it. It was too complicated, and he didn't think he'd be able to stand the condemnation in Samantha's pretty amber eyes when he told her about his role in Emily's death.

"It will probably be the only time for me, too," she said, surprising him. "I decided after Chad and the choice he made about not wanting anything to do with Timmy, that life alone would be preferable to one filled with heartache. Or worse yet, watching someone disappoint my child the way my father disappointed me."

It felt as if someone had reached inside his chest and squeezed his heart with a tight fist. How could anyone, no matter who it was, treat Samantha or Timmy as if they didn't matter?

Reaching out, Morgan pulled her into his arms. "That's one thing you won't have to worry about while you're here at the Lonetree, sweetheart," he said. His chest tightened further at the thought of her and the baby eventually leaving to face the world alone. "I promise I'll never hurt you, or Timmy, and you won't be lonely."

She stared up at him with guileless amber eyes. "At least for the next two years?"

"At least," he said, nodding as he lowered his mouth to hers.

He didn't want to dwell on the length of their upcoming marriage, or the reason for it. At the moment, the feel of her soft body against his, the scent of her lilac shampoo, and the sound of her soft sigh were sending his libido into overdrive.

Tracing her lips with his tongue, Morgan deepened the kiss to leisurely reacquaint himself with her sweetness, to explore the woman that in two days would become his wife. The thought sent heat streaking through his veins and caused his loins to tighten with need.

When she wrapped her arms around his neck and leaned into him, Morgan thought his knees were going to buckle. Her firm, full breasts pressed to his chest and the warmth of her lower body cradling the hard ridge of his arousal were almost more than he could stand.

Slowly running his hands up her sides to the swell of her breasts, he cupped the weight of them, then teased the hardened tips through the layers of her clothes. Rewarded by her tiny moan of pleasure, his body responded in a way that made him light-headed. Morgan didn't think he'd ever been as hard in his life as he was at this moment, for this woman.

Knowing that if things went much further, he wouldn't be able to stop, he broke the kiss and took a step back. As he gazed down at her, he decided that wasn't enough distance. She looked so soft, so sweet, that if he didn't move, and damned quick, he'd end up sweeping her into his arms and carrying her upstairs to his bed. And although he was more than ready for it, she wasn't.

"I…really should check on a new colt," he said, turning toward the back door. "If you need help getting that dress ready for Sunday, I'm sure Annie will be more than happy to lend a hand."

Without waiting for her response, he stepped out onto the porch and closed the door behind him. If there had been any doubt in his mind before, it had just been erased.

Taking a deep breath, he tried to get his body to calm down. Their marriage might not be a love match, but the attraction between them was too strong to be denied. There was no way the two of them could live in the same house, day in and day out, without the inevitable happening between them.

It wasn't a matter of if they made love. The question now was, when?

"I knew the first time I saw you and Morgan together that you were made for each other," Annie said, helping Samantha into Morgan's mother's dress.

"You did?" Samantha wondered how on earth her soon-to-be sister-in-law could have gotten that impression.

Annie nodded as she started fastening the tiny buttons that ran from below the waist at the back all the way to the shoulders of the dress. "It's the way you look at each other."

Samantha swallowed hard. She hated that she couldn't tell Annie the real reason behind her and Morgan's decision to get married. But they'd both agreed that the fewer people who knew their marriage was a sham, the better.

As Morgan had pointed out, it wasn't anyone's business but their own. But that still didn't keep Samantha from feeling guilty about not telling Annie.

"Have Colt and Brant made it back from Nashville yet?" she asked, hoping to change the subject. Both brothers had been tied up with a bull-riding event and couldn't make it home until that day.

"They arrived about an hour ago." Annie finished the last of the buttons and came around to stand in front of her. Tears filled her pretty green eyes. "Oh, Samantha, you look absolutely beautiful."

Staring at herself in the full-length mirror on the back of the closet door, Samantha sighed wistfully. If she'd had her choice of any wedding gown, she knew for certain she would have chosen this one. It was absolutely gorgeous.

With a simple scoop neckline, fitted bodice, cap sleeves, and floor-length skirt flaring from the waist, it was simple, feminine and elegantly traditional. Made of antique white satin overlaid with pure white lace it was everything that Samantha had ever dreamed of wearing for her wedding. That is before she'd stopped dreaming of ever being a bride.

"I think I look scared silly," she said, laughing nervously.

Annie nodded as she arranged a garland of white rosebuds on top of Samantha's head. "I don't think you'd be normal if you weren't nervous." She pinned the headpiece in place, then stood back to admire her handiwork. "Morgan is going to love seeing you come down the stairs in this."

"You think so?" A pang of longing shot through her. Maybe if she and Morgan had met at another time in their lives, and under different circumstances, then things could have been different.

"Absolutely," Annie said, grinning. "He's going to take one look at you and want to carry you back up here before the minister has a chance to perform the ceremony." Before Samantha could find her voice,

Annie reached into the shopping bag she'd brought upstairs with her when she first arrived. Pulling a box from the bag, she handed it to Samantha. "Since Morgan was in such a hurry to get you to the altar, I didn't have time to give you a lingerie shower."

Samantha frowned at the Sleek and Sassy Lady Lingerie Boutique logo on the top. "What's this?"

Annie gave her a sly smile. "Oh, just something to make your evening more…um, shall we say, interesting?"

Opening the box to peel back the layers of tissue paper, Samantha's cheeks heated. The skimpiest white lace teddy she'd ever seen lay nestled inside, along with a book on sensual massage and a bottle of scented oil.

"Oh, my!"

"I hope you like it," Annie said, sounding hopeful. "I wore one like this on my wedding night, and…" She blushed prettily. "I was really happy with Brant's reaction. Especially when I used the oil and gave him a massage."

Annie expected her to wear this for Morgan? Tonight? And to rub scented oil all over his body?

Samantha gulped. She felt warm all over at the thought, but she couldn't tell Annie that although they'd shared a few kisses that made her insides feel as if they'd turned to warm pudding, there wouldn't be any nights of grand passion.

A lump formed in her throat and an empty vacant

feeling filled her chest. She and Morgan had an agree-ment, and it was best if they stuck to it.

So why did the thought that they wouldn't be sharing everything a husband and wife shared make her feel so sad? So utterly alone? That's the way she wanted it, wasn't it?

"Thank you, Annie." She replaced the box lid, then set it on top of the dresser. "I think any man with a pulse would like seeing a woman in that."

When Colt punched the button on the CD player, and George Strait started singing about crossing his heart and promising that his love was truer than any other, Morgan's stomach churned like a cement mixer gone berserk. What the hell did he think he was doing?

Six years ago, he'd vowed never to get married—never to be responsible for another person's well-being. Yet, here he stood, waiting for Samantha to come down the stairs and join him in front of the fireplace in the great room so Preacher Hill from the Methodist church down in Bear Creek could pronounce them man and wife.

Reminding himself this was the only way to help her keep the land that was rightfully hers, Morgan reached up to put his index finger in the collar of his dress shirt. He gave it a tug in an effort to create a little more space between the restrictive top button and his Adam's apple. Why did a suit and tie always make a man feel like he had a noose around his damned neck?

"Relax, bro. Being married is the best thing that ever happened to me," Brant said as Annie appeared at the top of the staircase, holding Timmy. Grinning he asked, "Have you ever seen a woman prettier than my Annie?"

Morgan opened his mouth to tell his brother he sounded like a lovesick teenager, but the words lodged in his throat. Samantha stood at the top of the steps, her silky, golden-brown hair swept up in a cascade of loose curls, her whiskey-colored eyes gazing at him like he was the only man in the room. Wearing his mother's wedding dress, and carrying a single white rose, he'd never seen her look more beautiful.

He swallowed hard as he stared up at the woman he was about to marry. "Annie's almost as pretty as Samantha."

"I think I'm gonna puke," Colt muttered under his breath. "You two are about the saddest cases I've ever seen."

"Can it, little brother," Morgan said, unable to take his eyes off of Samantha as she and Annie descended the stairs. "You're lucky we didn't make you skip down the stairs scattering flower petals."

Colt snorted. "Yeah, like that would ever happen." He shook his head. "I'm never going to get as mooneyed over a woman as you two."

"Your day is coming," Brant warned, stepping forward to escort his wife and Timmy over to the fireplace.

Morgan's heart pounded hard against his rib cage and his knees felt as if they might fail him at any second when he moved toward the stairs to wait for Samantha. But the moment she reached the bottom step and trustingly placed her hand in his, a calm swept over him that he couldn't explain, nor did he want to.

"You look beautiful," he said, gazing down into her pretty eyes.

She smiled and Morgan could have sworn it chased the late afternoon shadows from the room. "I was just thinking how handsome you look," she said, touching the lapel of his black western-cut suit jacket.

"Are you ready for this?" he asked, tucking her hand in the crook of his arm.

She took a deep breath and nodded. "I guess so."

Leading her over to where Preacher Hill stood in front of the big stone fireplace, Morgan glanced at the baby sleeping peacefully in Annie's arms, then at Samantha. He was about to take on a wife and child. But instead of striking fear in his heart and sending him running like hell in the opposite direction as it would have six weeks ago, the thought filled him with a deep satisfaction that defied explanation or logic.

"Dearly beloved, we are gathered here today to join this man and this woman…" Preacher Hill began.

As the ceremony progressed, Morgan felt a twinge of guilt when it came time to repeat the traditional words that would make them husband and wife. He hated to lie about anything, but especially when it came to something as sacred as wedding vows. There was no doubt that he would honor and cherish Samantha. But he'd just promised to love her and stay with her until death.

He swallowed hard. Why hadn't they thought about

writing their own vows? They could have skirted around those issues.

But when he heard her promise to love, honor and cherish him in return, a satisfied warmth flowed through him. The thought of having her with him, loving him for the rest of his life lit the darkest corners of his soul. And at the moment, he wasn't about to remind himself that their arrangement was only temporary.

When the stoic, elderly preacher requested the rings, Morgan gave him the wedding bands that he'd made a special trip to Laramie to purchase the day before. Handing the smaller one back, the good reverend instructed him to put the ring on the third finger of Samantha's left hand and repeat the words that would make her his.

"With this ring—" he caught and held her gaze as he slid the shiny, wide gold band onto her trembling finger "—I thee wed."

"When did you get these?" she whispered, her eyes shiny with unshed tears.

"Yesterday," he said, bringing her hand to his mouth to press a kiss to the ring circling her finger.

Preacher Hill handed her the other wedding band, and as she slid it onto his finger and repeated the traditional words, a lone tear slowly trickled down her cheek. "By the power vested in me by God, and the state of Wyoming, I now pronounce you husband and wife," the man said. "Son, kiss your bride."

Samantha held her breath as Morgan reached up to

wipe the tear sliding down her cheek with the pad of his thumb, then drew her into his arms to seal their union with a kiss that made her insides quiver and caused her mind to reel from everything that had taken place in the last few minutes.

She'd just promised to love Morgan, to stay with him no matter what. How on earth would she be able to walk away from him in two years after pledging something like that?

"You might want to let her up for air," Brant said, laughing as he slapped Morgan on the shoulder. "Welcome to the world of the blissfully hitched, bro."

When Morgan lifted his head to smile at her, tiny electrical impulses skipped over every nerve in her body. If she didn't know better, she'd think he intended for them to...

"If this big galoot doesn't tow the line, just let me know," Brant said. He pushed Morgan aside to hug her and place a brotherly kiss on her cheek. "I'll be more than happy to kick his butt for you."

"I'll remember that," she said, smiling wanly.

The Wakefields were so nice she really hated deceiving them. But they had no way of knowing the marriage was only temporary, and not an everlasting commitment of love and devotion.

"My turn to kiss the bride," Colt said, shouldering Brant out of the way and making a show of really getting into the act. But when Morgan cleared his throat and sent a dark scowl his way, Colt grinned and lightly pressed his lips to her other cheek. "It's good to meet you, Samantha. Welcome to the family."

When her new brother-in-law mentioned the one thing that she'd always wanted—to be part of a family—she couldn't shake the deep sadness that washed over her. Although her last name had just become Wakefield, it was all pretend. She wasn't, and never would be, a real part of their family.

Morgan must have sensed her discomfort, because he put his arms around her waist to pull her close. "You and Timmy *are* part of us now, sweetheart," he whispered close to her ear.

"Thank you," was all she could manage as she fought to hold back her tears.

Once the minister filled out the marriage certificate, had Brant and Annie sign in the appropriate place as witnesses to the marriage and excused himself to drive back to Bear Creek, Annie took charge. Placing Timmy in his baby carrier, she instructed, "Brant, you and Colt watch the baby while I get everything ready in the kitchen." Turning to Morgan and Samantha, she added, "You two take a little time to catch your breath and get ready for pictures and cutting the cake."

"Pictures?" Morgan looked as surprised as Samantha felt.

"Cake?" She hadn't counted on Annie going to so much trouble.

Nodding, Annie grinned. "You'll want pictures to reminisce over when you celebrate your fiftieth anniversary. And it's not official until you smear cake all over each other's face."

Before Samantha found her voice to ask if Annie needed help in the kitchen, her new sister-in-law breezed down the hall and out of sight.

As Colt and Brant stared down at Timmy like they weren't quite sure what they were supposed to do, Morgan asked, "Are you doing okay?"

"I'm not sure," she said honestly. "It's hard to take in all that's happened in the last hour."

He smiled. "Feels like you've been hit by a train, doesn't it?"

She nodded, as she watched her two brothers-in-law gaze down at her son. "I just hate that we're deceiving them."

"Are we?"

Samantha sucked in a sharp breath and turned to stare at him. "What do you mean?"

"Everything's ready for the pictures and cutting the cake," Annie said, walking back into the room before Morgan could answer. "Brant, you get our camera. Colt, you're in charge of the baby."

"Me?" Colt sounded alarmed. "I don't know what to do with a baby."

"Take hold of the carrier's handle and bring him into the kitchen," Annie said, patiently. "Believe me, he won't bite."

"He might," Colt said, eyeing Timmy carefully. "He doesn't look like he likes me very much."

"You end up growing on people. Sort of like a

fungus," Brant said, laughing as he picked up the camera from the slate coffee table.

Colt looked insulted. "Thanks a lot. What kind of impression do you think that gives our new sister-in-law?"

"She'll get used to you, just like the rest of us had to," Brant said. "And don't worry about the baby biting. If he does decide to give you a little nip, it won't hurt. He doesn't have teeth yet."

"So now that Annie's pregnant you're an expert on babies, huh?" Colt groused as he picked up the baby carrier and followed his brother down the hall.

Morgan took Samantha's hand. "Come on. Let's get this over with so they'll leave and I can get out of this damned monkey suit."

Samantha didn't budge. "I think we need to discuss the issue of your questioning our deception."

"We'll talk later," he said, giving her a kiss that left her absolutely breathless. "Now smile, sweetheart. This is your wedding day."

Chapter 7

For the next half hour, Samantha felt as if she was living a dream. Morgan played the role of the attentive groom, while Brant, instructed by Annie, snapped so many pictures Samantha wasn't sure she'd ever be able to see again without spots dancing before her eyes.

"Time to cut the cake," Annie finally announced.

"Were you, by any chance, a wedding planner before you married Brant?" Samantha asked as Annie showed her and Morgan where and how to cut the cake.

"No, I was a librarian." Annie grinned as she added, "But one of my favorite books was *How to Plan a Fairytale Wedding.*"

Samantha laughed. "It shows."

Taking the decorative knife, her breath caught and heat coursed through her veins as Morgan covered her hand with his and they sliced the beautiful white wedding cake Annie had bought at a bakery in Laramie. Samantha tried to ignore the feeling.

But when they fed each other a small piece, and Morgan licked the icing from her fingers, there was no way she could dismiss the delicious fluttery feeling deep in the pit of her stomach. Nor could she deny the fact that every cell in her being tingled to life.

She had to get a grip on herself. It was as if she'd forgotten that this was just an act—a show for the benefit of his family.

After everyone had a piece of wedding cake, Annie enlisted Brant and Colt's help, and in no time they had everything put away and the kitchen spotless.

"Colt is spending the night with us," Annie announced as she tugged on his sleeve.

Colt frowned. "I am?"

"Yes, you are," Brant said, elbowing his younger brother in the ribs and treating him to a meaningful look.

"Oh, right." Colt's grin caused Samantha's cheeks to feel as if they were on fire. "Just in case you're tired and want to sleep in tomorrow morning, I won't be back until noon to get my stuff. After that I'll be taking off for Mitch's place."

Annie stepped forward to hug Samantha. "I'd offer to watch the baby for you, but since you're nursing, I know you can't be away from each other for that long."

Nodding, Samantha hugged her new sister-in-law back. "Thank you for everything, Annie. I truly appreciate your thoughtfulness."

"We're sisters now, and I was happy to do it." Lowering her voice, she added, "Don't forget to wear the teddy. I promise Morgan's reaction will be well worth it." Turning to her husband and brother-in-law, she motioned toward the door. "Come on you two. It's time we left the newlyweds alone."

No sooner had the three of them walked out the back door, than Timmy let out a wail, indicating that he wanted to nurse again.

Samantha was thankful for the excuse to have a little time to herself, in order to come to terms with all that had taken place. It wasn't every day a woman got married to one of the sexiest men alive, only to plan on spending her wedding night completely alone.

Lifting her son from the baby carrier, she started toward the stairs. "I'll come back down later and get the baby carrier."

"I'll get it," Morgan said, impatiently tugging on the knot of his tie. "While you're taking care of Timmy, I'm going to change into something that doesn't make me feel like I'm being throttled."

"I should change, too," she said, hoping Timmy didn't spit up before she could take off her borrowed dress. "This gown is beautiful, but—" She groaned as she suddenly thought of how much trouble it would be to get out of it. "Oh, no. I forgot to have Annie help me with the back."

Morgan shoved the necktie in one of the pockets of his suit coat and worked the top two buttons loose on his shirt. "I'll help you once we get upstairs."

Before she could think of some other way to get the dress unbuttoned, he took the baby carrier in one hand and guided her to the stairs with the other. Helping her climb the stairs without tripping on the long skirt, he opened the door to the room she shared with Timmy, then set the baby carrier on the window seat while she laid Timmy on the bed.

When he stepped up behind her, Samantha caught her breath and her stomach felt as if it did a somersault at the first touch of his hands at her shoulders. Having him unfasten the back of her dress seemed so intimate, so husbandlike.

"Damn, these things are little, and there's about a hundred of them," he said, his deep voice sending a wave of longing straight through her.

As he worked the buttons through the tiny loops, his fingers brushed her spine, and with each touch, heat streaked straight to the pit of her stomach. To distract herself, Samantha shook her head and tried to concentrate on what he'd said.

"I think there are only thirty or forty buttons," she said, trying not to sound as breathless as she felt. "But you're right, they are tiny."

When he reached the last few, the ones at the small of her back, his fingers lingered a bit longer with each one. Shivers of excitement shot through her and she found it extremely difficult to draw a breath.

What on earth had she gotten herself into? Had she lost her mind when she agreed to marry him?

Each time Morgan touched her, her body zinged to life and she was in serious danger of melting into a puddle at his big booted feet. How was she ever going to survive two years of living under the same roof with him and not give in to the sizzling tension between them?

"There you go," he said, his warm breath tickling the back of her neck and causing the heat inside of her to intensify.

Holding the dress to keep it from falling off her shoulders, she quickly stepped away from him. "Th-thank you."

His sexy smile and hooded sapphire gaze sent another wave of awareness skimming over every nerve in her body. "Samantha, we need to talk about—"

Impatient for his next meal, Timmy let them know that he was tired of waiting by wailing at the top of his lungs.

"He needs to nurse," she said, thankful for the interruption.

She had a good idea what Morgan wanted to discuss, and she needed time to collect herself. They were going to have to establish some ground rules to keep from doing something that would greatly complicate their situation.

To her surprise, instead of being upset that Timmy needed her, Morgan leaned down to tickle the baby's stomach. "I'll see you later, little guy." Walking to the door, he turned back to face her. "It's late. Do you think he'll sleep for a while?"

"I—" she swallowed hard "—think so."

Morgan nodded. "Good. We'll have plenty of time to…talk."

Once he'd changed into more comfortable clothes, Morgan carried his boots in one hand as he padded down the hall in his socks to Samantha's door. He'd been so turned on by the simple act of unbuttoning her dress, of feeling her soft skin beneath his fingers, he'd forgotten to tell her to meet him in his office after she got the baby down for the night.

He shook his head. It was important that they get a few things worked out about their arrangement. He needed to make it clear that although they were married, he wouldn't be responsible for any decisions she made concerning her or Timmy's welfare.

Tapping on the oak door frame, he waited a second then opened the door and walked into the room. "Samantha, I'll be down in my office when—"

He stopped short and his boots hit the floor with a loud clunk at the sight of her sitting in the rocking chair holding Timmy. She'd changed out of his mother's wedding gown and put on a pale yellow dress made of soft-looking gauzy fabric. But what held him riveted to the spot was the fact that the dress was open to the waist and the baby was nursing her breast. Morgan had never seen a more poignant sight in his entire thirty-four years.

"Morgan, what do you think you're doing?" Samantha asked, her startled movement pulling her nipple from Timmy's mouth.

The dark coral tip was wet and shiny, and Morgan couldn't have looked away if his life depended on it. "I..." He had to stop to clear the rust from his throat. "...wanted to tell you that I'll be waiting for you in my office."

His evening meal interrupted, Timmy protested loudly.

Morgan swallowed hard as he watched her guide her breast back to the baby's lips, then drape a small blanket over herself and the baby's face. Fascinated, he asked, "Does that hurt?"

She stared at him for several long moments, then slowly shook her head. "It did at first, but that was before I got used to breastfeeding."

He walked over to kneel down beside the rocking chair, then holding her gaze with his, he slowly reached up to move the soft blanket aside. When she didn't try to stop him, he glanced down to see Timmy's mouth working rhythmically to drink his mother's milk.

"I've watched thousands of animals nurse, but this is the first time I've seen a woman nurse a child." He'd never been one for putting his feelings into words, and he figured he should probably shut up now before he made a fool of himself, but the moment was so special, he had to let her know. "It's beautiful."

For the next several minutes they both remained silent as Samantha nursed the baby and Morgan watched.

"He's asleep," she finally said, her voice little more than a whisper.

Without asking, Morgan lifted Timmy into his arms

and cradled him to his chest while Samantha covered herself. "Do you want me to put him in the cradle?"

She nodded. "He should sleep until four or five tomorrow morning."

Rising to his feet, Morgan placed the sleeping baby in the cradle that had rocked three generations of Wakefield boys, then waited for Samantha to cover her son with a downy soft blanket. When she turned to face him, he thought he'd drown in the depths of her whiskey-brown eyes.

"Things have changed," he said, taking her left hand in his.

She stared at him for several long seconds before she lowered her gaze to their hands. "This isn't smart."

"Probably not." He ran the pad of his thumb over the shiny gold band circling her finger, reminding himself and her, that she was his.

"We agreed the marriage wouldn't be real," she said, lifting her head to look at him.

"Not really." He took her hands and placed them on his shoulders, then wrapped his arms around her waist to draw her forward. "*You* said the marriage would be in name only."

"And you agreed." She sounded breathless.

"No, I didn't." He leaned his forehead against hers. "I said it would probably be for the best. But technically, I never agreed to those terms."

Before she could respond, Morgan lowered his mouth to hers and once again tasted her sweetness, reveled in the feel of her soft curves against him. The spark that seemed to have been smoldering in his gut since the day they first met, ignited into a flame and tightened his lower body with a swiftness that left him dizzy. He'd never wanted a woman more in his life than he wanted Samantha.

Gently pushing his tongue past her lips, he stroked and explored her inner recesses. He loved the taste of her, the shy eagerness of her response when he ran his hands down to cup her bottom and draw her into the cradle of his hips. Her moan of pleasure at the feel of his arousal pressed to her soft lower belly sent his blood pressure up a good twenty points and had his heart hammering wildly against his ribs.

Lifting his head, he asked, "Can you honestly say we'll be able to live together for two years without making love, sweetheart?"

He watched her close her eyes for a moment, then opening them to stare up at him, she lifted her arms to encircle his neck and tangle her fingers in the hair at the nape of his neck. "We should try."

"Two years is a long time." He pulled her closer, letting her feel how much he wanted her. "Do you really want to keep this marriage in name only?"

She trembled against him. "I…I've probably lost my mind, but I'm not sure anymore."

"What do you really want, Samantha?" he asked, bringing his hands up to cup her full breasts.

When he teased the tips through the layers of her clothes, she sighed softly. "Kiss me again, Morgan. I want you to kiss me again."

"It'll be my pleasure," he said as he reached up to free her hair from the clip holding it off of her neck. "And I'm going to make damned sure it's yours, too."

Samantha's eyes fluttered shut as Morgan's mouth covered hers in a kiss that robbed her of breath, and what little sense she had left. She didn't want to think about how insane it would be to make their marriage real, or the fact that in two years, it would be over. The need to feel wanted, to be cherished by him as only a man can cherish a woman, was far stronger than the thought of the complications they would face later.

As Morgan ran his hands over her back, shivers of anticipation coursed through her. But when he plunged his tongue past her lips to claim her with sure, confident strokes, her knees began to wobble and she shamelessly clung to his solid strength for support.

Lifting his head to stare down at her with his incredible blue eyes, he smiled. "What do you want now, sweetheart?"

She took a deep breath as she tried to slow her rapidly beating pulse. "I don't think I want you to stop."

His deep chuckle sent a wave of goose bumps shimmering over her skin. "I don't think either one of us want that." He nuzzled the side of her neck, sending shivers of delight coursing to her very core. "Did the doctor put you on any kind of birth control when you went for your checkup?" he asked, his voice low and intimate.

"I...um, no. I hadn't planned on being married...let alone making love." How was she supposed to think with him so close, with his firm lips nibbling tiny kisses at the hollow behind her ear?

He raised his head to gaze down at her, and the look in his eyes sent her temperature skyward. "Don't worry, sweetheart. I'll take care of it." Giving her a quick kiss, he took her hand in his, switched on the baby monitor, then picked up the listening unit. "Why don't we go to my room?"

As she let Morgan lead her down the hall to his bedroom, her heart hammered inside her chest and she had to remind herself to breathe.

Once they made love, there was no turning back. Their marriage would be real and everything would be much more complex. Was that really what she wanted?

And what happened at the end of the two year requirement for her to gain control of her land? Was there a chance she and Morgan would stay together?

"It's going to be all right, Samantha," Morgan said as they entered his room. He switched on the bedside lamp, set the baby monitor on the table, then turned to cup her face with his large palms. "I'm not making any demands on you. If you want to call a halt to this right now, we will."

She searched his handsome features. God help her, she'd probably live to regret it, but she didn't have the strength to take him up on the retreat he'd offered her. Didn't even want to. She wanted his touch, the taste of his kiss and the warmth of his lovemaking.

"No," she said, surprised at how steady and sure her voice sounded. "I don't want to stop."

The heated look in his amazing blue eyes warmed

her all the way to her toes as he lowered his head and kissed her with a gentleness that brought tears to her eyes. "I promise you won't regret it, sweetheart."

When he reached up to unbutton her dress, his gaze held her captive and she had to force herself to breathe. "I think I'd better warn you…I haven't lost all of the weight I gained while I was pregnant."

She watched his eyes darken as he shook his head. "I like the way you look. A woman is supposed to have rounded curves."

Figuring he might as well be aware of all of her flaws, she added, "I also have a few stretch marks."

"I've got a few scars of my own, sweetheart." He worked the last button open, then trailed his finger up to her breasts. "You have no idea how extremely sexy you are, do you?"

"I've never—" when he released the front clasp of her bra, she had to stop and force air into her lungs "—thought of myself as sexy."

"You should," he said, pushing her dress and the straps of her bra from her shoulders. "You're the most desirable woman I've ever known."

As he cupped her breasts in his calloused palms, Samantha's heart rate doubled and she felt as if her insides had turned to melted butter. Closing her eyes, she concentrated on the feel of his rough hands on her body, the tingles of excitement that surged through her when he teased her nipples with the pads of his thumbs.

"Does that feel good?" he asked, kissing her forehead, her eyes and the tip of her nose.

"Y-yes."

She opened her eyes and bringing her hands up to the front of his chambray shirt began to unfasten the snaps. When she parted the shirt to reveal his well-muscled chest, her breath caught. Morgan Wakefield was perfect.

His chest muscles were well developed and the wall of his abdomen rippled from years of physical labor. A fine coating of black hair covered his chest, then thinned out to a fine line arrowing down to his navel and beyond. Samantha's gaze followed the stripe to where it disappeared below the waistband of his well-worn jeans.

"You're gorgeous," she whispered, placing her hands on the hard sinew. She ran her fingers over the thick pads of his pectoral muscles, lingering on the small flat disks that puckered and beaded from her touch.

Glancing up, the heat she saw in his blue gaze sent an answering warmth to the pit of her stomach and had her bare toes curling into the thick carpet. Without a word he lowered his head to kiss the slope of her breasts, then grazed each nipple with his tongue. Threads of desire began to wind their way through her and caused her breath to come out in short little puffs.

"You're the one who's beautiful," he murmured against her sensitized skin. He kissed the tips, then looked up at her. "I want to see all of you, Samantha."

His low, suggestive voice caused a delightful little flutter in her lower belly and made her knees feel as if they were about to fold. "I want to see you, too."

Smiling encouragingly, he slowly pushed her dress downward and in no time at all the loose garment lay in a pool of gauzy cotton at her feet. He placed his hands on her hips to steady her as she stepped away from it.

"My turn?" she asked, bringing her hands to the waistband of his jeans.

When he nodded, she worked the button through the buttonhole, then slowly, carefully pulled the metal tab down over the hard ridge of his arousal. Fascinated by the strength and power straining insistently against his white cotton briefs, she traced her finger along the warm bulge.

"Sweetheart, I'll give you all night to quit that," Morgan said with a groan.

"That sounds interesting," she said, wondering if that throaty female voice was really hers.

"Oh, I can guarantee you're not going to be bored." His low voice and meaningful look held such promise that goose bumps shimmied up her arms.

Before she could touch him again, he stepped back. Shrugging out of his shirt, he shoved his jeans and briefs down his muscular thighs, then removed his thick white socks. Straightening to his full height, he stood before her like a perfectly sculpted statue come to life.

Samantha didn't think she'd ever seen anything quite as magnificent as Morgan Wakefield. With impossibly wide shoulders, muscular arms and lean flanks, he looked like a Greek god. As her gaze drifted lower, her eyes widened and her breath caught. Make that an impressively aroused Greek god.

He closed the gap separating them, then giving her a smile that sent her temperature up a good ten degrees, he hooked his thumbs in the waistband of her sensible cotton panties, and quickly removed the last barrier between them. She suddenly felt shy and extremely vulnerable.

"Could we…turn off the lamp?" she asked hesitantly.

"Why, sweetheart?"

"I'm not exactly—"

He gently touched her cheek with one long, masculine finger. "I've seen you before, sweetheart. You're beautiful."

Samantha felt as if her cheeks were on fire. "You were supposed to forget the night Timmy was born. I wasn't exactly at my best."

Morgan shook his head. "I can't forget. It was one of the most meaningful nights of my life."

His answer shocked her. "It was?"

Smiling, he nodded. "I've always thought women were pretty special. But helping you give birth to Timmy left me with a deeper appreciation of a woman's strength and courage. I'm in awe of you, Samantha."

Before she could find her voice, he pulled her into his arms and the feel of him against her, the contrast of masculine hair-roughened flesh to smooth feminine skin caused her to forget anything she'd been about to say. A current seemed to flow between them, charging her with a need deeper than anything she'd ever experienced.

"You feel so damned good, I think I could stand here like this forever," he said, sounding out of breath.

She brought her arms up to circle his shoulders. "I hope you're strong enough to hold both of us upright because I think I'm about to collapse."

His deep chuckle sent a shiver of anticipation right to her core. "As good as it feels to hold you against me like this, it's going to feel even better for both of us when I'm inside you."

His candid comment sent a wave of longing pulsing through every cell in her being. Releasing her, he pulled the comforter and sheet back, then lifted her as if she weighed nothing at all, and laid her on his bed.

When he stretched out beside her, he gently ran his index finger down between her breasts, then continued on to her navel. "Are these the places you were talking about?" he asked, tracing the marks left by her pregnancy.

She nodded. "I hope they don't take too long to fade."

He propped himself up on one elbow, then leaned down to press his lips to each one of the uneven lines. "Wear them with pride, sweetheart. They're badges of courage."

The reverence in his deep voice, his firm lips tenderly touching her, caused her heart to fill with an emotion she wasn't quite ready to acknowledge. If she didn't know better, she'd swear she was falling for him.

Before she could fully comprehend the threat that might represent to her peace of mind, Morgan moved to gather her into his arms. His lips covering hers chased away all thought and quickly had her feeling as if the world had been reduced to nothing but this man and this moment.

He slid his calloused palm over her ribs, then down to her hip. A shiver of delight streaked up her spine. But when he moved his hand along the inside of her leg to find the moist heat at the juncture of her thighs, a pulsing need began to pool deep in the pit of her stomach. Parting her, he gently tested her readiness as he deepened the kiss.

Wanting to touch him as he touched her, Samantha ran her hand over his flat belly to his lean flank and beyond. When she found him and stroked him with the same infinite care, a groan of pleasure rumbled up from deep in his chest.

"Easy, sweetheart," he said, his voice strained. "It's been a while and I don't want this over with before we get started."

"Please—"

"Do you want me inside?" he asked, his gaze capturing hers as he continued to tease her.

"Y-yes," she said breathlessly. "Please make love to me, Morgan."

Giving her a smile that caused the empty ache of need within her to intensify, he arranged their protection, then moved over her. "I'm going to try to take this slow, Samantha," he said, propping himself up on his elbows. "But I want you so damned much, I'm not sure I'll be able to." He leaned down to give her a kiss so tender it brought tears to her eyes as he parted her legs with one muscular thigh. "The book said that some women find lovemaking uncomfortable the first time after giving birth." He brushed a strand of her hair from her cheeks with his index finger. "If there's even a hint of discomfort, I want you to tell me. You got that?"

His concern touched her in ways she'd never imagined, and if she could have found her voice she would have told him so. But all she could manage was a quick nod before he pressed forward and she felt the exquisite stretching of his body merging with hers. She bit her lower lip to keep from moaning her pleasure as she savored the feeling of being filled by Morgan.

"You feel so damned good," he said as he sank all of himself into her.

She watched his jaw tighten as he closed his eyes and she instinctively knew he was having to dig deep for the strength to maintain his control.

When he finally opened his eyes, he gathered her into his arms. "Are you all right, sweetheart? Am I hurting you?"

"It…feels wonderful," she said breathlessly.

"Are you sure?"

"I couldn't be more certain," she said, placing her hand along his lean jaw at the same time she tilted her hips into his. She watched his brilliant gaze darken at the movement. "Make love to me, Morgan."

He gave her a smile that made her feel like she was the most desired woman alive as he lowered his mouth to hers. Pulling back, then slowly pushing his hips forward, he set an easy pace and in no time Samantha felt the coil of need inside of her tighten, felt herself tense in anticipation of the mind-shattering release.

Morgan must have sensed she was close because he reached down to touch her tiny pleasure point, encouraging her to take everything that he offered. Without warning she was suddenly tumbling, free-falling through a mist of warm, wonderful sensations.

A moment later, she felt Morgan's big body stiffen, then shudder as he gave into his own climax. Wrapping her arms around his wide shoulders, she bit her lower lip and held him to her as she tried to fight the emotion building deep inside of her.

For her well-being, and for Timmy's, she couldn't allow herself to fall in love with Morgan Wakefield, couldn't let herself count on him returning her feelings. If she did, and he turned out to be like her father, or Chad, she wasn't sure she'd be able to survive the devastation of having him reject her.

Chapter 8

When Morgan finally found the strength to move, he started to lever himself away from her, but she hugged him tighter. "I'm too heavy for you, Samantha."

"I like the way you feel," she whispered against his shoulder.

Chuckling, he held her as he rolled to one side, taking her with him. "I like the way you feel, too." He kissed her cute little nose. "Are you okay?"

The tears filling her eyes scared him as little else could. "I'm...wonderful."

"Then why are you crying?" he asked, wiping a tear from her cheek. He wasn't sure, but he hoped like hell it was one of those times when a woman cried because something was meaningful to her.

"Making love with you was beautiful," she said, sending a wave of relief coursing through him.

He smiled. "You had me scared there for a minute, sweetheart."

The sound of an awakening baby suddenly filtered into the room from the monitor on the bedside table.

"Timmy may need to nurse some more," she said, starting to draw away from him.

Morgan shook his head as he rose from the bed and pulled on his briefs. "You stay here and rest. I'll go get the baby."

Quickly padding down the hall in his bare feet, Morgan entered the room where Timmy was raising nine kinds of hell. He grinned as he lifted the crying baby to his shoulder. Morgan liked the way Timmy smelled, the way his tiny body fit into the palms of his hands.

"Thanks for timing that just right, little guy," he said, gently rubbing Timmy's back.

When Morgan re-entered his bedroom, Samantha was sitting up in bed with the sheet tucked under her arms, her luscious breasts hidden from his appreciative gaze. "He's probably hungry," she said, holding her arms out.

"Wait just a second," he said, handing the baby to her.

She gave him a curious look. "Why?"

"You'll see." He gathered the pillows, propped them against the headboard, then sat down beside her. Pulling her onto his lap, he cradled her to his chest much as she cradled Timmy. "Are you comfortable, sweetheart?"

"Y-yes," she said, looking even more confused.

"Good." He smiled as he peeled the sheet back to

reveal her full breasts. "I'm going to hold you while you nurse Timmy."

Tears filled her expressive amber eyes. "You're a very special man, Morgan Wakefield."

"Nah, I just like holding you," he said, settling back against the pillows. He watched as she guided her nipple to the baby's mouth. "Samantha?"

"Hmm?"

"I want you to move yours and Timmy's things in here tomorrow morning," he said, surprising even himself. But the more he thought about it, the more it made sense. He wanted her with him—warming his bed, warming him.

She gazed up at him for endless seconds. "But our marriage isn't—"

"It is now," he said, smiling down at her.

He could tell there were several questions running through her mind. Truth to tell, he was probably asking himself the same things. But at the moment, he didn't have answers for either one of them. All he knew was that it felt right.

When Samantha yawned, he kissed the top of her head. "I'll move the cradle in here tomorrow morning."

She closed her eyes and snuggled against him. "We'll see," she said sleepily.

With his arms wrapped around her, Morgan gazed down at the woman and baby cradled in his arms. Both had fallen sound asleep. A possessive feeling like nothing he'd ever known filled his chest and made him want to protect and take care of them.

He sucked in a sharp breath and his heart began to hammer hard against his ribs. What had gotten into him? He couldn't be responsible for either one of them. He'd proven six years ago that his judgment was faulty. What if he made a wrong decision and jeopardized their welfare?

Closing his eyes, he leaned his head back against the headboard. What had he been thinking when he'd pushed Samantha to make their marriage real? Had he lost his mind and allowed his lust to override common sense?

He forced himself to breathe in, then breathe out. He'd blamed his wanting Samantha on the long, cold winter he'd spent alone in this same bed and the need for physical release. But in the past six weeks, he'd had more than one opportunity to make a trip down to Buffalo Gals, and he'd passed every time.

Swallowing around the fear clogging his throat, he opened his eyes to look down at them. Could he live with this woman and her child for the next two years without getting more involved than he already was?

When he first brought her home from the hospital, he'd tried to keep his distance. But that hadn't worked. He'd only ended up working himself into exhaustion during the day and spent every night lying awake, thinking about her sleeping right down the hall.

Would sharing his days with her, then making love to her every night get her out of his system? Or would it only whet his appetite for the life he'd always wanted, but couldn't trust himself to have? Would it only end up complicating everything in ways that he'd never be able to straighten out?

After Emily died, he'd vowed never to take on the responsibility of having a wife and family, of making the decisions that could mean the difference between life and death for them. He glanced down at his wife and her son. He'd promised to help Samantha get her land, and he'd be damned before he went back on his word. But could he live with them, play the role of husband and father, and still keep from investing himself emotionally?

Unable to come up with any answers, Morgan shook his head. He wasn't sure. The only thing he did know for certain was that he'd have to try. For their sake, and his.

Samantha nibbled on her lower lip as she emptied the dresser drawers in the room she and Timmy had shared for the past six weeks. Had she made the right decision about moving into Morgan's room?

Last night she'd become his wife in every sense of the word, but that would be ending once she met the terms of her grandfather's will. A lump the size of her fist clogged her throat at the thought.

"After we move the rest of your clothes, I'll put your suitcases in the storage room," Morgan said, returning to carry more of her things to his bedroom. He came up behind her to rest his hands on her shoulders. "After Colt finally shows up, we'll move the cradle, then go down to the machine shed and get the rest of your stuff from your car."

A delightful shiver slipped up her spine when he pressed his lips to the nape of her neck. "That's fine," she said, turning to face him. Searching his handsome face, she asked, "Are we doing the right thing?"

She held her breath when he remained silent for several long moments. "Samantha, I can't honestly answer that," he admitted. "I've made no secret of the fact that I want you." He smiled as he wrapped his arms around her waist. "And I can tell you want me. But I want you to know that even though you're my wife, you still have the freedom to make your own choices. I can't decide what's best for you and Timmy. I won't even try."

"I'm not sure I'm capable of that, either," she said, bowing her head. She suddenly felt very tired and unsure of everything.

He placed his index finger beneath her chin and lifted her head until their gazes met. "All I can promise you for sure is that I'll provide for you and Timmy, and I'll never intentionally hurt either one of you in any way."

She forced a smile. "At least for the next two years."

His expression suddenly unreadable, he slowly nodded. "At least."

They continued to stare at each other for what seemed an eternity, until the sound of booted feet climbing the stairs, followed by a succinct curse caught their attention. "Hey, Morgan, where the hell are you?" a male voice called.

"Down here in the guest room," Morgan answered.

He kissed the tip of her nose. "Do you still want us to move the cradle?"

Thinking of how gently he'd made love to her, how tenderly he'd held her while she nursed Timmy the night before, she found herself nodding. "Yes."

"What are you doing in here?" Colt asked as he walked into the room. He came to a halt, then looking sheepish, shook his head. "Don't answer that. I think know."

"You don't know squat, little brother," Morgan said, giving her a quick kiss before he released her. "We're moving Samantha and the baby into my room."

"How's my nephew today?" Colt asked, walking over to the cradle. "Still no teeth?"

At the reference to her son being his nephew, Samantha's chest tightened. As long as she was married to Morgan, Timmy had the one thing she'd always wanted for her child—he had a family he be- longed to.

"No, he still doesn't have teeth," she said, touched that her new brother-in-law already considered Timmy a part of the Wakefield clan.

"Come on, hotshot," Morgan said, clamping his hand down on Colt's shoulder. "You're going to help me with a couple of things before you take off for Mitch's."

Colt grinned. "Only a couple? You usually have a list of things you want me to do that's at least as long as your arm."

She watched as Morgan ushered his brother toward the hall. "Just wait until you drift in home again," he warned with a laugh. "The list will be twice as long."

When he reached the door, Morgan turned back to her. "Where do you want us to put the boxes from your car?"

"I'll need to sort through them," she said, trying to remember what they contained. Her and Timmy's clothes had been brought into the house weeks ago, so they wouldn't need to bring the boxes upstairs. "I think most of what's left are kitchen items. Could you put them in the pantry for now?"

Morgan nodded. "Will do."

"Come on, bro," Colt urged. "You can make moon eyes at your wife after I leave."

"You better watch your smart mouth, kid," Morgan said as he followed Colt out into the hall. "I might just have to kick your butt if you don't."

She heard Colt's laughter as the two brothers walked down the hall. "You and whose army?"

As she turned back to empty another dresser drawer, Samantha couldn't help but smile. She enjoyed listening to the good-natured banter between Morgan and his family.

"Samantha?"

At the sound of her name, she looked up to find Colt standing uncertainly at the door. "Where's Morgan? Is something wrong?"

Colt shook his head. "No, everything's fine. Morgan's on his way to the machine shed."

When he continued to stand just inside the room, she asked, "Was there something you needed?"

He shrugged. "I just wanted to thank you."

"For what?" She couldn't imagine why he thought he needed to express his gratitude. To her knowledge, she hadn't done anything that would warrant it.

"Sometimes Brant and I give Morgan a hard time, but he's a good man with a lot of heart. He doesn't think so, but he is." Colt cleared his throat before he continued. "Anyway, I just wanted to thank you for making him happy again."

Before she had a chance to ask what he meant, Colt turned and quickly walked back down the hall, leaving her to stare after him in total bewilderment.

"Is that the last of your clothes?" Morgan asked.

"I think so," Samantha said, looking around the room. She glanced over at the bright red-and-white striped box from the Sleek and Sassy Lady Lingerie Boutique sitting on top of the dresser.

"What's that?"

"Um…it's just…something Annie gave me," she said, her cheeks growing warm. In an effort to change the subject, she pointed to a box of disposable diapers. "Would you mind taking that to your room while I double-check the closet?"

He walked over, took her into his arms and gave her a kiss that left her breathless. "It's *our* room now, sweetheart."

Her stomach fluttered at the look in his startling blue eyes and the suggestive smile curving his firm male lips. "Right. Our room," she said, nodding.

Releasing her, he picked up the carton of diapers.

"After I put these with the other baby things, I'll be down in my office for a while. I need to get some paperwork done."

She nodded. "That reminds me. I need to make a list of places to call tomorrow about building estimates and funding for the camp."

"How's it going?"

"Slow." She sighed. "Everyone is either on vacation, or too tied up with other projects to come out to the ranch and give me estimated costs of renovating the house and barn, and building a couple of dormitory cabins."

"It'll all work out, sweetheart," he said, his smile encouraging.

"I hope you're right."

"I am." He started for the door. "After I get a few things caught up around the ranch, I'll see what I can do to help you."

Touched by his offer, she smiled. "Thank you. I'd like that."

After he left the room, Samantha stared at the empty doorway for several minutes. Morgan Wakefield was indeed a very special man and nothing like her father or Chad. They were selfish, self-centered men, who wouldn't think of offering to help with anything that didn't benefit them in some way.

But Morgan was different. He was kind, thoughtful and went out of his way to do for others—asking nothing for himself in return. He'd offered her his mother's wedding gown when he learned that she really didn't have anything appropriate to wear for the ceremony yesterday. She glanced down at the gold band on her finger. And he'd gone to the trouble and expense of buying wedding rings, so no one would suspect their marriage was anything but the real thing.

Sighing, she sank down on the edge of the bed. She only wished there was something she could do to show him how special she thought he was—something to make him feel as cherished as he'd made her feel in the past few days.

Samantha glanced over at the box Annie had given her the day before. Did she dare try the book and massage oil?

She rose to her feet and walked over to the dresser, lifted the red-and-white striped top and pushed the tissue paper out of the way. Moving the teddy to the side, she dismissed it completely. There wasn't much more to the undergarment than see-through lace and a couple of satin ribbons, and she didn't think she'd ever be able to work up the courage to wear something that provocative.

But Annie had said Brant loved the sensual massage she'd given him on their wedding night. Would Morgan protest his pretend wife giving him one?

Placing the soft, stretchy lace teddy back on top of the book and bottle of oil, Samantha folded the tissue back in place and put the top back on the box. She'd never in a million years have thought of giving a man a sensual massage.

Suppressing a nervous giggle, she shook her head as she tucked the box under her arm and walked from the room. Maybe if she tried really hard, she'd be able to work up the courage to try it sometime. But she wasn't sure she'd ever have the nerve to wear the teddy.

"Samantha?" Morgan tried to open the door to the bathroom adjoining their bedroom. It was locked. "Sweetheart, are you all right?"

He'd held her while she nursed the baby, as he had every night for the past week. But as soon as she'd gotten Timmy to sleep, she'd put him to bed in the cradle over in the corner, disappeared into the bathroom, and Morgan hadn't seen her since. He checked his watch. That had been half an hour ago.

His concern increasing, he pounded on the door. "Samantha, if you don't answer me, and damned quick, I'm going to break this door down."

"I'm fine, Morgan. I'll be out in a few more minutes," she said, her voice muffled by the thick oak panel separating them. "And keep your voice down. I don't want you waking Timmy."

He frowned as he unbuttoned and removed his shirt, then shucked his jeans and placed them on the chest at the foot of the bed. Walking around to the side, he sat down on the mattress and stared at the bathroom door. What could possibly take a woman that damned long for something as simple as a shower?

As he sat there contemplating the mysterious ways of women, he heard the lock being released. Glancing up, he watched the door open just a crack.

"Morgan?"

He was on his feet and across the room in a flash. "What is it, sweetheart? Are you sure you're all right?"

"Yes, I'm fine. I want you to do something for me," she said, sounding breathless.

"Name it." He tried to push the door open a little wider, but she held it firm.

"I want you to go lay down on the bed."

"You want me to what?" She had him scared about half-spitless and she wanted him to go lay down?

"Dammit, Samantha, what's going on?"

"Just do it, okay?"

"Women," he muttered as he walked back to the bed, shoved the pillows against the headboard, then leaned back against them.

"Are you lying down?"

"Yes," he said, blowing out a frustrated breath. He had no idea what she was up to, but the explanation had better be damned good.

The light in the bathroom went out a split second before the door opened the rest of the way, and Samantha stepped out into the room wearing a shy smile and a scrap of lace that revealed more than it hid.

Morgan sat bolt upright in bed, his eyes wide, his heart thumping his ribs like a bass drum in a high school marching band. "Wh-where…" He had to swallow around the cotton suddenly lining his throat and mouth. "…did you get that?"

"Annie gave it to me on Sunday, just before we got married." An uncertain look replaced her smile. "You don't like it?"

He grinned. "Hell, sweetheart, if I liked it any better, I think I'd probably have a heart attack."

Her easy expression returned as she walked toward him. "I really had no intentions of ever wearing it, but—"

"I'm glad you did, sweetheart," he said, meaning it more than she'd probably ever know.

He started to rise from the bed, but she shook her head and held up her hand. "Would you mind staying there?"

"Why?"

"Because it's taken me almost a week to work up my courage to do this, I'd like to finish," she said, her cheeks turning a pretty shade of rose.

"What do you intend to finish?" he asked, thoroughly intrigued.

He watched her bite her lower lip, then take a deep breath. "I'm going to give you a sensual massage."

Chapter 9

Morgan's heart took off at a gallop and his libido right along with it. "Sweetheart, are you trying to seduce me?"

Her cheeks colored a very pretty pink. "Well, no…I mean, I hadn't thought of it that way."

"It's fine with me if you are. Although, I don't think you can seduce the willing." Curious to see what Samantha had in mind, he grinned as he clasped his hands behind his head and leaned back against the pillows. "But I'm pretty easy to get along with. Go for it."

Her relieved expression caused his chest to swell with an emotion he forced himself to ignore. He wasn't ready, or willing, to acknowledge anything beyond the fact that his wife was standing before him in nothing more than a wisp of lace and ribbon, and one hell of a sexy smile. And she was looking at him like she fully intended to make him her next meal.

"Keep in mind that I've never done anything like this before, and that I'll have to learn as I go," she said, her throaty admission sending the blood rushing through his veins so fast that it left him light-headed.

"We're breaking new ground here for both of us," he said hoarsely. "You've never given a sensual massage, and I've never gotten one."

She toyed with the tiny satin bow between her breasts. "Do you want me to stop?"

"Hell, no!" He shook his head. "This is just starting to get interesting."

He watched her gaze travel from his face, down his chest to his stomach and beyond. The second she noticed the bulge of his arousal already straining at his briefs, her eyes widened.

"Real interesting," he said, unable to stop grinning. He had no idea what she intended to do next, but he was looking forward to finding out.

When she walked over to the side of the bed, he noticed a bottle in her hand. "What's that?"

"You'll see," she said, her smile sending a curl of heat to the pit of his belly. "But we have to establish a couple of ground rules first."

He made room for her to sit down beside him, then reached for her. "And those would be?"

She drew back. "You can't touch me until I tell you to."

"That's going to be difficult," he said, dropping his

arms and feeling as if air was in short supply. "What else?"

"I want you to keep your eyes closed."

This was getting more interesting by the second. "All right. Anything else?"

She gave him a look that sent his blood pressure off the chart. "I want you to concentrate on what I'll be doing to you and tell me how it makes you feel."

He swallowed hard. "You're determined to give me a heart attack, aren't you?"

"No, silly," she said, laughing. "This is supposed to heighten your senses and make you feel wonderful."

"Oh, I'm feeling pretty damned terrific right now as it is," he said, forcing himself to breathe. "And if my senses get any sharper, they could slice granite."

Her smile made the task of lying still all the more difficult. "I hope this makes you feel even better. Now, close your eyes."

When he did as she requested, a pleasant earthy scent drifted around him, followed by something liquid dripping onto his chest. "What is that stuff?"

"Light musk body oil."

"It's…warm." He had to concentrate to keep his eyes shut. "Feels good."

"Mm-hmm. I warmed the bottle in hot water."

She touched him with her soft hands, spreading the oil over his chest. But when she lightly massaged his pectoral muscles, then circled each one of his flat nipples with the tip of her finger, a shudder ran through him and he sucked in a sharp breath.

"Does that feel good?" she whispered close to his ear.

His muscles flexed and his eyes popped open. "If it felt any better I'd—"

She shook her head. "Close your eyes."

Frowning, he did as she instructed. "Now, I know you're determined to give me a coronary."

He loved the way her hands felt on his body. But he had a feeling before she was finished, he might end up certifiably insane.

As her hands drifted lower over his ribs, to his abdomen and his flanks, she asked, "What are you feeling now?"

Couldn't she tell? Hadn't she noticed how hard his body had become with wanting her?

He had to take a deep breath before he could manage to make his vocal cords work. "I think there's enough electricity running through me right now that I could light up Laramie and probably Cheyenne."

Her throaty laughter only increased the tension building inside of him. "Try to relax."

It was his turn to laugh. "Why don't you ask me to move a couple of mountains while I'm at it?"

"Impossible, huh?"

Shaking his head, he doubled both hands into tight fists to keep from reaching for her. "Never underestimate a man as charged up as I am right now. Just tell me which mountain, when you want it moved and where."

"I'll give that some thought," she said, taking one of her talented little hands away from his lower stomach.

He wondered what she was doing, but the sound of the flip-top cap on the bottle being opened quickly drew his attention. Where was she going to put the oil now?

It didn't take long to find out what she had planned next when he felt the warm liquid dribble over his legs. She placed a hand on each one of his shins, then started spreading the oil upward. His heart stalled. But when she moved her hands over his knees and up his thighs, his pulse took off at breakneck speed and the heat in his lower belly ignited into a flame. If she didn't stop, and damned quick, her hands were going to be dangerously close to—

His eyes snapped open and he swallowed hard. There was no doubt in his mind that she was going to kill him before the night was over. But, he decided as the back of her hand brushed the bulge of his arousal straining against his cotton briefs, he'd leave this world a very happy man.

Unable to lie still a minute longer, Morgan caught her hands in his and drew her up to face him. "Sweetheart, don't get me wrong. I'm loving the hell out of this seduction business. But I'm about to go into sensory overload."

Lying across his chest, she smiled down at him. "Don't you want me to finish?"

The air in his lungs came out in one big whoosh and a surge of need arrowed straight to his groin. "If you keep running your hands over me with that warm oil, things will be finished a whole lot sooner than either one of us really wants."

She glanced down his body at the evidence of his overwhelming desire. "Are you trying to tell me that I was successful at giving you a sensual massage?"

If he hadn't been fighting so hard to retain what little control he had left, he might have laughed. "I'd say it was a resounding success, sweetheart." Taking her into his arms, he rolled over to pin her beneath him. "I'll be more than happy to let you do it again any time you want. But would you mind if we put my complete surrender on hold for now and I took it from here?"

"Why?"

"Because I can't take any more of this." He pressed his lower body against her thigh as he lowered his lips to her ear. "I need to be inside of you, bringing you the same pleasure you're giving me."

"I'd like that," she said, shivering against him. Her warm breath teased the side of his neck, sending an answering shudder coursing through him.

The fire in his belly burned brighter, and unable to resist the lure of her soft lips any longer, Morgan traced their fullness with his tongue. When she sighed and wrapped her arms around his shoulders, he deepened the kiss to stroke her inner recesses and coax her into exploring him. Heaven help him, but he was addicted to the sweet taste of her, the way her reserved response quickly turned into passionate need.

Wanting to touch her, to hold her to him and bury himself deep inside of her, he ran his hands the length of her. The scrap of lace she was wearing looked fantastic on her, but he knew beyond a shadow of doubt that he'd like it better off of her. The only problem was, he couldn't figure out how to get her out of it.

He lifted his head to kiss the tip of her nose. "Don't

get me wrong. I like whatever this is you're wearing, but how the hell do I get it off of you."

"It's called a teddy." She kissed his chest, sending a shock-wave right through him. "There are two snaps below, at the—"

Before she could finish telling him where they were located, Morgan quickly found and released the tiny fasteners at the apex of her thighs. After he pulled the stretchy lace up and over her head, he removed his briefs and reached for the foil packet he'd tucked beneath his pillow earlier.

"Morgan?" She took the packet from him. "Would you mind if I—"

Blood rushed through his veins when he realized what she was about to ask. "Go right ahead, sweetheart," he said, lying back against the pillows.

He'd never had a woman help arrange their protection before and he found it was more exciting than he could have ever imagined. Her soft touch on his heated body as she rolled the condom into place almost sent him over the edge.

He reached for her once she had the prophylactic taken care of, but Samantha surprised him when she shook her head and moved to straddle his hips. Holding him captive with her smoldering gaze, Morgan thought the top of his head just might come right off his shoulders as her body slowly consumed his.

Closing his eyes, he gritted his teeth and placed his hands on her hips to keep her still. "Don't...move."

Heat and light danced behind his eyelids like some

kind of wild laser show as he fought for control. He'd never in his life been this hot, this fast. His body was urging him to allow Samantha to complete the act of loving him, but he ignored it. He wanted this feeling of being one with her to last forever.

The thought might have scared the hell out of him at any other time. But at the moment, Morgan didn't have the strength to fight it. Didn't even want to.

She leaned down to kiss his chest, his shoulder and his chin, then slowly, surely began to rock against him. His senses honed to a razor-sharp edge, he could tell by the tightness of her body and the passionate glow coloring her porcelain cheeks that she was as turned on as he was.

Holding her shapely hips, he helped her set a pace that quickly had them both close to the edge of fulfillment. Only when he felt her inner muscles cling to him, signaling that her release was imminent, did he abandon the last shred of his control and thrust into her a final time. Her moan of pleasure and the rhythmic tremors coursing through her triggered his own climax, and together they hurtled into the realm of complete and utter ecstasy.

The next morning, Morgan shuffled through the stack of files on his desk. When he came across the purchase option he'd had his lawyer draw up for the Shackley ranch, he tossed it aside. He'd have to shred it, along with some other useless papers. But that would have to wait.

He glanced at the calendar. It was time for his annual drive down to the cemetery just outside of Denver to pay his respects to the woman he'd promised to marry.

Every year since Emily's passing, on the day they were to have been married, he'd faithfully placed flowers on her grave and silently begged her forgiveness for his role in her death. But this year would be different. Today, he'd be making the trip to say his final goodbye to her.

He took a deep breath. He'd lain awake most of the night with Samantha nestled in his arms and he'd done a lot of thinking.

Emily was his past and it was time he let her go. She'd been his best friend as well as his lover, and he had no doubt that if they'd married, they would have made it work.

But for the first time in six long years, he felt ready to move forward and get on with his life. Samantha was his future now. He wanted her with him for the rest of his life, wanted to help her raise Timmy and share her dream of starting a camp for kids of the foster care system.

As he glanced out the window at the distant Shirley Mountains, he sucked in a sharp breath. Good Lord, he'd fallen in love with her.

The thought should have scared the hell out of him. But as the realization settled in, he smiled.

He'd first been drawn to her bravery and pride. She'd faced giving birth to her son in a ramshackle old ranch house with a depth of courage that had astounded him. Then, when she found out that he'd paid the hospital bill, she'd gathered her pride around her like a coat of armor and informed him that she'd cook his meals and clean his house in order to pay him back.

But as he'd gotten to know her better, he'd also learned how kind and caring she was. She was a wonderful mother to Timmy, and even though she had very little herself, she was determined to take her inheritance and turn it into a place where kids could briefly escape their emotional pain.

She'd even allowed him to feel as if he were a member of her little family when she let him hold her while she nursed the baby. And, if she'd let him, he wanted to be a permanent part of it. But he couldn't do that until he made the trip to Denver.

Smiling at the thought of them being a real family, he slowly rose from his chair and crossed the room. He needed to get on the road. The sooner he bid farewell to his past, the sooner he could get on with his future.

"Samantha?" he called as he walked across the foyer to the great room.

When he found her in the kitchen, he walked up behind her, wrapped his arms around her waist and pulled her back against him. He loved touching her, loved the way she melted against him. Hell, he just plain loved everything about her.

"Sweetheart, I have to go down to Denver today to take care of some unfinished business." He kissed the side of her neck. "Do you need me to pick up anything for you or the baby?"

She turned in his arms to give him a kiss that damned near knocked his size-13 boots right off his feet. "Would you mind picking up a couple of boxes of diapers?"

He shook his head. "Anything else?"

"I can't think of anything." She kissed him again. "How long will you be gone?"

He hated having to leave, when what he really wanted to do was take her upstairs and show her how much she'd come to mean to him, but he needed to say goodbye to an old friend. "I'll be gone most of the day." Giving her a kiss that left them both gasping for breath, he cupped her cheek with his palm. "When I get back, there's something we need to get settled."

She stared at him for several long seconds. "Could I ask what that would be?"

"You'll see." He kissed her again, then set her away from him. If he didn't put some distance between them, he wouldn't even make it as far as the truck, let alone take off for Denver. "I'll call you on my cell phone when I start home."

When he turned to leave, she asked, "Would you mind if I use the computer in your office? It will probably take most of the day, but I'd like to do an Internet search to find contractors for building estimates and possible sources of funding for the camp."

"Sweetheart, the Lonetree is your home now," he said, placing his Resistol on his head as he opened the back door. "You don't have to ask to use my office or anything in it."

Samantha felt warm all over when Morgan winked at her before closing the door behind him. She had no idea what he wanted to talk about, but she had a few things she needed to say to him when he got back.

Her chest tightened and she gave up trying to deny what she knew in her heart to be true. She'd fallen in love with her new husband.

Considering their agreement, it wasn't the smartest thing she'd ever done, but she wasn't sure she'd ever really had a choice in the matter. The question now was could he ever love her in return?

She knew he wanted her. Of that, there was no doubt. But could Morgan fall in love with her the way a husband loved his wife?

She wasn't sure. But she had every intention of finding out, because there was no way she could remain on the Lonetree Ranch if it turned out that he couldn't.

Strapping Timmy in the baby carrier, Samantha carried him downstairs, along with the folder containing her plans for building the camp. She needed to make some phone calls for estimates on building materials, as well as do an Internet search on Morgan's computer to see what kind of financial aid was available and how to go about obtaining it.

Entering the office, she set the baby carrier on the deacon's bench close to the desk, then settled herself in the big leather desk chair. The first thing she had to do was start making appointments with an engineer to come out and inspect the existing structures on her grandfather's ranch. If some of them could be renovated, it would cut down on the overall cost of getting the camp up and running.

Glancing over at Timmy, she smiled. "Now, all I

have to do is find where Morgan keeps the phone book. Any ideas?"

At the sound of her voice, Timmy waved his little fist in the air and smacked his lips around the pacifier in his mouth.

She laughed. "In other words, you're on your own, Mom."

The pacifier bobbled as if he agreed with her.

"It has to be here somewhere," she said, standing to search the floor-to-ceiling book shelves beside the desk, then the computer center behind it.

Finally spotting the directory under several legal-size files beside the keyboard, she reached to pull the book from beneath the pile. She sighed heavily when the entire stack of folders fell to the floor.

"Morgan will never trust your mommy in his office again," she said to her now sleeping son.

Disgusted with herself for being so careless, she bent to pick up the scattered papers. But her name on one of the documents caught her attention, and straightening, she scanned its contents.

Her heart skipped several beats and a chilling numbness began to fill her soul. Morgan wanted to buy her grandfather's ranch?

Her legs suddenly feeling as if they would no longer support her, she collapsed onto the chair behind the desk. Why would Morgan have a purchase option drawn up? Even before she learned of the new will, and the terms that had to be met to obtain the property, she'd never indicated that she wanted to sell. On the contrary. She'd told Morgan the first day about her plans to turn the ranch into a camp for foster children.

As she thought about the events of the past couple of months, tears filled her eyes, then ran down her cheeks. How could she have been so stupid?

After she'd explained about the camp, Morgan had avoided her like the plague. He'd left each morning before she got up and hadn't returned until well after she'd gone to bed each night.

But all that changed the day she met with her grandfather's lawyer and he informed her of the new stipulations placed on her inheritance. Once Morgan learned that the land would be turned over to the BLM if she wasn't married, he couldn't get her to the altar fast enough.

Her breath caught on a sob as she glanced down on the gold band circling her finger. What a fool she'd been.

When she questioned him about why he was willing to put his life on hold for the next two years, she'd taken him at his word and foolishly believed that he only wanted to help her hold on to the property. But instead, he'd married her simply because he'd known that once the land was donated to the BLM he'd never get his hands on it.

She scrunched her eyes shut at the emotional pain tightening her chest. Why had she been so quick to believe in Morgan? Hadn't she learned from her father and Chad that men couldn't be counted on for anything but heartache and grief? That they had their own agenda, that didn't include her?

Unable to sit still another minute, she rose to her feet, quickly picked up the remaining files still scattered on the floor and stacked them on the computer center. Turning back to Morgan's desk, she carefully laid the purchase option where he would be sure to see it, then with trembling fingers, removed her wedding band to place it on top of the document.

Tears blurred her vision and her heart felt as if it shattered into a million pieces when she picked up the baby carrier and started out of the office. As she closed the door behind her, the phone started ringing. She ignored it.

She didn't feel like speaking with anyone, nor did she have time. She had to get her suitcases from the store room and start packing to leave.

Morgan let the phone on the other end of the line ring until the answering machine in his office picked up. Frowning, he left another message for Samantha to call him, then depressed the end button. He'd been trying to reach her since leaving the cemetery three hours ago, but she still wasn't answering. Where the hell was she?

She'd told him this morning that she intended to spend the day working on plans for her camp. Fear gripped his belly as he stared out the windshield of his truck at the road ahead. Had something happened to her or the baby?

He pressed down on the accelerator at the same time he pushed the auto-dial on the cell phone. As soon as Annie answered, he asked, "Is Samantha over there at your place?"

"No. I tried calling her a couple of times today, but the answering machine picked up." His sister-in-law sounded alarmed. "Isn't she with you?"

The knot of fear twisting his gut tightened. "No. I've been trying to get hold of her since I left Denver."

"Where are you now? Do you need me to drive over there?"

"I'm only about six miles from home." He turned the truck off the main road and onto Lonetree land. "I'll get there before you could."

"Morgan, if you need us—"

"I'll let you know." As an afterthought he added, "Thanks, Annie."

"When you find out something, let us know if everything is all right." Annie paused. "I...have some bad news, Morgan."

His anxiety increased. "What is it?"

"Colt's friend, Mitch Simpson, was stomped by a bull last night in Houston." He heard Annie take a shaky breath. "He died in surgery a few hours later."

Morgan groaned from the deep sadness filling him. He liked Mitch and his younger sister, Kaylee. Everyone did.

"How's Colt taking it?" he asked, concerned. Colt and Mitch had been best friends since they'd competed against each other at the National High School Rodeo Finals in their junior year. Colt had to be devastated.

"He's taking it pretty hard—" Annie's voice caught. "But he's going to help Kaylee make arrangements for the funeral, then get Mitch's affairs settled before he comes home."

"Was Brant one of the bullfighters?" Morgan asked, knowing that if he was, his brother would blame himself for not taking the hit for Mitch.

"No, he didn't work the event." Annie sighed. "But he's feeling guilty because he wasn't. He said if he'd been there, he might have been able to do something."

It didn't surprise Morgan one bit that Brant regretted not being there. "Are you two driving down to Oklahoma for the funeral?"

"Yes, we'll leave in the morning."

"Take it easy and tell Brant I said to drive safely," Morgan said. "And give my condolences to Kaylee."

"We will. Don't forget to let us know about Samantha," Annie reminded.

"Will do," Morgan said, ending the call.

He tossed the cell phone onto the seat beside him and drove faster. Hearing about Mitch reminded him of how fleeting life was, and if something had happened to Samantha or the baby, he'd never forgive himself for making the trip to Denver, instead of staying home with her.

By the time he skidded to a halt at the side of the ranch house and killed the engine, Morgan already had his shoulder belt unfastened and the driver's door open. Jumping from the truck, he sprinted up the back porch steps, then threw the kitchen door wide. It crashed back against the log wall, splintering wood and shattering the window in the upper part of the door. He couldn't have cared less. All that mattered was finding his wife and son.

"Samantha?" he shouted.

Nothing.

He rushed down the hall, and taking the stairs two at a time, searched every room on the second floor. They were nowhere to be found.

Going back downstairs, he crossed the great room to the foyer. The door to his office was closed. He hoped like hell she'd taken a break from working on the camp plans to nurse the baby and hadn't answered because she didn't want to upset Timmy, or that she'd fallen asleep.

Morgan knew it was unlikely, but at the moment he was ready to grasp any explanation as long as Samantha and the baby were all right.

But when he entered the office, the knot in his gut tightened. Where the hell could she be?

As he started to leave the room, the late afternoon sun streaming through the windows glinted off something on his desk, causing him to turn back. When his gaze zeroed in on the reflective object, the air lodged in his lungs.

Forcing himself to walk over to the desk for a closer inspection, Morgan's heart felt as if it dropped to his boot tops. Samantha's wedding ring sat on top of the purchase option he'd had his lawyer draw up for her grandfather's land.

Chapter 10

As Samantha cradled her crying son to her, she glanced around the living room of her grandfather' run-down ranch house. Tears blurred her vision once again and she tried not to remember the last night they' spent here—the night Morgan had helped her give birth to the baby.

He'd been her rock—her source of strength and security that night. And she'd foolishly allowed it to continue, until she'd fallen in love with him.

Her breath caught on a sob. She'd been deeply hurt by her father's abandonment and Chad's refusal to have anything to do with Timmy, but both times she' gotten over it and moved on with her life. But she wasn't sure she'd ever recover from the devastation of Morgan's betrayal.

Why had she convinced herself that he was everything he appeared to be? Why had she allowed him to convince her that he truly wanted to help her keep her inheritance? And why had she allowed herself to fall hopelessly in love with him?

"What's wrong with Timmy?"

At the sound of the familiar baritone, Samantha turned to see Morgan standing in the doorway, looking much as he had the first time she'd seen him. His wide-rimmed hat pulled low on his forehead, his stance, the rigid set of his jaw, all spoke volumes about his state of mind.

She'd only seen him this way one other time. The night they met. He'd been angry then. He was angry now.

"This is private property," she said, meeting his dark gaze. "You're trespassing."

He shrugged. "So have me arrested."

Shifting the baby from the cradle of her arm to her shoulder, she nodded. "You can bet I will."

"What are you doing here, Samantha?" At the sound of Morgan's voice, Timmy's crying faded to a whimper. "Is the baby all right?"

Samantha detected the concern in Morgan's voice, and no matter how he felt about her, she knew he cared for her son. "He'll be fine. He's fighting sleep."

Morgan walked over to the fireplace to sit down on the raised stone hearth. "When Timmy goes to sleep, we'll talk."

"No, we won't."

"Yes, we will." He sounded just as firm as she had and from the determination etched on his handsom face, she knew he wasn't going to budge.

Swaying back and forth, she patted Timmy's smal back. "There's nothing to say."

"There's plenty to say." Morgan's scowl darkened "And by damn, Samantha, you're going to hear me out.

Turning to pace the room, she shook her head. "I won't do any good, so you might as well save you breath."

"Look, Samantha, I've had a hell of a day and I don' feel like arguing with you," he said, sounding tired "Just before I got home and discovered my wife and so had flown the coop, I got word that Colt's best friend Mitch, died last night after a bull-riding accident."

"Oh, I'm so sorry for Colt's loss," she said, he heart going out to her youngest brother-in-law. "I Colt all right?"

Morgan shook his head. "Annie said he's taking i pretty hard." Rising to his feet, he looked around "Where's the baby carrier? Timmy's asleep."

"Over by the couch." She kept her voice low, i order not to disturb her son.

Morgan walked over to take the baby from her, the went back to the couch to gently place her sleeping so in the baby seat. When he straightened to his full heigh he turned toward her. "Why don't we go back to th Lonetree to talk this out?"

She shook her head. "I'd rather not."

"Why?"

"I don't belong there," she said, her heart breaking. She'd come to love the Lonetree Ranch, almost as much as she loved its owner, and it broke her heart to think she'd never be going back.

Closing the distance between them, he towered over her. "That's bull and you know it. The Lonetree is your home."

"No, Morgan," she said quietly. "It never was."

"How can you say that, Samantha? You're my wife."

He reached for her, but she stepped back. She couldn't let him touch her. If she did, she wasn't sure she'd have the strength to resist him.

"Let's talk about that, Morgan." She folded her arms beneath her breasts. "Let's discuss the reasons behind your willingness to marry me."

His piercing blue gaze met hers head-on. "You were going to lose your inheritance and—"

"And what?" she interrupted, ignoring the pain caused by his duplicity and letting her anger take control. "You were going to lose any chance of getting your hands on the property?"

He shook his head. "No. *You* were going to lose what was rightfully yours and your dream of opening the camp."

Taking a deep shuddering breath, she met his dark gaze head-on. "Did you, or did you not, want to buy my grandfather's ranch?"

"I did." He had the audacity to smile. "But I don't anymore."

Her anger increased. "How silly of me to forget such an important detail. There's no longer a need to purchase the land, is there? It came as part of the package when you married me."

"Nope. This is your place." He took a step toward her, but she forced herself to stand her ground.

"Not for much longer." Tears filled her eyes again, but she blinked them away. "Once our divorce is final, it will belong to the BLM."

She watched his smile fade and a muscle begin to twitch along his firm jaw. "We're not getting a divorce," he said firmly.

"Yes, we are," she insisted.

"*No,* we're not." Morgan took a step forward. "We're going to stay married, in two years you're going to get the title to your land and start your camp for foster kids."

"I can't do that."

"Why not?"

"Because we aren't going to stay married long enough for me to get the land," she repeated.

He sighed heavily. "This is getting us absolutely nowhere. What do you say we start over?"

Her stubborn little chin came up defiantly. "What's the point?"

As she stared at him, he could see myriad emotions in the depths of her whiskey-colored eyes. He hated that his carelessness had hurt her and caused her distress, but he had to explain. Their future together depended on it.

Reaching out, he touched her cheek with his index finger. "Just hear me out, Samantha. Please."

"At this point, I doubt there will be anything you could say that will change things," she said, suddenly sounding tired. "But if it will get you to leave, then fine. I'll listen."

"Fair enough." He gave her what he hoped was an encouraging smile. "Do you remember the day you and Timmy came home from the hospital and I suggested that you sell this place?"

"Yes, but I thought you were talking about listing it with a Realtor." She walked over to the hearth to sit down. "You didn't tell me you were the one interested in buying the property."

"No, I didn't." Morgan paused. He needed to choose his words carefully. This was too important to have any more misunderstandings between them. "I had called my attorney to draw up the purchase option before I talked to you about selling it. But once I learned of your plans, I didn't see any reason to mention it. Starting a camp for kids is a much better use for the land than my just wanting to make the Lonetree bigger."

"Then why didn't you destroy the document if you didn't think at some later date you could convince me to sell?" she asked, looking doubtful.

"Because I'm a fool," he said, shaking his head at his own carelessness. "I had the attorney mail it to me so I didn't get it until a week or two after we'd talked. By that time, I was busy working from daylight until well after dark. I was so tired when it arrived, I opened the envelope, saw what it was, then tossed it on a stack of files and forgot about it. Then, when I ran across it this morning, I put it on a stack of papers I need to destroy."

"Okay, I'll accept that. But once you found out about my plans for the camp, you avoided me like the plague," she said, clearly unconvinced. "Then, when you learned that I was about to lose my ranch to the BLM because I wasn't married, you couldn't get me to the altar fast enough. Why?"

Her chin rose another notch and he couldn't help but smile. She was cute as hell when she was angry.

"You don't have a clue about the relationship between ranchers and the BLM, do you, sweetheart?"

"No, I…what does that have to do with anything?" She didn't look quite as certain as she had only moments ago.

"I could have had the land by the first of next year, if I hadn't married you."

"Oh, really?" She didn't look like she believed him. "And how would you have managed that?"

"All I would have had to do was contact the office in Casper and arrange for a long-term lease." He shrugged. "The land would have been mine for as long as I cared to pay for its use."

He could tell she was considering his explanation. "Then you really did marry me to help me keep my land?" she asked, her voice little more than a whisper.

Morgan nodded. "Among other reasons."

He watched the anger and hurt in her pretty amber eyes turn to bewilderment. "What other reasons?"

Taking a deep breath, Morgan knew the time had come to lay it all on the line. "I tried to stay away from you as much as possible because I couldn't keep my hands off of you," he said, hoping she'd understand. "You were everything I wanted, but couldn't have."

"What do you mean I was everything you couldn't have?" she asked, looking more confused than ever.

As he tried to find the words to tell her why he felt the way he had, he rubbed the back of his neck in an effort to relieve some of his tension. This was possibly the most important discussion he'd ever have in his entire life and he hoped like hell that he didn't blow it.

Deciding there was no better way to tell her about his past than straight out, he walked over to sit down beside her on the hearth. "Six years ago, I was engaged to be married. But a week before the wedding, I talked my fiancée into visiting her sister down in Denver while I caught up on chores around the ranch. She didn't want to go, but I insisted." He loosely clasped his hands between his knees and stared down at them. "While they were out shopping, she and her sister were caught in the cross fire between the police and a couple of thugs trying to rob a jewelry store. She…died instantly."

"Oh, Morgan, I'm so sorry," she said, placing her hand on his arm. "That must have been awful for you."

He nodded, but remained silent for several moments, drawing comfort from Samantha's warm touch. Covering her hand with his, he finished, "After that, I vowed that I would never make decisions for another person I cared about. No matter what the circumstances."

"It wasn't your fault, Morgan," she said, her voice filled with compassion.

"Whether it was, or not, I still felt responsible."

Samantha watched Morgan closely. She could tell that he'd been deeply affected by the loss of his fiancée. "Do you still feel that way?" she asked, quietly.

Turning to face her, he shrugged one shoulder. "I guess I'll always blame myself to a certain extent. But I finally feel ready to move on. It's the reason I made the trip to Denver today. I had to put flowers on her grave and say goodbye." He stopped to clear his throat. "I want us to stay together, Samantha."

Her breath caught, and for the first time since he walked in the door, hope began to blossom within her. "Why, Morgan? Is it just because you want to help me get my land?"

"No." She watched him glance down at his hands, then take a deep breath before he raised his head to look at her. "I want to hold you every night and wake up with you in my arms each morning for the rest of my life, Samantha. I already think of Timmy as my own son. I want to adopt him and help you raise him."

Tears filled her eyes and her heart skipped several beats. "Really?"

He nodded. "I also want to help you start your camp."

After all of the things he said he wanted for their life together, she was sure Morgan loved her. But she needed to hear the words. "Why?"

"Because I…love you," he said, his voice rough with

emotion. He reached into his shirt pocket to remove something, then taking her left hand in his, he slipped her wedding band back onto her finger.

When he wrapped his strong arms around her and buried his face in her hair, she felt as if her heart would burst with happiness. "Oh, Morgan, I love you, too."

He held her for several minutes before he spoke again. "I can't live without you, sweetheart. Please don't ever leave me again."

She shook her head. "Never."

Releasing her, he cupped her face with his large hands. "I want you to understand that even though we'll be a family, and equal partners in our marriage, I won't make any decisions, or try to persuade you to do anything you don't want to do."

Her chest tightened with emotion at the sincerity she saw in his brilliant blue eyes. He was such a good man, and one that she knew would never do anything to intentionally hurt or disappoint her, or Timmy, if it was within his power to prevent it.

"Morgan, darling, I hate to be the one to break this to you," she said, touching his jaw with her fingertips. "But you've been making decisions for me since the moment we met."

Frowning, he shook his head. "No, I haven't."

"Yes, you have." She couldn't keep from smiling. "You took charge as soon as you found out I was in labor and told me that I couldn't take myself to the hospital."

"That was different."

"How?"

"You were in no shape to drive."

"That's right. But you didn't give me a choice, did you?" When he slowly shook his head, she continued, "And what about your insistence that Timmy and I stay at the Lonetree with you, instead of coming back here?"

She could tell he considered her words before he finally spoke. "This place doesn't have heat, water or electricity. It wouldn't have been good for you or the baby."

"Once again, you were looking out for our welfare," she said, nodding. "You assessed the situation and *decided* it wasn't a good environment for us. You took care of us, Morgan."

He seemed to mull that over for a moment before he grinned sheepishly. "I guess I did, didn't I?"

She nodded. "Morgan?"

"What, sweetheart?"

"There's a few things that I want from our marriage, too," she said.

Giving her a quick kiss, he smiled. "Name it, sweetheart."

"Promise me that you'll continue to watch out for me and Timmy," she said, smiling.

Nodding, he ran his thumb over the gold band around her finger as his brilliant blue gaze met hers. "I'll protect you both with my life. Anything else?"

"How do you feel about having more children?" she asked. "I'd like for Timmy to have a couple of brothers and sisters."

His serious expression easing, he laughed. "Sweetheart, I'll be more than happy to give you all the babies you want. Is that all?"

She nodded, the love she felt for him blossoming inside of her with each passing second. "Take us home, Morgan."

He stared at her for endless seconds. "I love you, Samantha. Once I take you back to the Lonetree, I don't ever intend to let you go. This marriage will be forever."

"I love you with all my heart and soul, Morgan," she said, tears filling her eyes. "That's what I want, too."

Giving her a kiss that sent her heart soaring, he stood up. Then smiling, took her hand in his and pulled her up to stand beside him. "Forever, sweetheart."

She nodded as she smiled back at him. "Forever."

Epilogue

Two years later

"**O**ut, Daddy! Out!"

Morgan smiled as he unfastened the safety straps on Timmy's car seat and lifted him out of the truck cab. "Let's go see what Mommy's doing," he said, setting his son on his feet.

"Mommy! We here," Timmy yelled, racing toward the ranch house they'd turned into an office for Camp Safe Haven as fast as his short little legs would allow.

When he reached the steps, Morgan reminded, "Be careful and hold on to the rail."

Stepping out onto the porch, Samantha laughed

when Timmy knocked his black cowboy hat off when he raised his arm to take hold of the wooden banister. "How are my two favorite Wakefield men?"

"We here," Timmy said proudly.

Morgan grinned as he helped Timmy put his hat back on, then helped him up the steps. "We're doing pretty good. After Timmy coerced Uncle Colt into taking him for a horseback ride, he helped me feed Stormy Gal's new colt, then we went over to visit Uncle Brant, Aunt Annie and little Zach."

"It sounds like you've had a full morning," she said as she lowered herself into one of the rocking chairs by the door, then lifted Timmy onto her lap.

"You feeling all right?" Morgan asked, sitting in the chair beside her.

Nodding, she started rocking Timmy who looked as if he might fall asleep at any moment. "I'm fine." She grinned. "No backaches, no contractions, nothing."

When Morgan placed his hand on her rounded stomach, the baby inside kicked as if telling his father "hello." He laughed. "I see our little football player is still practicing his punting skills."

"He's definitely been active today," she agreed, rubbing the spot where the baby had poked her. "By the way, did you call to see if Kaylee Simpson would be interested in being the riding instructor when camp opens next week?"

"I e-mailed her, but she's not interested." He shook his head. "She said that she hasn't ridden in some time and doesn't intend to. She's out of school now and working as a physical trainer." He frowned. "I got the feeling she doesn't want to have anything to do with any of us."

"Do you think Brant would be interested in the job?"

Grinning, he nodded. "Since Annie is going to be the activity director, and here everyday, I'm betting he'll be here anyway."

"Go-o-o-d," she said, drawing out the word in a way that caused his heart to stall.

"Samantha?"

"What time is it?"

"Was that—"

He watched her focus her gaze on his truck for several long seconds. The hair on the back of his neck stood straight up. Unless he missed his guess, he was going to be a daddy again soon. Real soon.

When she blew out a deep breath, then turned to smile at him, he knew he'd never in his life forget how beautiful she was at that very moment, or how very much he loved her. "Morgan, I think we'd better take Timmy over to spend the night with Brant and Annie."

Rising to his feet, Morgan took their sleeping son in his arms and helped the woman he loved more than life itself to her feet. "Let's get going."

She looked absolutely radiant and he was once again struck by her calm, and the depth of her courage. "What's the matter, darling? Don't you want to deliver this baby like you did Timmy?"

"Sweetheart, that was a one time shot," he said, locking the office door and helping her down the steps.

"I'm more than happy to be your birthing coach, but that's as far as it goes. This time, you're going to be in the hospital with doctors who know what the hell they're doing."

"I love you, Morgan Wakefield," she said, placing her soft hand along his jaw.

He gazed at the woman who had given him everything he'd ever wanted in life—a family and a home filled with love and laughter. "And I love you, sweetheart," he said, turning his head to kiss her palm. "More than you'll ever know."

* * * * *

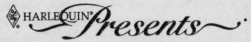

REQUEST YOUR FREE BOOKS

2 FREE NOVELS PLUS 2 FREE GIFTS!

Passionate, Powerful, Provocative!

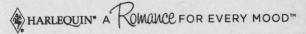

HARLEQUIN® A *Romance* FOR EVERY MOOD™

SUSPENSE & PARANORMAL

Heartstopping stories of intrigue and mystery—
where true love always triumphs.

Harlequin Intrigue®
Breathtaking romantic suspense. Crime stories that will keep you on the edge of your seat.

Silhouette® Romantic Suspense
Heart-racing sensuality and the promise of a sweeping romance set against the backdrop of suspense.

Harlequin® Nocturne™
Dark and sensual paranormal romance reads that stretch the boundaries of conflict and desire, life and death.

Look for these and many other Harlequin and Silhouette romance books wherever books are sold, including most bookstores, supermarkets, drugstores and discount stores.

SUSCAT

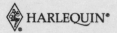
HARLEQUIN®

Showcase™

On Sale July 13, 2010.

Reader favorites from the most talented voices in romance

Save $1.00 on the purchase of 1 or more Harlequin® Showcase™ books.

SAVE $1.00 on the purchase of 1 or more Harlequin® Showcase™ books.

Coupon expires November 30, 2010. Redeemable at participating retail outlets.
Limit one coupon per customer. Valid in the U.S.A. and Canada only.